DEADL.
SECRETS

ALSO BY ROBERT BRYNDZA

DEADLY SECRETS

ROBERT BRYNDZA

bookouture

Published by Bookouture in 2018

An imprint of StoryFire Ltd.

Carmelite House
50 Victoria Embankment
London EC4Y 0DZ

www.bookouture.com

ISBN: 978-1-78681-428-9
eBook ISBN: 978-1-78681-427-2

This book is a work of fiction. Names, characters, businesses,
organizations, places and events other than those clearly in the
public domain, are either the product of the author's imagination
or are used fictitiously. Any resemblance to actual persons, living or
dead, events or locales is entirely coincidental.

For Riky and Lola

Man is least himself when he talks in his own person. Give him a mask, and he will tell you the truth.

Oscar Wilde

CHAPTER ONE

It was late on Christmas Eve when Marissa Lewis stepped off the train onto the platform at Brockley, moving with the drunken crowds to the footbridge. The first flakes of snow twirled lazily in the air, and the crowds were full of warmth and alcohol, eager to get home and start the festivities.

Marissa was a beautiful woman with blue-black hair, violet-coloured eyes, and an hourglass figure. She took pride in being the kind of girl your mother warns you about. She was coming home from the club in London where she performed as a burlesque dancer, and wore a long black vintage coat with an elaborate fur trim, heavy pale makeup, false lashes and a slash of scarlet on her lips. As she reached the steps up to the footbridge, a couple of young men up ahead turned back, greedily checking her out. She followed their eyes down and saw that the bottom half of her long coat had come undone, revealing, as she climbed the steps, a flash of the stockings and suspenders she wore for her act. She stopped to fasten the large brass buttons, and the crowds surged around her.

'I hope that's fake fur,' muttered a voice behind. Marissa glanced back to a bony young woman with her equally bony boyfriend. They both wore scruffy winter coats and the woman had long greasy hair.

'Yes, it's fake,' Marissa insisted, a dazzling smile masking the lie.

'Looks like real fur to me,' said the young woman. Her boyfriend stood staring with his mouth slightly open at the flash of lace and suspender as Marissa finished arranging her coat.

'Frank!' she barked, dragging him away and off up the stairs.

The fur trim on Marissa's coat *was* real. It had been a bargain from a second hand vintage shop in Soho. She'd bought it, along with the vanity case hooked over her arm.

Marissa climbed the remaining stairs and crossed the footbridge. The train tracks below gleamed in the moonlight, and a thin dusting of snow was starting to lay on the rooftops. As she neared the end, she saw the two young men had dropped back, and were waiting at the top of the stairs. Her heart began to beat faster.

'Can I help you?' asked the tallest, offering his arm. He was handsome, with red hair, and a smooth ruddy face. He wore a three-piece suit, a long tan winter coat, and his tan leather shoes gleamed. His friend was shorter, and dressed almost identically, but wasn't quite as blessed in the looks department.

'I'm fine,' she said.

'It's slippery,' he insisted, thrusting his arm up under hers. They were now blocking one half of the stairs down. She eyed him for a moment, and decided it might be easier to accept help.

'Thank you,' she said, and took his arm. His shorter friend wanted to take her vanity case, but she shook her head and smiled. The salt crunched underfoot as they climbed down, keeping Marissa sandwiched between them. They reeked of beer and cigarettes.

'Are you a model?' asked the tall guy.

'No.'

'What does M.L. stand for?' asked his shorter friend, indicating the letters printed on the vanity case.

'My initials.'

'And? What's your name?'

'I'm Sid, this is Paul,' said the taller guy. Paul grinned, showing large yellow teeth. They reached the bottom of the steps, and she thanked them, unhooking her arm. 'You fancy a drink?'

'Thanks, but I'm due home,' said Marissa. The guys were still blocking one half of the stairs, and a stream of people moved past beside them. They stood for a moment, waiting, weighing things up.

'Come on, it's Christmas,' said Sid. Marissa stepped away, putting the other commuters between them. 'Or we can give you a lift?' he added, pushing through them to join her. Paul followed, shoving a young lad out of the way. His beady eyes were both piercing and unfocused.

'No. Really. I must get home, but thank you guys. Have a Merry Christmas.'

'You sure?' said Paul.

'I am, thank you.'

'Can we have a picture with you?' asked Sid.

'What?'

'Just a selfie with us; we like a pretty girl and it gives us something to look at when we're cold and lonely in our beds at night.'

The way they stared at her made Marissa think of wolves. Hungry wolves. They came either side of her and leaned in. She felt a hand on her backside as Sid held out his iPhone, and took a selfie, and then another. His fingers began to work their way between her buttocks.

'Great,' she said, pulling away. They showed her the photo. She looked wide-eyed, but not as scared as she'd felt inside.

'You are really fit,' said Sid, 'are you sure we can't persuade you to come for a drink?'

'We've got vodka, Malibu, wine,' said Paul. Marissa looked back at the bridge, and saw there were still a few passengers crossing. She looked back at them and forced another smile.

'Sorry guys. Not tonight.'

She looked up at one of the CCTV cameras above them, encased in its plastic dome. They followed her gaze. Then finally seemed to take the hint, and moved off.

'What a stuck-up bitch,' she heard Paul say. She hung back, relieved, watching as they went to a car by the kerb, but averting her eyes as they glanced back. She heard laughter, doors slamming, and then the engine starting up. Marissa only realised she had been holding her breath when their car pulled away and left the station approach.

She exhaled, and saw the last few passengers were coming down the stairs. At the top was a tall, handsome man in his early fifties, with his wife, who was very pale.

'Shit,' she said under her breath. She hurried over to the row of self-service ticket machines and busied herself looking at one of the screens.

'Marissa! I see you!' said the woman's voice, thick with booze. 'I see you, whore!' There was a clatter on the stairs as the woman hurried towards her.

'Jeanette!' shouted the man.

'You leave us alone,' shouted the woman, reaching Marissa, but stopping short of making contact. She brandished a long finger, an inch from Marissa's face. 'You stay away from him!'

Her eyes were bloodshot and her face was red and puffy, and her scarlet lipstick had bled out into the smoker's lines around her mouth.

'Jeanette!' hissed the man, catching up and pulling her away. Although the couple were about the same age, he had a rugged, handsome face. It was a reminder to Marissa that time can be kinder to men.

'I do my best to keep out of your way, but we live on the same street. Our paths are bound to cross,' said Marissa, smiling sweetly.

'You're a bitch!'

'Been to the pub, Jeanette?'

'Yes!' she snarled. 'With *my* husband.'

'You look sober, Don. I would have thought you're the one who needs the beer goggles.'

Jeanette raised a hand to slap Marissa around the face, but Don grabbed it.

'That's enough. Why can't you keep your mouth shut, Marissa? You can see she's not well,' he said.

'Don't you fucking talk as if I'm not here,' slurred Jeanette.

'Come on, we're going,' he said. He led her away, almost like an invalid.

'Fucking prostitute,' muttered Jeanette.

'No one's ever paid me for sex!' shouted Marissa. 'Ask Don!'

He turned back with a look of sadness. She wasn't sure if he was sad for his alcoholic wife, or himself. He helped Jeanette to a car by the kerb, easing her into the passenger seat. As they drove away, Marissa closed her eyes at the memory of him. The times when he knocked on her door late at night, when her mother was asleep, and they stole up to her bedroom. The feel of his warm body against her skin as they made love...

When she opened her eyes again, she saw the last of the passengers had dispersed into the surrounding streets, and she was alone. Snow was falling heavily, and it caught in the arcs of the bright lights around the station concourse. Marissa emerged onto the station approach, and took a right down Foxberry Road. Christmas trees glowed in the windows of the houses, and the crunch of her feet on snow broke the thick silence.

The end of the road turned sharply to the right, and became Howson Road. She hesitated. It stretched away in darkness. Several of the streetlights were out, leaving just two to illuminate a five-hundred-yard stretch lined on each side with terraced houses. She had wanted to walk this with the other commuters from the last train; there were always at least a couple of people who took the same route, and it made the walk feel safer. However, Jeanette and the two creeps at the station had put paid to that.

Marissa hurried past shadowy alleyways and dark empty windows, speeding up to each pool of light. She was relieved when the Coniston Road came out of the darkness, it was brightly lit thanks to the school at the end. She turned left, and walked past the playground, before crossing the road to her front gate. It creaked as she opened it. The windows were all dark, and the tiny front garden was bathed in shadows. She had her keys ready, and was about to put them in the lock, when she heard a soft thud behind her.

'Jeez! You scared me, Beaker,' she said, seeing the sleek, dark body of the cat sitting on top of the wheelie bin beside the gate. She went over and scooped him up. 'Come on. It's too cold for us both to be out roaming.' Beaker purred and looked up at her with intense green eyes. She put her face against his warm fur. The cat seemed to give her a moment's grace, then squirmed in her arms. 'Alright, you little crap bag.' He jumped down and darted off through the hedge to the next garden.

Marissa reached up to put her key in the lock, but the gate creaked behind her. She froze. There was a faint scrape, and then a crunch of feet on the snow. She slowly turned.

A figure in a long black trench coat stood behind her. Its face covered in a gas mask, with a hood made of shiny black leather, tightly enveloping the skull. Two large round glass eyeholes stared blankly, and the drum, or breathing apparatus, elongated the face down to where it hung just above the chest. The figure wore black gloves, and in its left hand was a long, thin knife.

Marissa scrabbled to get the key in the lock, but the figure rushed at her, grabbing her shoulder, and slamming her back against the front door. There was a flash of silver, and blood sprayed across the glass eyeholes of the mask.

Her vanity case fell to the ground, and she reached up to her neck, only then feeling the terrible pain of the deep slash across her throat. Marissa tried to scream but there was only a gurgling sound and her mouth filled with blood. She put her hands up as the figure staggered and swung the knife, slicing through two of her fingers and the material of her coat into her forearms. She was unable to breathe and gasped for air, gurgling and spraying blood. The figure grabbed the back of her head and dragged her along the path, slamming her face first into the brick gate post. Pain exploded in her face, and she heard a crack of bone.

Marissa heaved and retched, no longer able to breathe air into her flooded lungs. She watched, almost detached, as this strange figure struggled to drag her across the ground, away from the gate post to the middle of the tiny garden. The figure tottered, and looked as if it was about to fall, but kept balance. With both hands, it brought the knife back down, slicing and stabbing at her throat and neck. As her blood pumped out over the blanket of snow, and the life left her body, Marissa thought she recognised the face through the large glass eye holes of the gas mask.

CHAPTER TWO

Detective Chief Inspector Erika Foster's alarm went off at 7 a.m., and from the depths of her bedcovers and blankets, a thin pale arm emerged and switched it off. Her bedroom was dark and chilly, and the streetlights shone through the paper-thin blinds that she'd been meaning to change for three years, but had never got around to asking her landlord about. She rolled over and pulled the covers off, then padded through to the bathroom, where she took a shower and brushed her teeth.

It was only when she had pulled on her clothes, pocketed her phone, wallet and warrant card that she remembered it was Christmas Day, and she was invited for Christmas lunch at Commander Paul Marsh's house.

'Shit,' she said, sitting down on the bed. She ran a hand through her short blonde hair. 'Shit.'

Most police officers would have seen this as a coup, an invite to spend Christmas lunch with the borough commander and his family, but for Erika, her relationship with Marsh was… *complicated.*

Erika had just completed work on a harrowing case, involving a young couple who had committed a string of murders. As part of their sick game, they had abducted Commander Marsh's two small girls, and Marsh's wife, Marcie had been attacked during the abduction. It had led to a fully-fledged man-hunt. Erika had been responsible for rescuing the girls, and she understood that Marsh and Marcie had invited her to say thank you, but she just wanted to move on.

Erika got up and opened her wardrobe, staring at the sparse rack of clothes, of which almost all were for work. Rooting through the neatly hung black trousers, sweaters and white blouses, she dug out a blue sleeveless dress. Turning to the mirror above her dressing table, she held the hanger up under her chin. Erika stood six-feet tall in bare feet. She had strong, high cheekbones, large brown eyes, and short blond hair which stuck up in wet tufts. 'Jeez, I'm scrawny,' she said, moulding the dress to her body, where once she'd had curves. She looked at the photo of her late husband, Mark, on the dresser. 'Who needs Lean Cuisine, eh? Being a widow does wonders for your waistline…' The bleakness of her humour shocked her. 'Sorry,' she added.

Mark had also been a police officer. Erika, Marsh and Mark had all trained together, but Mark had been killed four years previously, during a drugs raid. The photo of Mark was taken in the living room of the house that he and Erika had shared for fifteen years in Manchester. The sun streamed through the window, catching in his close-cropped blond hair to create a halo of gold. His face was handsome, his smile warm and infectious.

'I don't know what to say to Marsh and Marcie… I just want to turn the page and move on, without any fuss.'

Mark grinned back.

'Bah, humbug, eh? Is it too late to think up an excuse?'

Yes, his grin seemed to say. *Come on Erika, play nice.*

'You're right, I can't cancel… Happy Christmas.' She put a finger to her lips and pressed it against the glass.

Erika went through to the small kitchen/living room, sparsely furnished with a little sofa, a television, and a half-empty bookshelf. Perched on top of the microwave was a tiny plastic Christmas tree. It sat on top of the telly in years gone by, but since the advent of the flat screen, the top of the microwave was the only place it could go without looking ridiculous. She switched on the coffee machine, and opened the curtains. The car park and the road beyond were under a deep carpet of snow, glowing orange under the street lights. There were no people or cars, and she felt like the only person in the world. A gust of wind blew across the ground, skimming a dusting of snow across the surface to join the banked-up drift by the car park wall.

The landline rang as she poured her coffee, and she hurried through to the hallway and answered, hoping for a miracle and that lunch was cancelled. It was Mark's father, Edward.

'Did I wake you up, love?' he said, in his warm Yorkshire accent.

'No, I'm up. Merry Christmas.'

'Merry Christmas to you, too. Is it cold down there in London?'

'We've got snow,' she said. 'It's ankle deep, admittedly, but it'll be enough to make news headlines.'

'We've got four feet here. And over in Beverley, it's even deeper.' His voice sounded frail and strained.

'Are you keeping warm?'

'Yes, love. I've got the fire on, and I'm feeling a bit rakish, so I'll keep it on all day… It's a pity I won't be seeing you.'

Erika felt a twinge of guilt.

'I'll come up in the New Year. I've got holiday saved up.'

'Have they got you working today?'

'Not today. I'm invited for lunch at Paul Marsh's place with his family… After everything that happened to them, I felt I couldn't say no.'

'Who's that, love?'

'Paul; Paul Marsh…'

There was a pause on the line.

'Yes, of course. Young Paul. Has he had any luck selling that Ford Cortina?'

'What?'

'I doubt he'll get much for it. It's such a rust bucket. You can poke your finger through the body work.'

'Edward, what are you talking about?' said Erika. Marsh had owned a red Ford Cortina, but that was years ago, back in the early nineties.

'Oh, course. I'm being daft… I didn't get a very good night's sleep. How are things with them, after what happened?'

Erika didn't know what to say. She twisted the phone wire in her fingers. Edward was almost eighty, but always so sharp and on the ball.

'It's early days. I haven't seen them since…'

She heard the kettle whistle in the background.

'You give them my best, will you?'

'Of course.'

'I'll be off, love. I just need my morning cuppa, and to wake up. And open my presents. You take care, and happy Christmas.'

'Edward, are you sure everything's okay?' she started, but he'd hung up.

She stared at the phone for a moment, then went to the window. The Victorian manor house opposite was large and ornate, and like the rest of the houses on the street had been converted into flats. Several lights were now on, and she could see in one of the windows a couple with two small children opening their presents around a large Christmas tree. A woman in a thick coat struggled past on the pavement, her head down against the driving snow, pulling along a small black dog behind her. Erika went back to the phone and picked it up, then put it down again.

Erika got ready, and left the flat just before eleven. The snow was coming down thick, and there was a sleepy quality to the day, with all the shops closed, and she saw a few children playing outside, having a snowball fight.

As she drove past the row of shops by Crofton Park train station, the traffic began to thicken and slow, and then things ground to a halt. The windscreen wipers squealed as they cleared the dry snow. Up ahead she could see the flash of blue police lights. This cheered her a little; it made her think of work. The traffic crept forward, and just past Crofton Park School, one of the roads on the left was blocked by two squad cars and a line of police tape. Detective Constable John McGorry was talking to two officers by the fluttering tape. As Erika drew level, she honked her horn and they looked over.

'What's going on?' shouted Erika, winding down her window. A flurry of snow poured in, but she took no notice. McGorry pulled up the lapels of his long black coat and hurried over. He was a handsome young man in his mid-twenties, with dark hair which fell over his face with a floppy fringe. His skin was smooth and pale, and his cheeks flushed from the cold. When he reached her window, he swept back his hair with a gloved hand.

'Merry Christmas, Boss. Going somewhere nice?' he asked, noting that she was wearing make-up and earrings.

'Lunch… What's going on?'

'A young woman, found stabbed to death on her doorstep. Whoever did it went crazy on her, blood everywhere,' he said, shaking his head. The traffic in front started moving, and he stepped back onto the pavement, expecting Erika to drive off. 'Have a nice lunch; I was hoping to be off duty by now. You on tomorrow?'

'Who's the DCI on call today?'

'Peter Farley, but he's out at a triple stabbing in Catford. People don't seem to stop killing each other just because it's Christmas.'

The car in front pulled away, and a van behind sounded its horn. Erika thought how much more appealing a brutal murder scene was than Christmas lunch with Marsh. The van behind honked again. She put the car in gear and pulled up onto the pavement, causing McGorry to jump back. She grabbed her warrant card and coat and got out.

'Show me the crime scene,' she said.

CHAPTER THREE

Erika flashed her warrant card, and she and McGorry ducked under the police cordon. They started along the street, passing the rundown houses where neighbours watched from their doorsteps in various states of early morning dress, gawping at the police tape at the end of the road, and craning up the street to where uniformed officers milled around another police tape cordon.

Erika struggled to keep up with McGorry, finding the heels she'd put on for Christmas lunch had no grip on the icy pavement. She wished the weather was warm so she could take her shoes off and go barefoot.

'It's the worst day to close off the road; we've already had to turn people away who are coming to visit relatives…' He glanced back and saw Erika gripping a nearby wall as she carefully picked her way along.

'What?' she said, when she'd caught up, noticing McGorry staring at her.

'Nothing. You're wearing heels,' he said.

'Great work, detective.'

'No, you look great. I mean smart, really good…'

Erika scowled and went to move off, but slipped. McGorry grabbed her just as she was about to fall.

'Do you want to take my arm?' he asked. 'The house is a little way down the end.'

'Not really, but it might be quicker. And I don't want to go arse over tit in front of uniform.'

She grabbed his arm and they moved off at a slower pace.

'I wore heels, once,' said McGorry.

'You did?'

'Six-inch stilettos. When I was at Hendon, we did a charity Christmas show. I played Lady Bracknell in *The Importance of Being Earnest.*'

Despite her annoyance, Erika smiled as she picked her way through the ice.

'Six-inch stilettos? Isn't Lady Bracknell meant to be a staid and stuffy elderly Victorian lady?'

'I'm a size twelve. They were the only heels I could get for my feet,' he said, indicating his large shoes.

'How much did you raise for charity?'

'Four hundred and seventy-three pounds fifty…'

'Go on then, give me a bit of Lady Bracknell,' said Erika.

'*A handbag?*' he said, affecting an upper-class old lady vibrato.

Erika shook her head and smiled, 'I'm glad you didn't give up your day job.'

She let go of his arm as they reached another police cordon ballooning out in front of a terraced house near the end of the street. A low wall and a tall snow-topped hedge obscured the front garden, and through the open gate they could see a crowd of forensics officers in their blue paper Tyvek suits. The officer at the cordon peered at Erika's warrant card.

'A DCI has already been called. He's delayed, triple stabbing in Cat…' she started.

'Well, he's not here, and I am,' said Erika. The officer nodded and lifted the cordon. They went to the forensics van parked up on the pavement. Another uniformed officer, a stern middle-aged woman with a nose stud and cropped grey hair, handed them each a Tyvek suit. They took off their coats, draping them over the top of the van.

'Bloody hell, it's freezing, said McGorry, quickly stepping into the legs and pulling it up over his thin suit.

'It got down to minus twelve last night,' said the officer. Erika held on to the van, balanced on one foot, and pulled on the paper suit, but her left heel caught in the fabric and tore the leg as she pulled it up.

'Shit!'

'I'll bag that up; here's another one,' said the officer, handing her a fresh suit. Erika took it and pulled it on, but the same thing happened again. 'You should be in flats, especially on a day like this,' the officer said.

Erika shot her a look, and McGorry looked away politely as she took a third suit, and successfully managed to get it on over her heels. She zipped it up, and they both pulled up the hoods. They put on shoe covers which, again, Erika found tricky, but once they were ready they moved to the front gate and entered the tiny, cramped front garden.

Isaac Strong, the forensic pathologist, was working in the small space with two assistants. He was a tall, thin man in his early forties. The widow's peak of his dark brown hair poked out from under the hood of his Tyvek suit. He had long, thin eyebrows, which made him look constantly quizzical.

The blood-spattered body of a young woman was on her back under the bay window. Her long black coat lay open. The plummeting temperature during the night had frozen her spilled blood to the consistency of a ruby-red sorbet. Her throat had been sliced open, and this was where there was the most concentration of blood, stretching out in a pool underneath her. It saturated her thin green strapless dress, split up the left leg to reveal black stockings and suspenders, and it covered the bay window and sill above in a fine frosted spray.

'Morning, Merry Christmas,' said Isaac, shaking his head. His greeting hung awkwardly in the air. Erika looked back at the face of the young girl. Her face was frozen, figuratively and literally, in fear. Her lips were drawn back, and one of her front teeth was broken off close to the gum. Her eyes, though cloudy, were violet, and they were strikingly beautiful, even in death.

'Do we know who she is?' asked Erika.

'Marissa Lewis, twenty-two years old,' replied Isaac.

'Is that a formal ID?'

'Her mother discovered her body this morning, and there's a driving licence in her wallet.'

Erika crouched down and took a closer look. A square vanity case with the initials 'M.L.' was half-buried in snow by the hedge, and beside it was a black high-heeled shoe. They were both marked up with plastic numbers.

'Anyone touched the body?'

'No,' said McGorry. 'I was first on the scene with uniform. The mother found her and said she didn't touch anything.'

'Do you have a time of death?'

'The extreme cold is going to make it difficult,' said Isaac. 'Her throat was slashed with a very sharp blade, resulting in deep cuts and severing both carotid arteries on each side of the neck. You can see this led to rapid blood loss, and she would have bled out very quickly. On her right hand, the index finger is almost severed, and there are lacerations to the thumb, middle finger and arms, which indicates she put up her hands to defend herself.'

'There's no way out of the garden, apart from the gate, or through the front door,' said McGorry. Erika saw that in addition to the window, the front door had a fine spray of frozen blood on its faded blue paintwork.

'Are those her keys?' she said, noticing a bunch of keys with a heart-shaped keyring.

'Yes,' said McGorry.

Erika closed her eyes for a moment, imagining what it must have been like, overpowered by a knife wielding maniac in this small enclosed space. She opened them again, and looked at Marissa's face.

'Her nose is broken,' she said.

'Yes. And her left cheek. We also found her front tooth, embedded in the gate post,' said Isaac.

Erika and McGorry turned to look at the gate post, where a numbered marker was fixed halfway up. Clumps of snow clung to the brickwork. Next to it was a wheelie bin, and a recycling box stuffed with empty vodka bottles. Erika turned back to look at the house. The curtains were drawn, no lights were on.

'Where's the mother?'

'At the neighbour's house,' said McGorry, indicating a terraced house diagonally across the street.

'And we're sure the victim lives here? She wasn't visiting her mum for Christmas?'

'We need to check that.'

'We're going to have difficulties moving her,' said one of Isaac's assistants, who had finished clearing the snow from the blood-spattered legs.

'Why?' asked Erika.

He looked up at her – a small man with large, intense brown eyes. He indicated the vast pool of frozen blood spreading out from under the body.

'The blood. She's frozen solid to the soil underneath.'

CHAPTER FOUR

Isaac came to the gate with Erika. He looked up at the cloud hanging low and grey.

'I need to move her before the weather turns; there's more snow on the way,' he said. She looked back at the body, where Isaac's assistants worked carefully to dig her out of the frozen blood-soaked soil. Erika felt the same pang of horror and excitement she always experienced at the scene of a murder. So much in her life was out of her control, but she had the power to track down whoever had done this. And she would.

'When do you think you can do the post-mortem?'

Isaac blew out his cheeks. 'Sorry. Couple of days. I have a backlog; this is a busy time of year for suspicious deaths. And did I tell you? I've been moved. I'm working out of the morgue at Lewisham Hospital.'

'Since when?'

'Since the morgue in Penge has been sold to a developer. A big sign went up for Parkside Peninsula Apartments a few weeks ago, and we moved last week. It's causing all sorts of delays.'

'Parkside Peninsula Apartments, Penge,' repeated Erika, raising an eyebrow. Isaac raised one in return.

'Oh, and another thing,' he said. 'Blood spatter. The person who did this would have been covered in blood and carrying a weapon, but the drops of blood end abruptly at the gate.'

'You think they wiped the knife? Or had a vehicle parked by the gate?' asked Erika.

'That's for you to find out,' said Isaac. 'I'll keep you in the loop with the post-mortem.' He went back into the front garden.

Erika and McGorry changed out of their Tyvek suits, handed them in, then ducked under the police tape into the road. They buttoned up their coats against the cold. A large police support van had just arrived, and was attempting to park against the kerb. One of the police cars pulled out to make extra room, and it got stuck in the snow, its wheels spinning and squealing.

'So, we're looking at someone who had a car, potentially,' said Erika. 'They got in and drove away. But where?' Erika looked up and down the street. The house was on the end of the terrace, with an alleyway running along the side. It was overlooked by the back gardens of the houses in Howson Road, which ran parallel to Coniston Road. 'I want to get the house-to-house going ASAP. There should be plenty of people home on Christmas Day. I want to know if anyone saw anything, and I need the details of persons of interest in the area: violent offenders, anyone with previous or ongoing convictions.'

Two uniformed officers had come to help the squad car, and were giving it a push. The engine roared and the wheels spun.

'There's a railway bridge at the end of the next road, which leads over to the Fitzwilliam Estate,' said McGorry.

Erika nodded. 'Worth including in our H2H, but whoever goes in there needs to go easy.' She knew that the Fitzwilliam Estate, like many high-rise council buildings in poor areas, was known for trouble. She peered down the long alleyways running along each side of the terraces. 'And we need to check out if any garden gates back onto these alleyways…'

They stepped out of the way as the squad car broke free from the snow. It shot past, took a right at the end of the street, and parked outside the school opposite. The support van pulled into the gap by the kerb and turned off its engine. In the sudden silence came the click of a camera shutter. Erika turned to McGorry.

'Did you hear that?' she murmured. He nodded. They looked up at the surrounding windows, but couldn't see anything. There was a rustle directly behind. Erika turned and looked up into the branches of a tall oak tree across the road, next to the railings of the school playground. A young man who looked to be in his early twenties was slithering down the branches. He stepped onto the top of the metal railing lining the playground, and dropped down into the alleyway. He was scruffy, with long blond hair, and had a long-lens camera around his neck on a strap. He glanced at Erika and McGorry, then bolted for it down the snowy alleyway.

'Hey! Stop!' shouted Erika. McGorry headed off in pursuit down the alleyway, and Erika followed. The young man wore a long coat, which flowed out behind him as he ran. He jumped up onto the lid of a wheelie bin, and vaulted up and over a high wall with tall trees behind it. Seconds later, McGorry reached the wheelie bin, hitched up his coat and heaved himself up shakily. Erika tottered unsteadily along and reached the bin as McGorry grabbed hold of a branch of one of the thick, snow-covered evergreens and climbed up onto the lip of the wall.

'What's over there…?' she started, but he jumped off, and landed on the other side with a thud and a yell. The branches above the wall swayed, dislodging the snow, and then they were still. Erika heard more yelling, and instinctively reached for her radio in her pocket, but it wasn't there. She looked back down the alleyway, but the road with the crime scene appeared a long way off.

'Shit, if he's broken something…' she muttered, thinking how much paperwork there would be to fill in. Shaking the guilty thought away, she took off her heels and shoved them into the pockets of her long coat, before hitching the coat up to climb up onto the wheelie bin. The plastic lid creased and bent downwards with her weight. She hooked her leg up onto the brick wall, and grabbed a branch of one of the evergreens to steady herself, dislodging more snow on top of her head in the process. The ground was higher on the opposite side, and Erika dropped down softly onto a bed of soil and leaves between the wall and the thick row of trees. She slipped her shoes back on and walked out of the trees into a large, snow-covered garden. A gap in the middle was churned up with two sets of footprints, and there were two large sheds, a greenhouse, and a long polythene tunnel beyond. The garden's high walls muffled the sounds of traffic from surrounding streets.

McGorry was moving slowly towards the sheds. He turned to Erika and put a finger to his lips, pointing to the second shed in the row of two, closest to the house. She nodded. The house was large and crumbling. The sash windows were grimy, with peeling paint. A tall gate in one corner was blocked by overflowing rubbish bins. The back door to the house had a small roofed porch with steps down to the garden, which were covered in plant pots.

As Erika reached McGorry, from inside the house came a cacophony of clocks chiming the hour. The blond-haired lad appeared from behind the shed, and ran back to the wall. McGorry moved faster, tackling him to the ground. Erika hurried over to them, but lost one of her shoes in the process, and fell back into the snow.

'Calm down!' said McGorry as the lad fought, throwing punches and landing one in McGorry's face.

'Get off me!' cried the young man. He was wiry with a thin, feral face and bright blue eyes a little too far apart. Erika got up, losing her other shoe in the snow. McGorry was churning up the snow, struggling to keep hold of the young man, who kicked and flailed, and then got the upper hand, pushed McGorry's face into the snow. McGorry flailed and reached around, managing to get hold of the camera, and tightened the strap around the boy's neck. The boy released his grip on the back of McGorry's head, and grabbed at the strap tightening around his neck.

'Get back!' shouted a voice. 'Let him go!' A large, elderly woman in an orange onesie was at the top of the porch steps, holding a shotgun. Her grey hair hung past her shoulders, and she wore huge glasses that magnified her eyes. She aimed a shotgun at them, and advanced towards them through the snow.

Erika put up her hands. The elderly woman's eyes looked crazed, and she felt this situation has suddenly escalated to red alert. McGorry coughed and spat out snow, still holding the strap tight. The young man was scrabbling frantically at his throat.

'John. Let him go!' shouted Erika. McGorry let go of the camera strap, and the lad fell onto the snow, coughing. 'I'm Detective Chief Inspector Erika Foster of the London Metropolitan Police, and this is Detective Inspector John McGorry. We can show you our warrant cards, but you need to put the weapon down… Now.'

The woman looked anxiously between Erika and McGorry, but she didn't lower the gun.

'That is *my* son you are attacking, and you are trespassing on *my* property!'

'We are police, and your son was trespassing and photographing a crime scene,' said Erika. She wondered what the woman was capable of.

'Joseph! Come away from them!' the woman shrilled, still training the gun at them. Joseph coughed, and staggered over, his coat covered in snow.

'Elspeth!' shouted another voice. An elderly man emerged behind her from the back door. He looked like an eccentric university professor, and was wearing a long blue cape and a tatty skull cap dotted with sequins. He had a magnifying lens fixed to his head with a band, giving him one huge, staring eye. 'Elspeth, put that down at once!'

'Sir, we are police and we can show you identification,' said Erika, her heart beginning to race. She felt stupid for blundering into this situation, and she was aware she wasn't wearing any shoes. Her feet were numb from the cold. The man gently took the shotgun from Elspeth, and opened the barrel.

'It's not loaded,' he said, hooking it over his arm in the manner of a gamekeeper. 'And we have a firearms certificate.'

'My boy, my boy!' said Elspeth, who had gathered Joseph into her arms and was checking him over, running her hands over his neck and peering into his eyes. 'Did they hurt you? Are you okay?'

Joseph looked a little bewildered and shell-shocked.

'Why was that gun so easily to hand?' asked Erika. McGorry leaned breathlessly on his knees and spat out snow.

'If you join us inside officers, you can all get dry, and we can sort this out,' said the man.

CHAPTER FIVE

Erika and McGorry stamped their feet in the porch and brushed the snow off their coats. Then they were shown through to a warm, cosy kitchen. Elspeth fussed over Joseph like he was a small child, guiding him to one of the chairs at a long wooden table. McGorry moved to stand close to a blazing fire in the corner. The room was decorated like a country farmhouse kitchen, with a Welsh dresser, and a large green Aga from which a delicious smell of turkey was filling the room.

'There's a welt coming up already!' cried Elspeth, tilting Joseph's head to one side. He kept hold of his camera, and scowled at Erika and McGorry.

'Do take a seat, officers,' said the man, pulling out more chairs at the table.

'Can I see the certificate for your firearm,' said Erika, ignoring the chair.

'Certainly,' he said, leaning the shotgun by the fireplace and moving to a drawer in the Welsh dresser.

'It's a legal firearm,' insisted Elspeth, helping Joseph out of his wet coat and draping a towel around his shoulders. Erika noted he didn't want to let go of the camera, even when she was trying to get his arms out of the coat.

'What's your full name?'

'Family name is Pitkin. I'm David, this is Elspeth and Joseph. I take it you weren't expecting to be on duty today?' he said, looking up from rummaging in the drawer. He indicated Erika's soaked, misshapen shoes.

'No.'

'Were you headed anywhere nice?'

Erika realised she still had to tell Marsh she wouldn't be coming for lunch. She ignored him and pushed the thought to the back of her head.

'What do you do for a living?'

'I'm a horologist,' he said, tapping the magnifying lens strapped to his head by a leather band. 'I repair clocks and watches, although, to be honest, it's more of a hobby since I retired from the bar. Ah, here we are,' he said, pulling out a folded piece of paper.

'You were a barrister?' Erika said, her heart sinking.

'Yes. Thirty years.'

Erika took the licence and scanned the details.

'It's Elspeth's gun. I have my own. We like to shoot. It's a hobby, of course.'

'That seems in order,' said Erika, passing the licence back to him. 'But if it's a hobby, why was the gun so easily to hand?'

Elspeth looked up from peering at Joseph's neck. 'I have it in a locked cabinet in the back office! I saw you in the garden, creeping about. This isn't the nice area it used to be. There's drugs, and burglaries almost every other day… Look what you did to him! He's going to have a nasty bruise.'

'I'll also remind you, DCI Foster, of the law in Britain regarding self-defence, based on the principles of reasonable force being used?' said David.

'Does she brandish a double-barrelled shotgun, in broad daylight, to anyone she finds in the garden? Seems a bit excessive,' said Erika.

'Excuse me, I'm not going to be called "she" in my own house,' snapped Elspeth. 'I was going to offer you a piece of my coffee and walnut cake, to show no hard feelings, but I'm not going to now.'

McGorry turned away, suppressing a grin, but Erika didn't find the situation funny. What she wanted to do was to get hold of the camera Joseph was still clutching tightly, and return to the crime scene.

'A court will usually take into account the fact that being threatened in or at one's home is a frightening situation,' said David. 'The spirit of the law being that someone should have the right to defend themselves, their possessions, and those they are responsible for…'

'At no point was your son's or your wife's life in danger,' interrupted McGorry.

'Really? What's your name, young man?'

'John McGorry, Detective Constable.'

'Detective Constable John McGorry, why were you attempting an illegal chokehold on my son?'

'I wasn't…'

'Please don't lie. You were using Joseph's camera strap to restrain him about the neck. It's illegal to use chokeholds on suspects or members of the public. In years gone by, the police were trained in chokeholds, but I would think you're a little young and inexperienced…'

'I was merely…' started McGorry, his cheeks flushing with annoyance. Erika shot him a look to stay quiet.

'And your superior officer should know this too,' added David.

'I do know this,' said Erika. 'I can also tell you that if a police officer *does* use a choke hold, the officer may be able to present a justification for the use of force based on the circumstances. And based on the fact your son was attempting to suffocate my officer, by pushing his face into the snow, a choke hold in self-defence could be considered reasonable or necessary. Check online, this was detailed in a recent freedom of information act to West Mercia police.'

David tried, but failed to hide his annoyance.

'This still doesn't explain why you were pursuing my son?'

'Your son was trespassing at a crime scene.'

'Which isn't a criminal offence,' said David.

'He was taking photos of the crime scene…'

'Again, not a criminal offence.'

Erika paused and gave him a thin smile.

'He was evading a police officer.'

'Yes, and now we are all here and he will cooperate, within reason.'

'Your son may have information on his camera which could help our investigation,' said Erika. She felt foolish for giving chase, and now she was having to defend herself and McGorry to this retired barrister who was threatening to get the better of her.

'Where is the crime scene?' asked David.

'I can't comment on that.'

'They've found a body, up on Coniston Road,' said Joseph. He had a soft, cultured voice, almost speaking with received pronunciation.

'You found a body?' said Elspeth, who was still patting at his hair with the towel.

'No, mother,' he said, batting her away. 'The *police* found the body.'

'We're not at liberty to speak about an ongoing murder case,' said McGorry.

'You believe it's murder?' said David.

'Murder?' said Elspeth.

'It was Marissa Lewis; someone stabbed her to death on her doorstep,' said Joseph.

'That's speculating…' started Erika.

'No. I was there when her body was discovered.' Joseph pulled the camera into his lap protectively.

'Did you call the police?' asked Erika.

'I didn't have my phone.'

'But you took photos of the crime scene, before the police arrived?'

'You don't have to answer that, Joseph. We bought him a new lens for his camera, as a Christmas gift.' said David.

'If anyone round here was going to come a cropper, it would be Marissa Lewis,' said Elspeth, shaking her head.

'My wife is also speculating,' said David. 'Which is legal, is it not?' He was infuriatingly calm, and Erika took a deep breath.

'Of course it's legal, but could she – could you – explain?'

Elspeth draped the towel over the back of a free chair, crossed herself, and turned to Erika.

'Marissa Lewis has – *had* – a certain reputation, if you get my drift. A promiscuous reputation. She worked as a stripper.'

'You've seen her at work?' asked McGorry.

'Of course I haven't seen her at work! None of us have!' She glanced at David and Joseph, who shook their heads and looked at the floor. 'My hairdresser told me.'

Erika's eyes strayed to the loose, greasy grey hair hanging around Elspeth's shoulders, and wondered exactly what a hairdresser did for her.

'Who is your hairdresser?'

'Marissa Lewis's best friend, Sharon-Louise Braithwaite, is my hairdresser. At the Goldilocks Hair Studio by Crofton Park station. Marissa asked Sharon to put up a poster for one of her… *performances*, in the salon. It was a picture of her wearing nothing but stockings, suspenders and a bra!' Elspeth shook her head at the memory. 'I also heard from Sharon that Marissa had an affair with a married man who lived a few doors down, and she had several other blokes on the go.'

'Do you have the name of the married man?'

'Don Walpole. He has a wife, Jeanette. They're still together, despite it all.'

Erika turned her focus back to Joseph.

'So, you were in the tree opposite Marissa Lewis's house early this morning, and you took photos? What did you take photos of?'

'The sunrise,' he said, with a smarmy smile.

'You were up in the tree to capture the sunrise, but you remained in the tree after you saw there was a dead body in the garden opposite, and the road was closed off by police officers?'

'I only saw the body when I heard Marissa's mother scream.'

'What time was this?'

'I dunno.'

'We opened our Christmas presents at ten to seven,' said David. 'We had breakfast, and Joseph left around seven-twenty. Sunrise today was at 8.05 a.m.'

'It had just got light, so it was around that time when Marissa's mum came out of their house,' said Joseph. 'I don't wear a watch.'

'Do you know why Marissa's mother came to the front door?'

'No.'

'She probably had more bottles to put in the recycling bin; she's a drinker,' said Elspeth. 'It's not the nicest street.'

'There's been snow and thick cloud for the past few days. How would you expect to see the sun rise?' asked McGorry.

'If all photographers thought like that, they wouldn't take any photos,' said Joseph.

'You're a professional photographer?'

'The word *professional* is rather redundant. Would you say you are a professional police officer? Did you act professionally when you pinned me down in a chokehold?'

'Listen, you little sh…' started McGorry, taking a step towards him. Erika held up her hand.

'Joseph, stop wasting time, and answer our questions.'

'He doesn't have to answer any of your questions!' cried Elspeth.

'A young woman has been brutally attacked and murdered on her doorstep. She should be with her family this morning, but instead she's lying in the snow with her throat hacked open. The bones are broken in her face, and she may or may not have been sexually assaulted,' said Erika. 'Joseph doesn't have to answer any of my questions, but he could have information that helps our investigation.'

Joseph looked uncomfortable for the first time, and shifted in his seat.

'Okay, I did watch stuff for a bit, then the police arrived really fast. Then they closed off the road. I didn't know what to do. When I climbed up that tree, it wasn't a crime scene, but by the time I stepped back down, it was.'

'Did you photograph the body?'

'No.'

'Can I look through the photos on your camera?'

'No. It's a film camera,' he said, holding it up. Erika moved over to him and saw that it was a vintage model, and had no digital screen. She went to take it, but before she could, Joseph flipped it over, opened the back and whipped out the roll of film. He pulled out the negative, and dumped it on the table.

'There. No photos to process. All gone.'

Erika stared at him. He had an odd face, both vulnerable and hard. He stared at her, defiantly.

'I think we've been more than cooperative, officers,' said David. 'Now if that is all, we'd like to get on with celebrating Christmas.'

Erika and McGorry left through the front door. It had stopped snowing and the road was busy with cars. When they turned and looked back, the house looked oddly out of place: a crumbling, sagging structure, sandwiched in a gap between the smart, upright row of terraces.

'It's like it's been dropped from above,' said McGorry.

Erika put her hands in her pockets and hunched down against the cold, as they started back down the alleyway towards Coniston Road.

'I'm going to have to write all this up,' she said.

'What about the chokehold?'

'They haven't said they're going to complain, but that doesn't mean they won't. You're a bloody idiot, John. Why the hell did you let it go that far?'

'He was lashing out, I was trying to… calm him down, stop being hit. It was instinctive. And you said all about that freedom of information request, that I can justify a choke hold.'

'He could still complain, and cause problems. You need to be on the ball. You have to always think about the consequences of your actions.'

'That's impossible.'

'Of course it's bloody impossible, but that's part of being a police officer. You can't let yourself get into a situation where you are using unnecessary force.'

'I'm sorry,' said McGorry, his face flushing.

'It's okay. We live in a shitty time, John. Everyone takes offence at everything, and you're presumed guilty, at all times. Be smart. Think. I'll do my best to steer my report away from it…'

They were now back in the alleyway and level with the high wall leading back over to the Pitkins's garden. Erika spied something behind the wheelie bin and stopped.

'What?' asked McGorry.

She crouched down, and using a small, clear plastic evidence bag from her pocket, she picked up a small, black plastic cylinder. She stood and held it to the light. She fiddled with the bag and managed to get the small lid of the plastic tube to come off inside the bag.

'A camera film,' she said, smiling at him.

'Used?'

'I hope so. I saw his camera before he yanked out the film. He'd only taken one photo on it.'

'You think he used a whole film when he was up in the tree, then changed it?' said McGorry hopefully.

'We'll know for sure when we get it developed, and the tube tested for prints,' said Erika.

CHAPTER SIX

When Erika and McGorry arrived back at Coniston Road, the house-to-house was underway. Uniformed officers were moving up and down the street, knocking on doors, and several were talking to neighbours on their doorsteps. It had started to snow again, and despite the early hour, just before 3 p.m., the light was starting to fade. The police presence was at odds with the Christmas lights in the windows.

They stopped off at the support van, where Erika asked McGorry to get the roll of film fast-tracked through forensics and developed. She left him to work on it, and when she emerged from the van, a small black body bag was being wheeled through the narrow gate posts on the post-mortem trolley. There was a brief pause as everyone stopped and watched. Erika thought how small it looked. Isaac nodded to her as it was loaded into the van, and the doors closed. She felt a wave of exhaustion and depression approaching, but she forced herself to keep it at bay. She took a deep breath and welcomed the distraction of an officer with a short blonde bob of hair, wearing a long blue winter coat, who had just arrived on the scene.

'I'm Detective Constable Tania Hill, I'm the family liaison officer,' she said, offering her hand.

'What do you know about the case so far?' asked Erika.

'I just saw the body of the young girl. I've never seen so much frozen blood,' she said, pulling the lapels of her coat around her face. 'The mother is, apparently, very vulnerable. Low income, serious health issues with alcohol.'

'She's with the neighbour; I'm glad you're here. I'd like to talk to her,' said Erika.

They crossed the road to a smart house with brand new UPVc windows and a small square of concreted-over front garden. Erika rang the bell. The door was opened by a small, middle-aged lady wearing a red velvet tracksuit and gold slippers. Her snow-white hair was neatly clipped in a pixie cut, which looked at odds with her lined face. In her left hand, she held a cigarette.

Erika made the introductions and they held up their warrant cards.

'What's your name?'

'Who's asking?' said the woman, with almost comedic defensiveness. Her voice had a deep smoker's growl.

'I am,' said Erika.

'The name's Joan Field.'

'Can we please come in?'

Joan stood to one side. The dark blue carpet in the hallway was immaculate. 'Shoes off,' she added.

'Can I call you Joan?' asked Tania.

'No, I'd prefer Mrs Field.'

'I'm the family liaison officer,' said Tania, placing her shoes by the bannister. 'I'm here in a support capacity, to bridge the gap between Mandy and the police investigation.'

Joan looked her up and down. 'Bridge the gap? Isn't that fancy talk for answering the phone?'

Tania ignored the dig.

'Where is Mandy?'

'In the kitchen.'

They followed her, passing a living room which contained a heavy red velvet three-piece suite and a small silver Christmas tree, but which was otherwise devoid of any ornaments or photographs and didn't looked lived-in. At the back of the house was a small kitchen, looking out over the snowy garden. It was clean, but cramped. The ceiling and the walls were yellow from nicotine. A frozen turkey, still wrapped in plastic, floated in the sink.

Marissa Lewis's mother, Mandy, was a huge woman, her vast frame swathed in a grubby pink tracksuit. She sat at the table, her enormous buttocks spilling over either side of a wooden chair. Erika's eyes strayed to the old trainers Mandy was wearing, which had been cut up the middle to accommodate her swollen feet. Her face was pale, and her eyes bloodshot and watery.

'Mandy Trent?' she asked.

'Marissa weren't adopted. We're blood,' said Mandy, seeing Erika's surprise at her appearance. 'She got her father's name, and I changed mine back when he fucked off… Marissa got the slim genes from him.' Her voice was loaded with bitterness.

'I take it you both want tea?' said Joan, moving to the kettle.

'Please,' said Erika. Tania nodded and they each pulled up a chair.

'Mandy. I'm here as your family liaison officer,' said Tania, placing a hand on her arm. 'This will be a very hard time for you, and I'm here to help, and to explain what happens next.'

Mandy lit up a cigarette and blew the smoke in Tania's face.

'What happens next? You want to take me to see her body? It was her.'

'Are you up to answering some questions?' asked Erika.

'I found her outside the front door, this morning, when I took out the rubbish. Just lying there, quiet and still, but the blood. There was so much of it.'

'Can you remember what time?'

'Eight-ish.'

'Marissa lived with you?' asked Erika.

'Yeah. She's paid me housekeeping since she was sixteen.'

'Do you know where Marissa had been last night?'

'She had a dancing gig, don't ask me where. She has – had – a lot of them. She was a burlesque dancer, worked in clubs all around the West End. A few nights a week.'

'And you heard nothing last night; you didn't hear her return home?'

'No.'

'Did you expect her home at a certain time?'

Mandy shook her head. 'I've done my job rearing her, she's an adult…'

'What time did you go to bed?'

'I nodded off about ten-ish, I think.'

'You didn't hear anything?'

'Like what?'

'Screaming, sounds from the front garden. A vehicle?'

'No.'

'Marissa's front door key was still in the lock outside when you found her?'

'Yeah. I told the police that.'

'Were you in the living room until 10 p.m.?'

'Yeah, I was watching telly. It was shit. They used to show decent stuff on Christmas Eve.'

'How long had Marissa been working as a burlesque dancer?' asked Tania.

'Three or four years. She's been doing well for herself, always had bookings. Though she don't make much money from it – didn't. She'd pay me housekeeping and then borrow it back three days later.'

'The gear costs a packet,' said Joan, as she took cups from the cupboard. 'Props, costumes she used for dancing. Big feather fans, head dresses. Mandy even moved to the back bedroom, so she'd have more room to store it all, didn't you?'

'The back bedroom's nearer the loo, and I put her housekeeping up,' clarified Mandy, as if she didn't want it on record that it was a nice gesture. Erika couldn't work out what was going on. Mandy seemed so matter-of-fact about Marissa's death. Joan came over with mugs of tea.

'Did Marissa have a serious boyfriend?' Erika asked.

Mandy exhaled cigarette smoke with a long, silent chuckle.

'They never seemed to hang around long enough to get serious. A lot of the local lads used to sniff around, and she had a few admirers who'd watch her dance, buy her presents…' Erika and Tania exchanged a look. 'I don't want to speak ill of the dead, but my daughter was a right slag. She slept with two blokes on this road, both married. And there were all sorts of lads coming and going, and those were the ones I knew of.'

'Who were the married men?' asked Erika.

'Don Walpole, lives at number 46 with his wife. Marissa was shagging him a few years back, when she was sixteen…'

'The rumour is, he was sleeping with her before her sixteenth birthday,' interjected Joan, with a knowing nod.

'Don Walpole ain't no kiddy fiddler, Joan. He just did what any bloke would do when it's offered up on a plate. Marissa was an early developer, by the time she was fourteen she looked twenty,' said Mandy, lighting another cigarette with the stub of the old one.

'And the other married man?'

'Ivan… Whatsisface…'

'Stowalski,' said Joan.

'Yeah. He's Polish. Got a few quid in the bank, so I think that's why she liked him. He's certainly not good looking. Pale and washed-out as anything, he is. He's been around for a few months.'

'Do you know when she last saw him?'

'No. He rang the bell a few weeks ago, but he didn't come in.'

'Marissa worked full-time as a burlesque dancer?'

Mandy shook her head. 'No. She also did a few hours a week as a carer for an old lady, in Hilly Fields over the way.'

'What's her name?'

'Elsa Fryatt,' said Joan. 'She's ninety-seven. Very posh, despite the name Elsa. Lives in one of the big houses overlooking the fields.'

'Marissa was onto a nice number there,' said Mandy. 'All she did was took her shopping; she got herself insured on the old girl's car. It wasn't proper caring work. I think she liked having Marissa around, much like a woman likes a bit of rough in a bloke. I think she finds common people quite entertaining.'

'What about her friends?' asked Erika.

'I would think most of her friends are dead, didn't you hear? She's ninety-seven.'

'No, I meant Marissa,' said Erika.

Mandy exhaled smoke and took a big gulp of tea. 'The girls she works with on the burlesque circuit are a bunch of bitches, that's what Marissa used to say, but she's got a friend she's had since school. Works up the hairdresser, Sharon-Louise Braithwaite.'

'The Goldilocks Hair Studio?'

'Yes, that's it.'

'Could I ask you to make a list of the clubs where Marissa worked?'

Mandy's bottom lip trembled and she wiped at her eyes.

'Bloody hell, I can't think straight to make lists, and all this talking in the past tense: worked, lived…'

'We can get to that later,' said Tania, touching Mandy's arm.

'When can I go back to my house?' she said, pulling it away.

'The forensics officers are inside to make sure there isn't any other evidence that can help. We will let you know as soon as we've completed our investigation,' said Erika. 'Would you like Tania to find you somewhere to stay?'

'No, I'll stay here, with Joan,' said Mandy. Joan nodded, but she didn't look too thrilled.

CHAPTER SEVEN

'What did you make of that?' asked Erika, pulling up the collar of her coat, as she and Tania left Joan's house.

'Grief displays itself in different ways,' said Tania.

Erika frowned.

'Leave it out, don't give me hot air. You see a lot of grieving relatives. There was real hostility there.'

'From both of them, although I think Joan was being led by Mandy. Mandy wears the trousers, and had the most dislike for her daughter.'

'Not everyone that gets murdered is loved by their relatives.'

'You think the mother is a suspect?'

'Everyone is a suspect. I want forensics to take a look at her clothes, and I'd like swabs taken from under her fingernails...' Erika beckoned to a young uniformed officer, who looked worried as she crossed the street to the front gate. 'What's your name?'

'Kay Hornby, PC Kay Hornby, ma'am,' she said.

'I need you to grab one of the CSIs and bag up the clothes and get fingernail swabs from the victim's mother, Mandy Trent.'

'Yes, ma'am... Erm, I have a spare pair of trainers in my car,' she said, noticing Erika's heels, which were soaked and on the verge of disintegrating. Erika looked down at the young woman's feet, clad in black shoes.

'What size shoe are you?'

'A six. They're not stinking gym shoes. I use them for driving. It was just a thought, ma'am.' She looked worried, as if she'd overstepped the mark.

'Thank you. I'd appreciate that,' said Erika.

'Absolutely, ma'am. I'll just run and get them.'

Erika's phone buzzed in her pocket. She pulled it out and moved off along the street.

'Where the hell are you?' said Marsh. 'It's almost four o'clock!'

'Sorry. I was called to a crime scene. A young woman killed on her doorstep on Coniston Road, near Crofton Park.'

'You weren't on call today.'

'I'm helping out, loads of officers have taken leave over Christmas…'

'I know that!'

'I'm just explaining to you why I'm here.'

'I was expecting you for lunch.'

'I know, I'm sorry. I won't be coming. I've got presents for the girls, so I'll arrange to drop them round later…'

'I said: I was expecting you for lunch.'

'That's an order, is it?'

'No. I just wanted to see you; Marcie and the girls wanted to see you…'

Marsh paused. The silence went on, and then Erika realised he had hung up on her. She put the phone back in her pocket, feeling guilty. She crossed the road to the support van, where Kay was waiting with a pair of pink and white running shoes.

'Thank you,' said Erika.

'There's socks too, in the shoes.'

Erika took off her ruined high heels and Kay held onto her arm as she pulled on the socks and trainers. 'Ahh, that's so much better. Thank you.'

McGorry came out of the van. He noticed Kay and smiled and raised an eyebrow.

'I'll get the shoes back to you later today,' said Erika.

'That's okay, take as long as you need with them,' said Kay, and she went off to the forensics van, giving McGorry a curt nod.

'Haven't you got a girlfriend?' asked Erika, seeing McGorry glance after her.

'Yeah,' he said, seeming a little annoyed.

'You know, not every young female officer has to fall for your charms.'

'I dunno what you're talking about.'

Erika rolled her eyes. 'Come on, let's get to it.'

A police officer was stationed at the front door. The body of Marissa Lewis had now been removed from the front garden, leaving a vast pool of frozen blood. Snow had been cleared from the path, and the course of the blood spatter was marked with small yellow numbers.

The house was messy inside, with dated furniture and overpowering smells of damp and fried food. There was a tiny Christmas tree in the living room, and the kitchen was overflowing with dishes and grime. Stairs led up to a dingy landing, where the ceiling sagged. Doors led off to a bathroom and two bedrooms. Erika and John pulled on latex gloves. The bedroom at the front had a bay window looking out over the road, busy with police activity. The room looked freshly painted, and was neat and tidy with new furniture and a beautiful flowered bedspread. Three tailor's mannequins lined one of the walls, and they were dressed in feathered costumes, one with a black corset. A set of shelves on the opposite wall contained seven wigs on polystyrene heads, and a dressing table under the window was covered in make-up. A row of high-heeled shoes in different colours were neatly lined up in front of a fitted wardrobe.

'Does she toast marshmallows on the gas fire?' asked McGorry, moving to a small fireplace and picking up one of several thin metal rods with blackened marshmallow shapes on the end, which were leaning up against the grate.

'I think they are used for fire eating,' said Erika, peering at them. There were a couple of framed photos on the wall. In the first, Marissa lay in a huge champagne glass, wearing see-through pink lingerie. In another she wore black stockings, suspenders and nipple tassels, and held one of the flaming rods close to her mouth. The final framed photo was a publicity poster, where Marissa lay on a chaise in a silver bodice, surrounded by muscled young men in underwear. A huge header read:

A NIGHT WITH MISS HONEY DIAMOND
JULY 14TH 2017
BETHNAL GREEN WORKING MEN'S CLUB

'That must be the name she performs under, Miss Honey Diamond,' said McGorry.

Erika noticed a diamond shape embroidered in gold on the bodice of the black corset on the second tailor's mannequin. 'This diamond logo is the same as it is on the poster. It's also embroidered on the other two costumes,' she said, looking at the other two mannequins.

'A diamond for Miss Honey Diamond,' said McGorry, coming over to run his finger over the stitching.

'We need to check if this is a brand of clothing, or if it's been stitched on afterwards. And our first port of call – along with phone records –should be her social media.'

'Forensics said there wasn't a laptop or a PC in the house,' said McGorry. 'There wasn't a mobile phone, and they didn't find one on her body.'

'So her phone is missing.'

Erika went to the wardrobe and opened it, seeing more of Marissa's burlesque clothes. Two additional bras were embroidered with the diamond logo. There was also some civilian gear: jeans, jumpers, a few 'conventional' dresses and shoes. Tacked to one of the wardrobe doors were several pictures of Dita Von Teese performing burlesque, and one of her lying in a giant martini glass.

They moved back out along the landing, past a grotty little bathroom, to a small bedroom at the back of the house. It was nothing more than a box room, sparsely furnished with a single bed and a wardrobe. The bed was covered in bin bags full of clothes and towels. Perched on the windowsill was a hairbrush and some face cream. On the radiator was an enormous pair of greying knickers.

'Jeez,' said McGorry, holding them up. Erika gave him a look, but didn't say anything. 'She gave up the best bedroom for Marissa and her stuff?'

'She said she charged her extra housekeeping.'

'Doesn't look like she sleeps in here.'

Erika saw that the plastic bags had a layer of dust.

'She said she was in bed around 10 p.m.'

'Did she mean she slept on the sofa?' asked McGorry. They came back downstairs and went into the living room. The sofa under the bay window was covered in a creased duvet and a pillow. On the floor was an empty litre bottle of cheap own-brand vodka and two empty tubes of Pringles.

'She didn't say that she sleeps on the sofa,' said Erika. She went to the window. It was grimy with dirt and condensation, and the spray of Marissa's blood. There was a single pane of glass, and a freezing draft was blowing through the rotten window frame, and they could hear very clearly the noise from the road outside.

'Maybe she was too pissed to remember,' said McGorry, indicating the empty bottle of vodka.

Erika heard the door of the support van slam, and the crunch of snow as someone walked past on the road behind the hedge. She wondered if the killer had been lying in wait.

'I wonder if Marissa had the chance to scream,' said Erika, more to herself than to McGorry.

CHAPTER EIGHT

Erika and McGorry came back to the police support van, where a group of six officers were taking a quick break. They had been chatting away, but fell silent when they saw Erika.

'Don't mind me,' she said.

'Refreshments have arrived, ma'am,' said one of the officers, indicating the table in the corner with an urn and a cluster of pre-packaged sandwiches.

'Thanks. What's your name?' she asked.

'PC Rich Skevington, ma'am.'

Erika and McGorry grabbed a sandwich each and filled paper cups with steaming coffee. The sound of the coffee hitting the paper cup was loud in the silence. Erika looked around. She didn't recognise any of them; they all seemed so young.

'Who can give me an update on the house-to-house?' she asked, ripping the plastic off her sandwich and taking a bite.

'We haven't been able to get an answer from Don Walpole and Ivan Stowalski. We're waiting on their mobile phone numbers,' said Kay, the young officer who'd lent Erika her shoes.

'What about the rest of the street? Are people being helpful?' asked Erika, washing down a mouthful of the dry sandwich with a gulp of coffee.

'Half the houses are empty, but the locals who knew Marissa Lewis also knew about the affair she had with Don Walpole and that she was sleeping with Ivan Stowalski behind his wife's back.'

'The jury's out as to whether or not Ivan Stowalski's wife has left him,' said Rich. 'Their next-door neighbour, a beady-eyed old girl, says they're both up north for Christmas visiting his family. We've also been on the lookout in gardens and dustbins for the victim's mobile phone, in case it's been dumped, but nothing so far.'

'How are the team getting on over at the Estate?'

'I've just come back,' said another young male officer. 'We spoke to the usual suspects. A couple of lads said they'd heard of Marissa Lewis.'

'How do you mean, "heard of"?' asked Erika.

'They said she's had a reputation in the past for being the local bike – their words, not mine. One of them has a record, did three years for rape. The other has a record for assault, GBH. Both of them say they have an alibi, they were out until 6 a.m. this morning at a club in New Cross Gate, H20. They told us to check the club's CCTV.'

Erika rolled her eyes.

'*Haitch 20.* I know it. I've lost count of the times we've requested CCTV from them. Okay, get someone on it…' She took another bite of the sandwich. 'What the hell is in these sandwiches?' she said, through a mouthful.

'"Festive Christmas dinner sandwiches", that's all they had at the petrol station,' said Rich.

Erika spat a mouthful out into the packet. 'I can see the appeal in turkey and cranberry, even some stuffing, but who puts roast potato in a bloody sandwich?'

Erika dumped the rest of the packet in the bin. She looked around at the team, who had averted their eyes, not wanting to risk her wrath. Every other officer her age had taken leave to be with their family or other halves. She missed the continuity of the officers she regularly worked with. Detective Inspectors Moss and Peterson, and Sergeant Crane. She wondered fleetingly if they were having a good Christmas. She was pleased that McGorry was with her, but he was still a relative newbie – and even he had volunteered to stay, risking the wrath of his girlfriend waiting at home.

Her phone rang. It was a number she didn't recognise, so she came out of the van. It was now dark, and the cold air caught at the back of her throat.

'Hey Erika, this is Lee Graham.'

'Hi, Merry Christmas,' she said.

'Merry Christmas to you too. I've drawn the short straw today, and I'm in the lab.'

Erika liked Lee. He was a forensics and computer expert in the Met police, and they had worked together on a few cases. There had been a frisson of flirtation between them, but nothing more. She wondered now if he was single, and if that was the reason he had decided to work on Christmas Day.

'To what do I owe the pleasure?' she asked.

'Unfortunately, this isn't a personal call. I saw your name on an urgent request for developing a camera film.'

'Yes. How soon can you get it done?'

'It's already done. I've scanned them in, and I'm just emailing the photos over to your work email. I'll get the hard copies over by snail mail.'

'Thank you. I should buy you a drink sometime.'

'Here's hoping,' he said.

Erika heard her phone beep. 'I think I just got your email.'

'Okay, I'll let you go. Merry Christmas,' he said and rang off.

She opened his email and scrolled through the attached photos. They were mostly taken from the tree opposite Marissa's bedroom. There was a series of photos taken at night through Marissa's bedroom window, where she was fresh out of the shower and wearing a towel, then naked and pulling on her underwear. There were also three photos, taken from above, of Marissa's body lying in the snow. And three more at a lower angle, which looked like they were taken at ground level, close to, or inside, the front garden.

'Joseph Pitkin, you lying little shit,' said Erika. She walked over to the front gate of Marissa's house, where the frozen blood in the front garden was rapidly being covered by fresh snow. She could see up into the tree, with its thick bare branches. 'Was that your regular spot, to spy on her, Joseph?' Erika looked at the photos again, and saw that Lee had included a message at the bottom of the email:

The owner of this camera uses ILFORD DELTA 100 Professional 35mm film. They could be using a darkroom to process photos. Lee.

She was about to return to the van, when she caught an acrid smell of burning plastic. She looked around, and saw that at the end of the alleyway leading down to Joseph Pitkin's house, smoke was rising into the sky.

Erika hurried down the alley towards it, the smell growing stronger. By the time she reached the back wall of the Pitkins's house, thick black smoke was billowing into the air from behind the line of evergreens. She climbed up on to the wheelie bin, finding it much easier in the borrowed trainers, and pulled herself up onto the wall. Through the trees, she could see Joseph in his long coat, huddled over a burning oil drum. On the snowy ground beside him was a box of papers. He picked up a handful and dumped them into the drum, a shower of sparks and flames floating up into the dark sky. The windows in the house behind him were dark, and he was only lit by the glow of the flames.

Erika dropped down softly onto the strip of earth between the wall and the line of trees and stepped through. Joseph heard her feet crunch on the snow as she came towards him.

'Stop what you're doing. Right now,' she said. He grabbed at a spade propped up against the oil drum, but she moved faster and grabbed it from him. She thought he would attempt to run, but he sank back onto the snow with his head between his hands as she put in a call to McGorry.

CHAPTER NINE

'Loads of these photos are of Marissa,' said Erika, sifting through the box of photos on the snow beside the oil drum. She held up a black-and-white shot of Marissa performing in a burlesque gig. McGorry was picking up several which had dropped onto the snow. The fire inside the drum had died down, but it still beat out warmth into the cold evening.

'Talk about a Kodak moment!' said McGorry, holding up a photo of Marissa striking a pose on a stage wearing knickers and nipple tassels, and removing a long black glove with her teeth.

'I don't need silly comments. Just bag them up,' said Erika. She looked back at the house. The lights were now on in the kitchen, and two uniformed officers were standing over Joseph, who was sitting in a chair. One was talking to him, the other was taking notes, and Joseph was crying. 'Do you think those tears are real?'

'He is a mummy's boy,' said McGorry.

Joseph had now lost his cool, and was pulling at his hair. He stood up, shouting at the officers. One of them pushed him roughly down into the chair, which almost toppled over, and started shouting back. Erika pulled off her latex gloves and lit up a cigarette. They weren't able to salvage anything from the fire, and inside the drum was a blackened lump. She needed to move fast, and make up her mind whether or not she wanted to bring Joseph in for questioning. He had told them his parents had gone round the corner to visit their friends for a quick Christmas drink. She checked the time. It was coming up to 8 p.m. She took a deep drag on her cigarette, and her phone rang. She moved down to the end of the garden, and saw it was Marsh. As she silenced the ringing phone and put it back in her pocket, she accidentally dropped the lit cigarette. It rolled across the snow and under the line of trees. She pulled her phone back out and activated the torch, training it under the trees. She found the cigarette, tucked under one of the evergreens, still lit. She also saw that a small square of soil had been disturbed towards the end of the row of evergreens. It hadn't been like that earlier in the day. She called back to McGorry to bring the spade propped up against the oil drum.

'Look,' she said, when he joined her. 'The ground wasn't disturbed when we came over the wall this morning. Get digging.'

She trained the light on the ground as McGorry began scraping at the soil. He only had to dig down a few feet before he uncovered something small and grubby, wrapped in plastic. Erika pulled on a fresh pair of latex gloves and squatted down beside the hole. She shook off the soil, and gently started to unwrap several layers of plastic bags, thinking she was going to find a block of cannabis resin. The final layer of plastic uncovered an iPhone with a pink bejewelled case. Written across the back in clear Swarovski crystals was the name, '*Marissa*'.

'Bloody hell,' said McGorry.

'Indeed. Let's bring him in for questioning,' said Erika. She checked the iPhone was switched off, and slipped it into a clear evidence bag.

They came back to the house, and went into the kitchen. David and Elspeth Pitkin had just arrived home.

'What is the meaning of this intrusion?' said David, still wearing his thick winter coat and grey bobble hat. Elspeth went to Joseph and started to examine his tear-streaked face.

'What did they do to you?' she said. He stared blankly at her.

'Mr and Mrs Pitkin. Did you have a nice evening?' asked Erika, smiling sweetly.

David turned to her. 'What is this?'

'Your son was burning photos of the murder victim in your garden.'

Elspeth shot a look at her husband, but he ignored her.

'It is not illegal to take photographs; we've already been over this, DCI Foster.'

'It is illegal to steal a mobile phone from a dead body and then bury it in the garden.' Erika held up the mobile phone in the evidence bag. 'It's called withholding evidence.'

'How do we know you didn't plant it there!' cried Elspeth, her voice cracking with emotion.

Erika nodded at the two uniformed officers. 'Joseph Pitkin, I am arresting you on suspicion of withholding evidence…'

'NO, NO, NOT MY BOY!' cried Elspeth, moving to block the two officers.

'…Withholding evidence pertaining to a murder enquiry. You do not have to say anything; but it may harm your defence if you do not mention when questioned something which you later rely on in court. Anything you do say may be given in evidence.'

'He was with us all last night! He didn't go out!' insisted Elspeth, reaching to grab at Joseph. One of the uniformed officers moved her to one side and handcuffed Joseph with his hands behind his back. 'Don't you touch me! Don't you assault me!' she screamed. David looked on, his face ashen.

'Please, officers, my son is very vulnerable,' he said.

'Get his phone,' said Erika. One of the officers reached into Joseph's coat and pulled out a smartphone. She handed it to Erika, who switched it off and put it in a clear evidence bag. 'I want this house searched, top to bottom. And as you are aware of the law, Mr Pitkin, you'll agree that your son has given me enough cause to search without a warrant.'

'Please! Don't lock him away. Please!' cried Elspeth. David had to hold her back, as Joseph was led away.

CHAPTER TEN

The custody suite at Lewisham Row police station was down in the basement, and separated from the rest of the offices in the station by a thick steel door. Erika had been a police officer long enough to remember that it used to be called 'the cells'. However, the fancy term didn't hide the fact that this was a dank and depressing part of the station: a thin corridor lined with big steel doors with hatches, painted a deep pea-green colour.

Ray Newton was the custody sergeant who was on duty. He was a small, rotund, balding officer with a thick moustache, and he was waiting for them when Joseph was led up to the desk by two uniformed officers.

'He's had a full body search,' said Erika. 'And we're waiting on word about a solicitor.'

'Right, young man,' said Ray, pulling out a clipboard and handing him a pen attached to the desk with a thick piece of string. 'We have to fill out some paperwork, so the officers are going to remove your handcuffs. I don't want any funny business. You treat me well, and I reciprocate.'

Joseph's mood flipped, and he started thrashing about with his arms still cuffed behind him.

'You! You're fucking cunts!' he screamed, trying to turn around and see Erika and McGorry.

'That's enough!' said Ray.

'They stitched me up! I've done nothing! NOTHING!'

'We'll leave him with you,' said Erika, indicating to McGorry that they should go.

They came up the stairs, through the thick doors, and into the main part of the station. They stopped at the vending machines by the stairs.

'That's a first, being called the C-word on Christmas day,' said McGorry.

'Makes you feel all cosy and festive, doesn't it? Like you're beside the fire with a glass of something warm.'

'You want to let him sweat in the cells overnight?' said McGorry.

'I want to wait till morning to question him,' corrected Erika. 'Kay is working on unlocking the phones upstairs.'

Her phone rang and she had a brief conversation with one of the officers at the Pitkin house.

'They found an improvised darkroom upstairs, in a small cupboard in Joseph's bedroom, but there were no photos,' she said when she came off the phone.

'Burned them before we got to him,' said McGorry.

'Kay is trained to forensically examine electronic devices. I want to know what's on his phone and Marissa's, before we question him. Let's hope there's something.'

'They're a bit of a weird family, aren't they? The posh ones always are a bit odd. Is he really stupid enough to have buried that phone, with Marissa's personalised case still on it?'

'Don't underestimate how stupid people can be. I also want to run his prints against the ones we found on the plastic film holder in the alleyway.'

'What about all those photos of Marissa Lewis? Do you think she knew he took them?' asked McGorry.

'He probably bought a ticket to her show.'

'Then why burn them?'

Erika shook her head, feeling exhausted.

'We need to confirm the phone was registered to Marissa, and see if we can get any more information about Joseph. Has he got a record? Etc.' She selected her coffee, and they were silent as the cup dropped out and it began to fill and steam. 'Mandy Trent was pretty open about who Marissa associated with. She didn't mention Joseph. I'll get Tania, the FLO, to ask her again.' She took her cup from the dispenser.

'We don't have enough to charge him with her murder. And he has an alibi,' said McGorry.

'From his mother.'

'We've got nothing that places him at the scene last night.'

'Yet. Nothing *yet*. Post-mortem, forensics, everything is still left to play.'

McGorry yawned as he put money in the machine and selected coffee. Erika studied his tired face as the machine filled his cup. 'You should go home and get some rest. I want you here when I question him tomorrow morning.'

They both sipped their drinks, then spat them back in the cup.

'What the bloody hell is that?'

'Oxtail soup,' he grimaced.

'Did you press the coffee button?'

'Yeah.'

They dropped their cups into the small bin by the machine. Erika pushed more change in, and selected a white coffee. When it was done she put the cup to her nose.

'That's bloody oxtail soup as well. They close down the canteen, and leave us with nothing but oxtail soup!'

'They must have filled the machine up wrong,' said McGorry.

Erika rolled her eyes and dropped the second cup in the bin.

'What is it with this country? Potato sandwiches, and oxtail bloody soup! I've never met anyone who actually eats oxtail soup, yet in the world of second-rate vending machines that's the third option after tea and coffee!'

'You can buy it in tins…'

'What?'

'Oxtail soup. My Nan has a cupboard full of tins of oxtail soup. She loves it.'

Erika looked at him and grinned.

'Go on, bugger off home, have your Christmas dinner. I'll see you tomorrow,' she said.

Erika went up to her office on the fourth floor. It was tiny, with barely enough room for a small desk, a chair, and a bookshelf. Kay was working at a laptop with Joseph's smartphone plugged into it.

'Sorry, the coffee machine is buggered, and there's nothing in the staff kitchen,' said Erika. 'How are you getting on?'

'The iPhone is password protected. You'll have to get it sent to the Cyber Crime Unit, and even then, they probably won't have any luck. It's virtually impossible to hack into an iPhone. I can also see from the IMEI number that this was a pay as you go phone.'

'Which will make the phone records harder to track down. Shit.'

'The good news is that Joseph Pitkin's smartphone isn't password protected.' Kay indicated a window on the screen with all the downloaded files. 'I've just pulled off a load of video files.'

Erika's mood brightened and she pulled up a chair. Kay started to click down the list of image and video files; some were very short, of a tabby cat on a summer's day stretching on the windowsill outside Joseph's bedroom, another of Elspeth, red faced and taking a huge plaited loaf of bread on a tray out of the Aga, another of the tabby cat in the garden, amongst the flower pots, chasing after a red admiral butterfly in that playful-yet-lethal way cats enjoy.

'All very charming,' said Erika. When Kay clicked on the next video, the sound blared out from the computer, making them jump. Distorted music played, and the video was a blur of colour until it came into focus. Marissa Lewis was on a small stage in a crowded club. Behind her was a red velvet curtain. The video was taken a little further back in the audience, and some people's heads were visible. Marissa's dark hair was set in pin curls, and she wore bright red lipstick and huge lashes. She was slowly unbuttoning a long black coat, and then she let it drop to the floor. Underneath she wore a 1950s-style pink silk satin corset, stockings, suspenders and towering heels. The video seemed to tremble as she went through her act, stripping down to underwear and nipple tassels. Marissa took a bow to applause and sashayed off the stage.

'Blimey, she was good,' said Kay.

'I thought her act would be sleazy, but this is – well, professional burlesque,' said Erika. They clicked through photos of the same evening, of Joseph standing with Marissa among the tables in the club. They were posing for the camera; someone else must have taken the pictures.

'Do you think it looks like Marissa knows him?' asked Erika, as Kay clicked through six almost identical shots: Joseph with his arm slung around Marissa's waist.

'He looks like the creepy fan you want rid of. Why did he need six photos? By the sixth she looks like she wants to get away,' said Kay.

'When are these dated?'

'Almost a year ago. Last January.'

Kay clicked through more photos of the same evening, of Marissa talking to other guests and posing for photos, then a couple of blurred ones as she went to the bar. Then the background changed. The next few photos were dark, and illuminated with a flash.

'When is this?' asked Erika.

'The time stamp shows the same day, same time.'

'Looks like backstage.' There were photos of what looked like a dressing room. It was empty, with a large mirror surrounded by lights. There were close-ups of a rack of burlesque clothes; a pair of lacy black knickers discarded on the floor. A hand holding them up to the camera. There was a diamond symbol sewn into the fabric.

'Honey Diamond,' said Erika. 'That diamond symbol was embroidered on Marissa's burlesque costumes.'

Abruptly, the photos then changed to a video of Marissa Lewis's house. It was taken high up, at night, looking down into the window of Marissa's bedroom. It started off shakily, and they could hear wind distorting the phone's microphone. Marissa came into focus, walking around the bedroom in a towel. She went to the dressing table and picked up a brush, dragging it through her wet hair. Then Marissa dropped her towel, and was naked. The video zoomed in closer and lost focus. When it came back into focus, Marissa was staring out of the window, directly at the camera.

'Shit,' came Joseph's voice, above the wind distorting the microphone. He kept the camera trained on her. She stood, very still, watching. Then she cupped her breasts, and ran her hands down the front of her body. She stopped above her pubic hair, and waggled a finger and pulled the curtains together. The camera stayed on the glowing curtains for a moment, then the video ended.

'She knew Joseph was watching her?' said Kay.

'She knew someone was watching her,' said Erika. Kay clicked on another video, which showed the same view, at night. This time, Marissa's bedroom was brightly lit, and she entered the room with a tall, older man. Marissa made sure they both came close to the window, and the camera caught his face. Kay ran the video forward, as they moved to the bed, starting to kiss and undress each other. The video was the longest on the phone, ten minutes in total, and it zoomed in as the couple had sex on Marissa's bed. 'We need to get a clear image of that man's face, and find out who he is. When was this taken?'

'December 14th, this year. Do you think she knew they were being filmed?'

'Or she asked Joseph to film,' said Erika. She rubbed her tired eyes and sat back in her chair. 'What did you make of him?'

'In the short space of time I was there? He seemed scared, but clingy with his mother.'

'He's ticking all the boxes so far. He was obsessed with Marissa. He stalked her, and spied on her. He stole Marissa's mobile phone, and photographed her dead body. But I need forensics. I need DNA if I want to really nail him and make an arrest.'

*

In the basement of Lewisham Row, all was quiet in the custody suite. The long line of cell doors was propped open, ready and waiting for any offenders Christmas night had yet to offer. Only the cell door at the far end was closed. Ray, the custody sergeant, got up from his desk, and went to do his fifteen-minute check, his polished shoes squeaking on the floor. He opened the metal hatch on the closed door, and shone his torch inside. Joseph Pitkin lay on a bed in the corner.

'You alright, lad?' he said.

Joseph shrank away, and turned to the wall.

'Yeah, great,' he murmured. He flinched as the metal hatch slammed shut. He shifted on the bare bed in the darkness, trying to get comfortable, silent tears rolling down his cheeks.

CHAPTER ELEVEN

Four miles away in Sydenham, a cold wind screamed down Walpole Road, pushing the snow in drifts up against the walls of the terraced houses. Diana Crow left her friend Fiona's house just after 11 p.m., wincing at the cold. She'd stayed longer than she'd intended, but Fiona had insisted that she saw the end of the Christmas film.

Diana put her head down, and hurried along the dark snowy street to the main road. Despite the cold, her face felt hot after four glasses of sweet sherry. She waited for a small Fiat to drive past before she crossed. Snow had been falling heavily all day, and the pavement and road had merged into one. She carefully picked her way across, and slowed, feeling around in the snow for where the kerb began on the other side. She stepped up onto the pavement and shivered. It was so quiet. Every window was lit, but the curtains were clamped shut. It was only a few minutes' walk home. Fiona had told her to call a taxi, but Diana thought it a ridiculous extravagance to pay good money for a thirty-second taxi ride, three streets away.

As she passed by the train station, the streetlight was out, and the short station approach was shrouded in darkness. There were no cars on the road now, and she picked up the pace as she approached the railway underpass. The air was damp, with a nasty smell of urine. She pulled the lapels of her coat up over her mouth. The pavement was dry in the underpass, and her footsteps echoed, breaking the silence. The pavement on the other side, lit up by the orange streetlight, seemed far away. She hurried on, and had almost reached the light, when one of the dark walls seemed to bulge out. A tall figure moved out from the shadows and blocked her path.

She stopped, and couldn't move. Afterwards, she would ask herself why she hadn't turned and run – she had been less than sixty seconds away from her front door – and why she hadn't fought back, or shouted out for help? Instead, she stood there, paralysed with fear as the tall figure came closer. Loomed over her. He moved with a soft creaking sound, and as her eyes adjusted a little to the dark, she saw he wore a gas mask. The two large eyeholes were blank, and rubber material stretched up and over his head like a hood. Vapour streamed out from the large breathing drum hanging down. White squares were painted on the drum, and it looked like a grotesque smiling mouth. There was a faint chemical smell about him as his breathing quickened, and she saw that his coat was open and he was exposing himself, masturbating with a gloved hand.

Diana opened her mouth to scream, but it was cut short when he grabbed her by the throat and pinned her to the cold bricks, his powerful leather-gloved hand tightening around her neck. It was all so quiet, and she gagged and choked, wishing she would pass out. Just as the edges of her vision started to go black, he loosened his grip enough for her to take a breath, then his hand tightened again.

Outside the underpass, the road remained empty. The snow fell. Everything was quiet and still.

CHAPTER TWELVE

Erika arrived home late to a cold flat. In the two years she'd lived there, she hadn't got around to figuring out how the timer on the boiler worked. The first thing she did when she got in was flick on the heating, and she kept her coat on until it started to warm up.

She then ran a bath, with the water boiling hot, almost too hot to bear. The scalding water helped her to block things out, and made her forget about work, but despite the hot water, she couldn't shake off the image of Marissa Lewis's body lying in the snow. A crime scene always tells a story, and the small front garden in Coniston Road told of a violent struggle. The sheer volume of blood, caking Marissa's body and the surrounding snow. Her shoe, left lying close by; her vanity case, broken on its side, the contents spilling out into the snow. Her keys still dangling in the lock of the front door. If Marissa had reached her door a few seconds earlier, would she have been able to turn the key and get safely inside?

Erika found it a struggle, the balance between feeling sorrow for a murder victim, and shutting it out. To stay sane, it was easier to dehumanise a dead body, and think of the person as an object: a thing, or a piece of evidence. Erika could never do that, though, any more than she could come home from work and live a normal life. She didn't have anyone to come home to. Since Mark's death, she had been involved in a relationship with her colleague, Detective Inspector James Peterson, and for a time he had been someone she could come home to – or more precisely, she would go to his place and they would watch television and eat takeaway and laugh. Then Peterson had been badly injured in the line of duty: shot in the stomach, on Erika's watch, at the climax of an abduction and murder case. His subsequent battle to recover and return to work had driven a wedge between them. It had been a messy end to a promising relationship. And she was left alone again, for endless evenings with her thoughts.

The image of Marissa Lewis's tooth embedded in the brickwork of the gate post swam into her head. She closed her eyes, but it was still there: broken off, close to the gum, and daubed with a smudge of red lipstick. Erika opened her eyes and added fresh hot water to the bath. Her usually pale legs were an angry red from the heat. In her mind's eye, she saw Marissa's blood-spattered legs in the picture taken from high in the tree. The folds of her long winter coat, open in the snow. Then she saw the crime scene, and Isaac crouching down beside the body. The thin material of the dress hitched up to expose Marissa's underwear. The underwear had been spotless. There had been no blood, and a neat strip of pubic hair had shown through the sheer material.

Erika yanked out the plug, and stepped out, wrapping herself in a towel. She hurried through to the living room, where she had her laptop and the case file laid out on the coffee table. The lights were off, and the curtains were still open. Snow was falling again. It made a dry rustling sound as it hit the glass. She went to her computer and clicked through the photos taken by Joseph. First, the ones high up in the tree, and then the close-ups.

'You sick little shit,' she murmured, flicking between the two different perspectives and zooming in. 'You lifted up her skirt when you came down from the tree...'

Erika's phone rang, making her jump. She checked the time and saw it was just after 11 p.m. It was Edward, asking if she had enjoyed lunch.

'I didn't go in the end. I was called out to a crime scene,' she said. 'Very sad. A young girl, murdered on her doorstep.'

'Oh. Do you want to talk about it?'

'Not really. It's too dark and gruesome for Christmas. Did you have a good day?'

'I had a bit of a party, as it turns out,' he laughed. 'Kelly from down the road popped over with her mother, Shirley. They brought over a big lasagne and Monopoly. It was Manchester Monopoly. Guess where the most expensive street is?'

'Coronation Street?'

'No. I thought the same. It's the Lowry on Salford Quays. It's the same price as Park Lane on the London version. I don't think you can win Monopoly unless you fork out for the best real estate.'

'Listen to you, saying things like "real estate".'

'And that's why I won. I was a proper little tycoon!'

He sounded normal, nothing like the confused old man from that morning. In the background, she could hear the television.

'I'm glad you had a nice day,' she said.

'I've just been over to the graveyard. And it was snowing, but over on the hills it was clear and the moon was up. Is it right that I thought it was beautiful?'

'It is.'

'I didn't want Mark to be on his own on Christmas Day…' His voice trembled and broke on the end of the phone. 'It's so hard, him not being here.'

'I know,' she said, wiping her eyes.

'There's 'owt we can do about it, is there?'

'No.'

There was a long silence, interrupted by tinny laughter from Edward's television in the background.

'Oh well, I just wanted to check on you, lass, and wish you goodnight.'

'Thank you.'

'Merry Christmas. I'll phone you soon.'

'Merry Christmas,' she said. The laughter on his television cut out, and Erika was back in the silence of her flat, the snow against the windows. She closed the curtains and flicked on the lights. Her phone rang again. This time it was Kay.

'Sorry it's late, ma'am, but I found something on Joseph Pitkin's phone, amongst the files.'

'That's okay. You're still working?' asked Erika, impressed.

'I was just going over the downloaded files, and I found some files on the hard drive which had been deleted. I managed to recover some of them. They're troubling.'

'Pornography?'

'No. Pictures and video of Joseph. I'm sending them over now.'

Erika came off the phone and opened the email. There were six photos. Joseph was naked, lying on his back, and fastened with leather straps to a wooden table, by his neck, arms and thighs. His eyes were bloodshot and wide with fear. The hand of an unknown man gripped him by the throat, making the tendons on his neck strain. Erika clicked on the video file. It showed the same scene as the photos, and looked like it was filmed with a mobile phone.

'Please, please! Let me go. I won't say anything. I won't tell!' Joseph pleaded, wincing up at the bright light on the phone camera.

'You won't tell. Do you want this video sent to all the people you know?' said a voice. It had been electronically distorted. The hand appeared and grasped Joseph's genitals, and he screamed out as the hand twisted them. 'I have your address,' said the voice. 'I have your phone. You say anything, I send this to everyone in your contacts... Friends. Family. Everyone.'

The camera angle jolted, and moved to show a table with a row of sex toys. The disembodied hand picked up the largest, and went back to Joseph, who tried to close his legs, but they were spread and strapped to the table.

'NO!' he screamed. 'NO!'

Erika muted the sound, and had to force herself to watch the rest of the video.

CHAPTER THIRTEEN

Erika arrived at Lewisham Row police station just after 8 a.m. The construction work around the centre of Lewisham, which had started when Erika was first assigned to South London, was almost complete. Several high-rise blocks of luxury apartments now dwarfed the eight-storey police station. The cranes were still on the snowy morning, and on one there was a Christmas tree, lit up.

It had been a sleepless night. The images of Joseph had haunted her dreams. In the photos, he appeared to be a victim, but she needed to question him about his role in Marissa Lewis's murder, and there was still so much information she didn't have: post-mortem results; DNA; the murder weapon hadn't been found. Erika felt uncomfortable about it, but the photos of Joseph could be used as leverage.

At 9 a.m., Joseph was brought into Interview Room 1 by two uniformed officers. He wasn't cuffed. He looked pale, and had dark circles under his eyes. A bleary-eyed solicitor in an expensive pinstripe suit filed in with him. He didn't seem happy that he'd been called in to work on Boxing Day. He introduced himself as Henry Chevalier, and sat next to Joseph.

Erika sat on the opposite side of the table with an equally tired-looking McGorry, who Joseph eyeballed with hatred.

'It's 9.04 a.m. on December 26th, 2017,' said Erika. 'Present for the interview is DCI Erika Foster, DI John McGorry, Joseph Pitkin and his legal representation, Henry Chevalier.'

Henry leaned over and whispered something in Joseph's ear. He didn't react, but nodded. Erika opened one of the grey cardboard files she had stacked on the table and took out hard copies of the photos which had been developed from the roll of film.

'Joseph. Can you tell me if you took these photos?' She spread them out across the table. For a split second, Joseph's eyes registered shock, then he sat back and folded his arms.

'My client has chosen not to answer this,' said Henry.

Erika went on, 'This is from a roll of undeveloped film in a small plastic tube we found in the alleyway behind your parents' garden. I believe it fell out of your pocket when you climbed over the wall.' Joseph crunched up his face in a scowl. 'We lifted prints from it. A thumb and forefinger, and they match yours. I'll ask you again. Did you take these photos?'

Joseph looked at Henry, who nodded.

'Yeah, I took them.'

'Photos of a dead body,' said Erika.

'We can see the photos,' said Henry. Erika picked up one, a close-up of Marissa's blood-spattered face, her eyes wide. Frozen with fear.

'This photo is taken from high up, in the tree opposite Marissa's house.' Erika held it up to Joseph and he looked away. 'You'll see her skirt is down over her thighs.' She picked up another. 'But in this photo, taken up close, her dress has been lifted to expose her underwear. Did you touch the body, Joseph?' He shook his head. 'We've also recovered videos from your mobile phone, which show you had quite an unhealthy obsession with Marissa Lewis. You filmed her covertly when she was in her bedroom, and on one occasion when she had sex with another man.'

Joseph was now shaking, and his face had drained of blood.

'I didn't kill her.'

'What did you do, then?' asked McGorry, sitting back and folding his arms. 'Have a fiddle with her as she lay dead? You took the opportunity to dip your fingers into her knickers when she wasn't able to object?'

'Officers, I would appreciate a more respectful line of questioning,' said Henry.

Erika gathered up the photos and put them away. She opened another cardboard file. 'I have your PNC record. You served six weeks in a youth detention centre when you were fourteen. You attacked a boy at school with a broken bottle. The surgeon managed to save his eye.'

Erika held up the photo of a young, dark-haired boy from the file. An ugly purple line of stitches ran from his left eyebrow and across his eyelid.

'I was defending myself. He hit me,' said Joseph.

'Then why not hit him back? Instead, you smashed a glass bottle and ground it into his face. Bit of a psycho thing to do,' said McGorry.

'Can I ask if you are planning to charge my client?' said Henry. 'And if so, what are you planning to charge him with? He served his time for what he did. He also has an alibi for the time when Marissa Lewis was killed.'

'From his mum and dad,' said Erika.

'My client's father is a former Queen's Counsel with an impeccable reputation. He states that Joseph was at home all night and didn't leave the house until the next morning.'

'Do they all sleep in the same bedroom?'

'That's a ridiculous question.'

'Is it? The murder scene was less than two minutes from Joseph's house. He's already shown that he likes to hop over the back wall. He could have made it there and back in a very short space of time.'

'*Could* being the operative word. Detectives, do you have any concrete evidence?'

'We have taken DNA samples from the victim's body. I also have officers searching the Pitkin house. It's just a matter of time,' said Erika.

'Yes, eleven hours and counting.'

'I have the right to extend custody for another two days.'

'I would advise against that,' said Henry softly, with a steely sense of finality. His eyes bore down at her from across the table.

'Is that a threat?'

'Of course not,' he said, with a fake smile. 'Do you think I would threaten you, in a room full of cameras, where a transcript of our conversation is being recorded? Are you, DCI Foster, feeling paranoid?'

'No. It's probably just caffeine withdrawal.' She smiled.

'Our coffee machine is on the blink,' said McGorry. 'Whatever button you press, oxtail soup comes out.'

Henry rolled his eyes. 'How is this relevant?'

They ignored him. McGorry looked at Erika. She pulled the third and final cardboard folder from the pile, and took out the photos of Joseph, naked and strapped to the table, and a still image from the video file. She lay them out on the table and they both sat back.

They weren't prepared for the reaction. What little colour Joseph had left drained from his face, and his hands started to shake uncontrollably.

'Hang on. Why weren't these photos disclosed to me?' said Henry.

'We recovered these photos and an explicit video file from your mobile phone, Joseph,' said Erika. 'Who is the person who did this to you? Did he send you the files?'

Joseph shook his head and stood up, his chair crashing back onto the floor. He vomited spectacularly across the table. Erika just managed to pull two of the folders out of the way, and they all leapt back.

'Christ!' shouted Henry, recoiling at the pile of saturated paperwork he held, before dropping it onto the floor.

Joseph stood very still, and hunched forward, a long line of drool hanging from his mouth. They all stood in shocked silence. Suddenly, he lunged at Erika, screaming with bared teeth.

'You fucking bitch!' he spat as McGorry held him back, pinning his arms to his sides. 'Where did you get them? How? How did you get them? He's nothing to do with this! NOTHING! He'll kill me!'

'Who? Who will kill you?' said Erika, pivoting out of the way as Joseph kicked out at her. 'We need some help in here!' she shouted, turning to the camera mounted in the corner of the interview room. Seconds later, two uniformed officers came rushing in, and they helped to pull Joseph towards the door. 'Who? Who will kill you? Give me his name and all this will be over.' Joseph was dragged out of the interview room, kicking and shouting. 'Give me his name, I can protect you!' The door slammed.

'Boss,' said McGorry, putting a hand on her arm. 'The interview's over.'

Erika looked at McGorry and the solicitor, and the mess across the table, and she came back to her senses.

'Yes.'

'Jesus Christ,' said Henry, picking up his bag from the corner of the room, and seeing where he'd been caught with vomit on the sleeve of his jacket. 'Jesus fucking Christ!' And he left. Erika and McGorry stood in shock.

'We know one thing for sure. He had a big Christmas lunch,' said McGorry, wrinkling his nose.

CHAPTER FOURTEEN

Erika and McGorry were joined in the corridor outside the interview room by Kay, who had been watching from the observation suite next door. She had with her a bunch of paper towels.

'What the hell just happened in there?' asked McGorry, taking one and dabbing at the sleeve of his suit. 'Yuck, this is all I need today.' He gingerly took off his jacket.

'I got to him. I hit a nerve,' said Erika. She absently took the offered paper towels, and saw she had managed to remain unscathed.

'We don't know that those photos and the video have anything to do with the Marissa Lewis case. This looks like revenge porn,' said Kay.

'I've got to get rid of this jacket, I won't be a sec, Boss,' said McGorry, holding his jacket between thumb and finger and hurrying off.

'Revenge porn is about scorned lovers, and exposing. No. Whoever it is on that video is blackmailing him not to talk,' said Erika.

'We can't use past trauma as leverage.'

'I was so bloody close.'

'How? How can we be close to something completely in the dark to us, ma'am?'

Erika turned to her. 'You need to make sure that interview room is cleaned properly,' she said, handing back the paper towel. 'And don't call me ma'am.'

*

Erika came back up to her office. She put in calls to Isaac, and forensics, but they both told her they wouldn't be able to come back with anything until the next day. She then called the officer who was following up on the house-to-house in Coniston Road, and he told her that the two men who had been involved with Marissa, Don Walpole and Ivan Stowalski, had still not been made contact with. He did, however, have the contact details for Marissa's friend, Sharon-Louise Braithwaite, who worked at the hair salon. Erika thanked him and wrote down the number. She was about to call her when there was a knock at her door.

'What?'

It opened and McGorry stuck his head round.

'Alright, Boss. The doc has examined Pitkin. There's nothing wrong with him physically. Blood pressure okay, temperature okay, no infection, but he's recommended to the custody sergeant that Pitkin gets a couple of hours' rest and the chance to calm down before we attempt to interview him again. He's still in quite a state.'

Erika looked at her watch. It was coming up to midday.

'I've got five hours before I have to decide whether or not to keep him in custody for another couple of days. I'm no closer to being able to charge him… You know you can come into my office; you don't have to hang around in the doorway!' she snapped. McGorry came inside and shut the door behind him.

'Okay, direct question. Do you think he did it?'

McGorry shrugged. 'I dunno if he's got it in him. The person who did it went batshit crazy. Hacking at her with a knife. They would have been covered in blood. And what about the trail of blood from the crime scene? He doesn't have a car. We haven't found a murder weapon.'

'Who do you think is blackmailing him with the photos?'

'Could be a man or a woman. Judging from his reaction, I think it's a man. You can see in the photos that he's not a willing participant, or if he was at the beginning, he wasn't by the time he was strapped in and naked. He was being overpowered physically. He looks terrified. And of course, he yakked all over the interview room when he saw we had the photos and video.'

'He could have been working as a rent boy,' said Erika. 'No, the family is well off.'

'He was signing on at the Jobcentre.'

'There's too many questions surrounding him, and you're right, he did look frightened in the video. We should tread carefully. Whoever this person is, they have the power to terrify him.'

CHAPTER FIFTEEN

Four floors down, in the custody suite, Joseph lay on the single bunk in the harsh light of the cell, staring at the tiny window. His face was ashen, and he was almost catatonic with fear. He had been checked over by a doctor, cleaned up, and put back in his cell. He wore dark jeans, ripped at each knee, and a thick dark sweater. His belt and shoes had been taken from him.

He could hear voices echoing in the corridor. A group of young lads had been arrested and brought in, and were making a noise, shouting and swearing at the custody sergeant.

How did they get those photos? he thought. *I deleted them. He told me if I kept my mouth shut, no one would see them.*

Joseph saw the face of the man he knew as 'T': a wide, handsome face with a high forehead. Piercing eyes. He had thought they were friends, and T had trusted him enough to show him what he kept in the basement.

'This is where I play,' he'd said.

The basement was dark, with a low ceiling and bare, stained concrete floors. The air was hot and stank of sweat. There were wooden stocks, a cage and leather restraints. Pornography, cut out from magazines, covered the walls. Joseph wasn't shocked by the nudity or sex. What chilled him were the faces of the women and men in the pictures who were being dominated. There was genuine fear in their eyes, and some of them were bleeding.

'Are they real?' he'd asked.

T had nodded, smoothing his hands over his crotch, and he came towards Joseph.

'I have to go,' Joseph had said, making a dash for the door.

'Stay for one more drink,' said T, reaching out and grabbing the back of Joseph's shirt, catching the material in a powerful grip. Joseph, eager not to appear scared, and to diffuse the situation, said yes. That last drink had been spiked, and he'd woken up naked, and tied up. Unable to move.

He didn't know how long it had lasted. The fear that he was going to die had been bad enough, but looking into the eyes of a person who ignored your screams, who seemed to get excited by your pain, was terrifying. The final image that burned into his mind was of the gas mask. He could still smell it, the filthy sweat mingled in with rubber and amyl nitrate.

He was strangled to the point of unconsciousness several times and woke up as T was reviving him with mouth-to-mouth. He didn't remember the photos being taken, but he remembered the video… The bright light from the phone camera. He'd got them in an email a day later, with a note:

I have these photos locked away. So long as you keep your mouth shut, they'll stay that way.
T.

And now the police knew, and if the police knew they would follow it up. Did they have the note too? Would they tell his parents, and who else would find out? Joseph put his hands between his thighs and began to sob and rock himself. Blind terror flashed through his body again and he retched, but there was nothing left to come up, just bile. He reached up to wipe his mouth and his fingers caught on the rip in the left knee of his jeans.

He jumped as the hatch opened and the noise at the end of the corridor became clearer. The lads were still shouting, but now from inside their cells.

'You alright, lad?' came the custody sergeant's voice. Joseph turned on the bed and looked over, making himself nod. The hatch slammed shut again, and the shouting receded a little. Joseph set to work with his fingers, widening the tear in the knee of his trousers and tearing off a long strip of the material.

*

The commotion had died down outside the cells, and all the men in custody were locked up when the custody sergeant did his next check on Joseph Pitkin fifteen minutes later. When he opened the hatch, he couldn't see where he had gone, as the single bed was empty.

'Son, you alright?' he asked, shining the torch over the steel toilet and sink in the far corner. The hatch was high up on the door, so when he saw the piece of material hooked into the tiny joint which made up the hinge of the hatch, he panicked. He reached a hand inside and felt the thin line of taut material and then the top of Joseph Pitkin's head. 'Shit! Shit!' he cried. He ran back down the corridor to the desk, and hit the emergency alarm. It rang out, echoing along the corridor as he grabbed the keys and ran back to the door. Once he had it unlocked, he had to push against the weight of the body against it. His colleague, a female officer in her mid-fifties, came running down to help him as he got the door open, then pulled it back. Joseph hung from the back of the door, a couple of feet off the floor, suspended by his neck with a strip of denim. His face was bright purple, and his eyes were wide open and bloodshot. 'Get him down, quick, get him down!' he cried. The female officer had thought to grab a pair of scissors, and she cut the improvised noose. The custody sergeant lay Joseph down and loosened the strip of material. His colleague didn't say anything as he started to perform CPR, continuing for several minutes, pumping Joseph's chest and blowing into his mouth at intervals.

She knew that he was dead. She had seen it so many times before.

CHAPTER SIXTEEN

Superintendent Melanie Hudson stood at just over five foot, with short blonde hair and soft grey eyes, but her eyes and elfin frame belied a steely determination.

She was settling down for an afternoon of television and a box of chocolates with her husband and young son when the call came through that a young man had died in custody at her police station.

She drove straight to Lewisham Row, and was able to attend the scene as Joseph Pitkin's body was taken out. She heard statements from the two custody officers, and then she came up to her office. When she rounded the corner into the corridor, she found Erika waiting on the chair outside.

'Have you been sitting here in the dark?' she said, reaching up and flicking on the lights with her elbow.

'It helps me think.'

She put down her bag and unlocked the office door. Erika followed her inside.

'Start from the beginning, and tell me everything,' she said, indicating the seat opposite her desk.

Erika outlined everything that had happened with Joseph, from when she was first on the scene at Coniston Road, discovering him watching the crime scene, and the subsequent arrest when they found the photos and video.

'I'll need to review all video that you have from formal interviews. I also want a full written report from you. And from McGorry. Is there anything you want to tell me?'

Erika looked at the floor.

'Joseph's father is a retired barrister... When we chased him, at the end of the chase, McGorry got involved in a tussle – well, a fight – with him. He was trying to stop him getting away... He held him by the strap that was around his neck.'

'Define "held"?' said Melanie.

'The father, David Pitkin, said that he thought it was a chokehold.'

'Was it a chokehold?'

'It was in the heat of the moment. Joseph was throwing punches, he was on top of McGorry. John was acting in self-defence.'

'But was it a chokehold?'

Erika scratched her head. 'Yes. Bloody hell, yes.'

'For how long?'

'I don't know. A few seconds, ten seconds.'

'You understand that there will be a full investigation as to why Joseph Pitkin hung himself. He was on suicide watch.'

'Why are suicide watch checks every fifteen minutes? A lot can be achieved in fifteen minutes. He tore off strips of his jeans, for God's sake!' Erika wiped tears away from her cheeks. She sat up and took a tissue. 'I want to inform the parents.'

'No. That's not a good idea.'

'He was in custody because of me.'

'He was in custody because you had compelling evidence to arrest and question him. You have also had conflict with the family; they need someone impartial. I will go and inform them with a family liaison officer.'

'I wasn't aware he had any mental health issues. I don't have his medical records, but he was examined by a doctor after our first, explosive interview, and the doctor was satisfied that he could be interviewed again, after a break. We didn't get that far. He was a key part of my investigation...'

'Okay. I need you to take the rest of the day off,' said Melanie.

'I'm off the case?'

'No. I need to look over the interview footage, and I need to talk to the custody sergeant, and the arresting officers. I also need a written statement from you with all the details. I also want to talk to McGorry.'

Erika got up. 'Okay.'

'Just hold on, sit down.'

Erika sat back in her seat.

'What?'

'I'm going to say something you're not going to like, but I want you to hear me out.'

'Yes?'

'You've been through a lot this year, Erika. It's barely a week since you came off the murder-kidnap case.'

'It's ten days…' Erika closed her eyes. It had been a harrowing case, involving a young couple, Nina Hargreaves and Max Hastings, who had committed a string of murders and robberies across London. The press, inevitably, had made a Bonnie and Clyde-style story out of it, and then Commander Marsh had made a fateful statement to the press, denouncing the two killers.

Marsh had thought he had been smart, giving them an ultimatum, but what he'd given them instead was a face and a name. It hadn't taken long for Nina and Max to dig around in his personal life, and discover that Marsh's wife came from a wealthy family, and that they had two young daughters.

They'd attacked Marcie when she was at home alone, and Nina Hargreaves had duped the nursery into thinking that she was the girls' new nanny. This was when the case escalated to a full-blown kidnapping. Against all advice, Marsh and Marcie had paid a ransom of £200,000 – but it had only ended when Erika had managed to track Nina and Max down to where the twins were being held in a remote location on Dartmoor, in the south of England.

The subsequent bloodbath, where Max and Nina had turned on each other, was still imprinted on Erika's mind. She'd rescued the twins, who were physically unhurt, but the emotional scars would take a long time to heal.

'Erika! Erika!'

She opened her eyes. Melanie was looking at her with concern. 'What happened there?'

'Sorry. I'm tired, and still a bit shocked. Not only is it tragic when someone so young takes his own life – he was a key witness.'

Melanie took out her wallet and removed a card, handing it to Erika.

'Dr G Priestley. Clinical Psychologist,' she read, looking up at Melanie. 'Is this for me?'

'Yes.'

'You think I'm crazy? Unbalanced?'

Melanie put up her hand. 'No, I don't. And before we go any further, I want to add that Dr Priestley is my doctor. I see him once a week.'

'Therapy?'

'Yes.'

Erika didn't know what to say, and she looked down at the card again.

'What is this? A referral? I come off another successful case and stop two multiple murderers and rescue the daughters of the borough commander, and I'm not congratulated, I'm put in therapy?'

'Erika. No. This is me talking to you as a friend, or a colleague, privately. This is nothing to do with the Met, or any case, or the suicide of Joseph Pitkin. You are one of my finest officers, and I am confident that you will be back shortly and continuing work on this murder case, but this is what I want from you. It's my duty to report if any of my officers are struggling with the pressures of work.'

'You're going to report me?'

'No! Listen to what I'm saying, you bloody idiot!'

Erika looked up at her and smiled.

'Sorry…' started Melanie.

'No, it's okay. I'll take being called a bloody idiot over bullshit corporate language…' She held up the card. 'This is your therapist?'

'Yeah.'

'Do you mind me asking why you…?'

Melanie took a deep breath and sat back.

'My first pregnancy was twins. I carried them to full term, had the baby shower, had the excited family and husband waiting in the delivery room to hold our babies… They were both stillborn.' She took a deep breath and wiped a tear from her eye. 'The doctors didn't know why. I have no family history of stillbirth. It was a textbook pregnancy. The lack of reasons why it happened were devastating. I lost my faith, and I almost lost everything else. It almost destroyed me.'

'I'm so sorry. When was this?'

'Ten years ago, but it was a long journey to come back to normality. Of course, I never think I'll come fully back from that place, but life is good now. So, I'm talking to you as a friend, with no judgement. Don't crash and burn, Erika. The job isn't worth that much. I don't want to tell you how to live your life, but I am not against you. As I said, you are one of my best officers and I want you to stay that way. I want you to go on and keep doing what you're doing, but you need to make sure you are in the right frame of mind.'

Erika looked down at the card again. 'Can I think about it?'

'Sure, just don't think about it for too long. In the meantime, go home and get some sleep. I'll call you. And send in McGorry.'

Erika came out of the office, and closed the door. McGorry and the custody sergeant were both waiting on chairs in the corridor. They both looked in shock.

'How did it go?' asked McGorry, blowing out his cheeks.

'OK. Just tell the truth, as it happened. I had to mention the chokehold on Joseph. I said it was in self-defence. I'll be putting it all in my report.'

'Jeans, his jeans,' muttered the custody sergeant, shaking his head in disbelief.

'You did your job,' said Erika.

'It's not enough, though,' he replied.

She briefly put her hand on his arm, and nodding goodbye, she left the station. When she got into her car, she saw that the Christmas presents for the twins were still on the back seat. She started the car and headed for Commander Marsh's house.

CHAPTER SEVENTEEN

Marsh lived on a smart road of large detached houses near Hilly Fields, which had a stunning view of the London skyline. The sun came out just as Erika found a parking spot outside, and it gave the snowy streets a golden hue. She hoped the Marshes were out, so she could leave the presents on the porch, but when she got to the front door she could hear the television blaring. She took a deep breath and grasped the large iron door knocker. It crashed loudly against the wood.

A moment later, Marsh opened the door. He was a handsome man in his mid-forties with short-cropped blond hair. He looked pale and drawn, and like he'd lost a lot of weight.

'Erika,' he said, surprised. She held up the presents.

'I know I'm a day late, but I wanted to give these to the girls, and apologise for my no-show.'

Marsh went to say something, but Marcie appeared in the hall behind.

'You made it. Merry Christmas,' she said, giving Erika a hug. 'How are you?'

Marcie was a beautiful woman, but she too had lost too much weight. Her usually glossy black hair was long and lank, and she wore heavy pale make-up, which didn't quite disguise the two black eyes and swelling from the broken nose, still healing after the attack.

'I'm fine,' said Erika, feeling awkward. She and Marcie went back a long way. They'd never had an easy relationship, until Erika had rescued her two small daughters.

'Come on, inside, out of the cold,' Marcie said, rubbing Erika's shoulders. 'That coat isn't very thick; you need more than a leather jacket in this weather!'

They took her through to the living room, which was stiflingly hot. An open fire was blazing, and next to it was a huge Christmas tree. Marcie's father, Leonard, was snoozing in an armchair in one corner, and Marsh's father, Alan, was asleep in another armchair by the tree.

'Do sit down,' said Marcie. 'I'm just putting out a buffet lunch. I've got cold meats and cheeses, and some broccoli and stilton soup.'

'Lovely,' said Erika.

'Can we get you a drink? Champagne?' said Marsh.

'Paul, keep your voice down. They're sleeping!' scolded Marcie in a stage whisper.

'My voice is the same level as yours,' he hissed.

'No, you were bloody loud… Come and help with the food. Do excuse us, Erika.'

They left the room. Erika looked over at the two old men, red-faced and snoozing. Marcie's dad, Leonard, was tanned and well-dressed in casual blue slacks and a checked shirt with a cravat. Alan was scruffier, in old jeans and a yellow woollen jumper. Leonard shifted in his chair, coughed, and sat up, taking a moment to get his bearings. With an almost comic double take he noticed Erika.

'Hello.'

'Hello.'

'I know you, don't I? You're that lady police officer,' he said. His voice was posh and plummy. 'Ulrika, isn't it?'

'Erika Foster, Detective Chief Inspector.'

He got up awkwardly and came over and held out his hand, smiling. His false teeth looked unnaturally white against his tanned skin. She took it and they shook, and then he swooped in and kissed her on both cheeks.

'We're very grateful for what you did, for Paul and Marcie, and the twins. Thank you,' he said, continuing to pump her hand.

'I was just doing my job.'

'Bloody awful business. I saw the news report; they had to blur out the pictures of Max Hastings's body.'

'Yes…'

Leonard was still shaking her hand.

'Paul tells me the girl fired a distress flare at him – blew his whole head open, brains all over the place? Do you think the twins saw it?'

'Yes, I do think so.'

'My grandfather survived the trenches during the First World War. He had shell shock, of course. He remembered young lads having the backs of their heads blown off by shrapnel fire… Course, these days we're all encouraged to have therapy; back then they suffered in silence…'

Alan woke up. He took a moment to come around, and smacked his lips and rubbed his eyes. He was an older version of Marsh, with a craggy face and full head of short-cropped grey hair.

'Alan, this is Ulrika, the police officer who caught those murdering bastards!'

'Hello, it's Erika,' she said, pulling her hand away from Leonard's grip.

'Ulrika… That's a Swedish name. Did you used to do the weather?' asked Alan, with dead-pan seriousness.

'The weather?'

'Poor old git is losing his marbles,' murmured Leonard, tapping the side of his head.

'I heard that!' said Alan. 'Is she the district nurse?'

Thankfully, Marsh came back into the room with a tray of champagne.

'Dad, this is Erika. Erika Foster. We trained together in Manchester,' he said. Alan nodded, but looked none the wiser.

'Were you at lunch? Was she at lunch, Paul?'

'No dad, Erika has just arrived,' said Marsh, speaking slowly and loudly. There was an awkward silence. Leonard picked up the remote and switched on the TV. There was a cacophony of noise as *The Sound of Music* came on the screen. The von Trapp children were marching down the stairs. 'Let's go through to the kitchen,' Marsh added in a low voice. Erika smiled at the two old men, now engrossed in the film.

'Sorry about that. Dad's getting a bit confused. It's been quite a frustrating Christmas. I keep having to repeat everything,' said Marsh as they went along the hall and into the kitchen. 'Leonard's fine, he just doesn't listen. He's in his own world.'

'Who doesn't listen?' asked Marcie as they came into the kitchen. She was laying out a beautiful buffet on the long kitchen table.

'Your father.'

'At least my father knows what day it is.'

'That's a bit harsh,' snapped Marsh.

'It's an observation. He should be in a home. It's been very stressful having him here. There's nothing wrong with my father. If you remember, he won Trivial Pursuit yesterday.'

Erika looked down at her champagne glass, wanting to be out of the firing line.

'I'm not saying he's going the same way as mine. I'm saying he's bull-headed, and the way he talks to your mother…'

'My mother can be just as bad.'

'Why else did she go out today? I wish I'd gone out!'

Marcie looked at him. She had tears in her eyes.

'Maybe I should go,' said Erika.

'No, please stay,' said Marcie, dabbing at her eyes with tissue. Marsh stood beside her, trying to control his anger.

Sophie and Mia came into the kitchen, breaking the mood. They were two tiny, identical four-year-olds, dressed in matching purple velvet dresses with thick cream tights and pink hairbands in their long dark hair. They saw Erika and wordlessly came to her and gave her a hug. Erika put her glass down and crouched to hug the two little girls, smelling their hair against her cheek. In the warm, bright kitchen, what had happened all seemed surreal, and so long ago.

'We're so pleased to see you,' said Sophie, taking the lead.

'I'm pleased to see you, too,' said Erika. They all looked at each other. Mia nodded solemnly; her big brown eyes were so expressive. Erika felt rotten that she had missed coming for lunch the day before.

'I brought you both presents. They're a bit late, but Merry Christmas.' She gave the two bags to the girls, and they pulled out the wrapped gifts and tore off the paper excitedly. The first was a Blingles Glimmer Studio Sticker Maker set, and the second was a Fashion Headbands set, with options to make your own hairbands in different colours and with flowers and glitter. 'I got two different things, but I remembered how much you two like to share,' said Erika.

Both girls had genuine faces of wonderment and excitement.

'Oh. Girls, what do you say to Erika?' said Marcie.

'Thank you, Erika!' they both said.

'You didn't already get them for Christmas? My niece and nephew are around your age, and they said these were really good presents.'

'No, we haven't got them, and they are the best presents, EVER!' cried Mia, giving her another hug.

The girls looked up at Marcie. 'Mummy, get the thing,' said Sophie. Marcie went to the kitchen counter and picked up a small gift-wrapped box. She handed it to Sophie, then Mia grabbed the corner and they both handed it to Erika.

'We got this for you,' said Mia.

Erika pulled the paper off a small jewellery box. When she opened it, inside there was a necklace with a small silver cross.

Marcie took the box and undid the necklace, and Mia lifted the short hair at the back of Erika's head so that they could put it on.

'This is a beautiful gift,' said Erika to the girls, then looking up at Marcie and Marsh. They smiled. The twins then pulled out two new iPhones from the pockets of their dresses, and with their tiny hands they expertly swiped through their screens.

'These were presents from Mummy and Daddy,' said Sophie. 'They want us to be in contact with them, always, because of what happened.'

They held their phones up to Erika and showed her the picture they'd taken of her in the necklace. She looked gaunt and almost translucent; against the white fridge, she was so pale.

'You look pretty,' said Sophie.

'But you look like you could do with some food,' said Mia. Luckily, this broke the atmosphere and they all laughed.

'Girls, go and wash your hands,' said Marcie.

Erika waited until the girls had left the room. 'How are they doing?' she asked.

Marcie and Marsh looked at each other. 'Surprisingly good, all things considering,' said Marcie. 'Sophie is much stronger. She's been the one who looks after Mia.'

'They keep disappearing off into corners to talk to each other in their own made-up language,' said Marsh.

'There's no manual for what to do. I'm taking them to see a therapist in the new year,' said Marcie.

'How are you both doing?' asked Erika. They looked at each other, as if seeing that they were a couple for the first time. They hesitated.

'Taking each day as it comes,' said Marsh, and he patted Marcie on the leg. She twisted out of his way.

'Come on, let's eat,' she said.

*

Erika drove home later that evening. The gift from the girls brought her great comfort, and she kept reaching up to touch it on her neck. For once, she was relieved to come home to an empty flat. The atmosphere at Marsh's had been so hostile, and despite the size of the house, it had seemed claustrophobic with all their guests.

Erika was just pouring herself a vodka over ice when her phone rang. It was Melanie.

'I've been through everything to do with Joseph Pitkin, and at this stage, I can only say it was a tragic accident.'

'Okay. Did you tell his parents?'

'Yes. As expected, they were devastated.'

'Do they blame me?'

Melanie sighed. 'I'm not going to answer that. But they obviously see this whole situation very differently.'

'Did you ask them about the photos and the note from the person called T?'

'No, Erika. I didn't…' Melanie was silent on the end of the phone for a moment. 'I do need you back at work tomorrow, though. I'm giving you a bigger team for the Marissa Lewis murder case. Get a good night's sleep.'

When Melanie had hung up, Erika went to the living room window. The lights were out, and she stared at the dark snowy street. A fox moved into the glare of the orange streetlight, pausing with its feet in the snow, its sleek body rippling under the light. It was waiting, checking out her building and whether it could ransack the dustbins. Erika watched from the shadows.

'Come on. It's safe, make a dash for it,' she said. The fox crept forward slowly into the car park, past the white humps of the snow-covered cars, towards the rubbish bins, which were no doubt groaning with leftover food. 'That's it.'

There was a creak from upstairs and a light went on in the window, illuminating a large square of the dark car park. The fox turned and dashed off, disappearing into the shadows.

CHAPTER EIGHTEEN

Dark winter nights in the suburbs of London were always exciting for the man who liked to call himself 'T'. He would leave the house under cover of darkness, dressed in black, with the leather gas mask stowed in one of the large pockets of his long coat.

The sprawl of South London stretched for miles, and every time he felt lucky to find an area he had never seen before amongst the rows upon rows of terraced houses, dark alleyways, small tucked-away parks and scrubland. The suburban areas of South London were mostly free of CCTV cameras. The train stations only had them in the lit areas.

He believed his face was the true mask. It was an ordinary face, not quite the guy next door, but acceptable enough. In all the months he had been doing this, the only mug shot the police had was of the gas mask.

It always struck him how little people noticed in plain sight. Commuters were experts at not seeing. They just wanted to get to work and were eager to return home. They rarely engaged. Eyes blinkered. Almost afraid that they might have to get involved with the world around them. The unemployed, the drunkards, and the homeless were the ones you had to watch out for. They were differently tuned to their surroundings, and not just passing through from A to B. They were stuck in plain sight, forced to conjure the tools for their survival from a barren landscape. They were the expert watchers, instantly aware of who they could squeeze some change or a spare cigarette out of, and who wanted drugs.

The good news for T was that no one took any notice of the homeless. No one who mattered. It would have been far easier to pick off a homeless person. Offer them a few quid to follow him into a dark corner. For a fiver, he could do almost anything he wanted, depending on how desperate they were.

But that would be no fun. It was fear that he enjoyed, finding someone clean and upwardly mobile. Finding a nice, well-dressed, tax-paying pillar of society and ripping them out of their nice little bubble. There was always a look in their faces when he cornered them, as if to say: *This kind of thing doesn't happen to me. It happens to other people. Bad people. I'm good.*

The gas mask had its practical purpose, but it also added a sensory wow. The feel of the tight leather hood, the goaty smell of his own stale sweat, mixed with the smell of animal hide. The way the thick glass eyeholes distorted his vision, and slightly magnified the faces of his victims.

Tonight, he would just be a spectator. The snow added an extra layer of protection. Muffling sounds. He would watch and wait. He never knew their names, but he did like to crack their routines. That was another thrill. To work out when they left the house. What time they left for work, what time they came home. People could be such creatures of routine. Even at Christmas.

Learn their routine, and the rest was easy.

CHAPTER NINETEEN

The next morning, Erika arrived early at Lewisham Row, and went down to the tiny kitchenette on the ground floor, next to the cloakrooms used by uniform officers. She was staring at an open cupboard full of mugs when two young officers came in still wearing their stab vests.

'Morning, ma'am,' they said in unison. They looked surprised to see her.

'Morning. What's the cup situation? Do these belong to anyone?'

The young man, who was shorter than Erika, reached up and took out two mugs, handing one to the young woman, who seemed embarrassed to make eye contact.

'No one uses the flowery ones, ma'am,' he said. Erika took one out of the cupboard, and there was an awkward silence as the kettle came to the boil then clicked off. No one moved.

'Go on, go first; you've earned it,' she said. The young man spooned coffee from a large catering tin and filled their mugs. 'Was it a rough night?'

He nodded. 'The usual nightmare around kicking-out time from the pubs. The young teenagers seem to get more drunk and abusive around holidays.'

'And we were called out three times by people who thought they'd seen the gas mask attacker,' said the woman.

'Gas mask attacker?' said Erika.

'Yeah. It's been in the local news in the past few weeks. You haven't heard?'

'No, I was pre-occupied with another case.'

A guy wearing a gas mask has been assaulting women and men. He likes to target train stations, early in the morning, or late, after the last train has gone.'

'How many victims?'

'Five, going back to the middle of November.'

'Does he rape them?'

'Not all of them. His first two victims were strangled until they passed out, and when they woke up he was gone. The local news put out an appeal for information yesterday morning, after a woman was attacked on Christmas Day, next to Sydenham train station.'

'She was less than a minute from her front door,' the man said.

'So we've had call-outs all night from people who think they've seen or heard something. They were all false alarms,' the woman added.

They took their tea and left. Detective Inspector Moss then came into the kitchen, wearing a huge winter coat. She was a short, solid woman. Her flame-red hair was dotted with melting snow, and her pale face was covered in a sea of freckles.

'Morning, Boss. How was your Christmas?' Moss undid the buttons on her coat and took out a mug.

'It was…'

'You worked, didn't you?'

Erika nodded. 'On the murder case I'm about to brief you about.'

'Did you get a nice lunch?'

Erika shook her head. 'I had my first, and last "Christmas dinner" sandwich.'

Moss pulled a face. 'I had my first and last Christmas pudding smoothie. And my brother Gary came to stay with his wife and kids.'

'How many?'

'He's just got the one wife.'

'Very funny.'

'Three kids.'

'Do they get on with Jacob?'

Moss rubbed her eyes and filled her cup with boiling water.

'Yeah, they just don't get on with each other, and they're at that age: seven, eight, and nine. It was pandemonium. Our house is too small. And during Christmas lunch, the kids asked about the L-word.'

'Lapland?' said Erika.

Moss grinned and stirred milk into her coffee. 'Ha, ha. No. Lesbians. Namely, me and Celia, why we are married, how we are married, and how we managed to give birth to Jacob. Celia managed that of course, but there were a million questions. We didn't even get around to telling the jokes inside the Christmas crackers. It was all fine, but not the conversation I expected to have.'

Erika went to say more, when a tall, handsome black officer came into the kitchen. He stopped when he saw Erika and Moss.

'Alright. Morning,' he said, recovering his composure. It was Detective Inspector Peterson.

Moss looked between Erika and Peterson, trying to work out what to say. 'Bloody hell. He's finally back at work!'

He nodded and flashed his warrant card, giving them a big grin which made his serious face goofy.

'You're looking much better,' said Erika. It was a surprise to see him. A nice surprise, she realised. 'Did you have a good Christmas break?'

'It wasn't a break really; it was more of a countdown so I could get back to work… It turned out to be… Well, it was one of the best Christmases ever.'

'Care to elaborate?' asked Erika, wondering if he had met someone else, and then wishing she hadn't asked.

'This is officially my first day back at work,' he said, changing the subject. There was an awkward silence.

'You've picked a good day. I'm briefing in five minutes down in the main incident room. Don't be late.' Erika picked up her mug and left.

*

Moss and Peterson stood in silence for a moment. Moss went to the door and checked Erika was out of earshot.

'Did you see her over Christmas?' she asked.

'No.'

'Are things going to be okay with you two? I can't be stuck in the middle of two of my favourite people.'

'Am I one of your favourite people?' he grinned.

'Sometimes. Depends. You should have called her on Christmas Day. I know you two have broken up, but she ended up working. She was meant to take the day off… You know she's a lonely old bird, and I mean that in the nicest sense. I invited her over to mine, but she didn't want to intrude.'

'I was going to go over and see her, and then something… happened,' said Peterson. 'I'm still trying to process it.' He smiled and shook his head.

'I can see by your face that it was something good?' said Moss.

He went to the door and closed it. 'Make me a cup of coffee, and I'll tell you,' he said.

CHAPTER TWENTY

The meeting was held in the largest incident room on the ground floor of the station.

Erika stood in front of a huge map of London, which was three metres square, the maze of roads blending under the North and South Circular and the M25 forming increasing circles around central London, and the thick blue lines of the River Thames snaking across the centre. Twenty officers and civilian support staff had been called to work on the Marissa Lewis case, and it was the first time since Christmas Day that they had all been called back to one place.

The team included officers Erika had worked with before: Sergeant Crane, a pleasant-faced officer with thinning sandy hair; Moss and Peterson, who she noted were still getting coffee; McGorry and Kay, who were sorting out their desks – they both nodded and smiled at Erika as she passed. Detectives Knight and Temple were working with PC Singh, a small and fiercely intelligent officer, to collate the information about the case onto the whiteboard.

Superintendent Hudson slipped into the briefing and closed the door, taking a position perching on a desk at the back. She nodded and smiled.

'Good morning, everyone,' started Erika. 'I hope you all had a good Christmas, and sadly it's over all too quickly…' She went to an ID picture of Marissa Lewis, taken from her passport. 'Twenty-two-year-old Marissa Lewis was murdered on the doorstep of her house on Coniston Road in South London. I'm still waiting on details of the post-mortem, but time of death has been estimated as late on Christmas Eve…' The door opened, and Moss and Peterson filed in, carrying their mugs of coffee. Moss mouthed an apology to Erika, so did Peterson, and they took their seats next to a photocopier underneath the long line of windows looking out over the corridor. 'Thanks for joining us. I didn't know it took that long for instant coffee to brew.'

'Sorry, Boss,' said Moss, looking mortified. Peterson stared down guiltily at his mug.

Erika went on, 'Marissa Lewis was slashed repeatedly with a sharp serrated blade.' Erika indicated the pictures on the white-board, the close-up photos taken of the injuries on the dead body. 'At this stage, we don't have a murder weapon. But we do know from early forensic reports from inside the house that the crime scene was confined to the area in the small front garden. There is no evidence of blood spatter, or Marissa's blood inside the house. We're also waiting on more detailed results from forensics, and on the post-mortem…'

'Does that rule out Marissa's mother being involved?' asked McGorry.

'No. It just means if she did kill Marissa, she would have cleaned herself up, and disposed of whatever she was wearing before going back into the house. No one is being ruled out this early in our investigations. Everyone is a suspect.'

Erika went on to explain everything that had happened with Joseph Pitkin, and his suicide the day before in custody. There was a moment of silence. Suicides in custody were a terrible reminder of how vulnerable prisoners could be.

'At this stage, we are still treating Joseph Pitkin as a person of interest to this case. I feel that we need to arm ourselves with more evidence before we ask his family for any more informa-tion. We have video and photo evidence, taken from his mobile phone, that he had some kind of relationship with the victim. On several occasions, mostly at night, he filmed her covertly, when she was at home, in her bedroom. I believe that at some point she became aware he was filming her. We need to establish if this was something she encouraged, or if there was a reason why she allowed him to film her. There is a video of Marissa having sexual intercourse with a man who matches the description of a neighbour called Don Walpole.'

Erika indicated some stills taken from the video, which were being pinned up to the board.

'Don Walpole is married, in his early fifties, and is believed to have had a relationship with Marissa when she was a teenager. He also lives on Coniston Road. Another neighbour, again from the same street, is Ivan Stowalski. He also was involved with Marissa in a sexual relationship. He is in his mid-thirties, Polish, but lives in the UK with his wife. Marissa was a burlesque dancer who performed in clubs around London. She was also a carer for an elderly lady, who lives in Hilly Fields, just around the corner…'

As Erika was talking, Detectives Knight and Temple were working with PC Singh to put up photos from the case files.

'Marissa's mother is also someone I would like us to look at closely. She told us that she sleeps upstairs in the back bedroom, and that this was where she slept on Christmas Eve. But when we looked round the house, we saw that the back bedroom hasn't been inhabited for some time. The bed was covered with old clothes and a layer of dust. We found bedding on the living room sofa, which is on the other side of the single-glazed and poorly-insulated window where Marissa was stabbed and killed.'

Erika paused and let everyone digest this. She went on, 'Christmas and Boxing Day have slowed things down, hampering our ability to do a house-to-house. Thank you to everyone here who talked to neighbours, but we are going to have to go back and do it all again. I'd like backgrounds on Marissa Lewis and the neighbours I've mentioned, and anyone else you discover who was part of her life. Friends, family, colleagues, burlesque clubs. We are still working on getting into her iPhone to access emails and social media. We've requested her phone records. A request was also put in yesterday for any CCTV footage covering the area around Coniston Road, and from Brockley train station. We need to know if she took the train home after her burlesque gig on Christmas Eve, which is the normal mode of transport she used. Sergeant Crane will now be tasked with delegating tasks. We need to go back to the beginning and we're playing catch up from the Christmas break.'

The room sprang to life, and Erika went over to Moss and Peterson.

'Sorry, again, Boss,' said Moss.

'Welcome back, James,' said Erika. She seemed to take him off-guard.

'Thanks,' he said, standing up.

Several other officers and support staff came and patted him on the back, and welcomed him back before they dispersed around the incident room.

'You look good. I mean, you've put a lot of weight back on,' Erika said, correcting herself. 'You look like your old self again.'

'I still need to put on a few more pounds,' he said, opening his jacket and hitching up his trousers. 'But I'm feeling back to normal.' He slapped his flat stomach.

'Leave it out, you're putting us all to shame!' grinned Crane, slapping his own beer belly.

'Speak for yourself!' said Moss, grabbing at her ample stomach. 'I'm just big boned.'

'Okay, okay you lot, let's focus. I figured that as you've only just returned to work, you'd want to stay desk-bound and ease yourself in?'

Peterson nodded. 'I'll need a new login for Holmes; I'm told mine is no longer active, cos I've been off for so long.'

'OK. Get Crane to put in a call about your login.' Erika smiled at him and he smiled back, their eyes locking for a moment. Then he looked away. 'Moss, I want you with me; James, I want you to work on building us a profile of Marissa Lewis, and work to untangle her life.'

He nodded and went off, leaving Erika with Moss, who had been watching her.

'What?'

'Nothing. Things seem cool between you, which is… Cool. Where are we going?'

'I want to talk to Marissa's best friend.'

CHAPTER TWENTY-ONE

Erika arranged to meet Sharon-Louise at the Brockley Jack pub, a little way down from the hair salon where she worked – which was still closed on the 27th of December. It was snowing again as they drove through Crofton Park, but the temperature had warmed up a bit, turning it to slush on the road. They passed the train station, a Co-Op and some shops, before seeing the sign for the Goldilocks Hair Salon.

'Why do hair salons always go for pun-tastic names?' asked Moss, peering in at the garish white-and-gold interior decor as they passed. 'When I was growing up, I used to go to "Herr Kutz", but the owner wasn't German. And during my training at Hendon, there was a "Curl up and Dye".'

'Is that relevant?'

'Don't you have that in Slovakia? Hairdresser names with puns?'

'No.'

'The clientele is often working class – nothing wrong with that, of course – but they're ladies who like to look after themselves. I bet it has lots of regulars who like a gossip, not like a central London stuck-up place.'

'You think this Sharon-Louise likes a gossip?'

'Hairdressers hear everything,' Moss said. 'Don't you end up saying far too much when you get your hair cut? I know I feel obliged to chat.'

'When I get my hair cut, which is not that often, I ask them not to talk to me,' said Erika.

'I bet you do,' muttered Moss with a grin.

Erika only noticed an old lady step off the pavement at the last minute and had to slam on the brakes, throwing them both forward. The car came to a screeching halt, less than a foot from the old lady, who, unfazed, continued to push her battered old shopping bag across the road. She had long grey hair, and for a moment Erika's heart quickened, thinking it was Elspeth Pitkin, but when the old lady turned she saw she was much older, with the compressed mouth of someone with no teeth.

'Jeez that was close,' said Moss.

The old lady reached the pavement on the other side, and stepped up. For a moment Erika saw Joseph, lying in his cell, the noose tight around his neck. His face waxy and swollen. There was a honk from behind.

'You okay?'

Erika nodded. They pulled into the car park of the Brockley Jack. At just after 10 a.m. it was empty, apart from a couple of cars.

It was quiet and warm inside the pub, apart from an old man sat up at the bar, watching the TV with a pint on the go. A large young girl sat tucked away in a corner booth. She waved, and they went over.

'Hi. I'm Sharon-Louise, but you can call me Sharon,' she said, getting up and shaking hands with them. She had long, sleek honey-blonde hair with streaks of pink, and wore a wraparound dress with a flower pattern. Her face was round and wide, and she wore a pair of small, round glasses. She had an orange juice on the table.

'You alright for a drink?' asked Moss.

'Yeah. I could murder some crisps… I don't mean… Oh shit, not murder.'

'It's okay,' said Moss. 'What flavour?'

'Tomato sauce or prawn cocktail,' she said. Erika asked for a juice and Moss went off.

'I didn't sleep last night, after hearing about Marissa.' Sharon took out a tissue and lifted up her glasses, dabbing delicately at her eyes.

Erika took the chair opposite. Moss returned a few minutes later with orange juices and crisps, and took the seat next to Sharon.

'Who told you about Marissa?' asked Erika.

'My mum got a phone call from someone she knows on Coniston Road... It's bad enough that I had to say goodbye to her, but I thought I'd see her again one day...'

She broke down, pulling out a scruffy ball of used tissue, lifting her glasses again to dab at her eyes.

'Sorry. It's just too much to believe... And look, everything is going on as normal. The Christmas decorations are still up, happy music is playing. Makes you think that no one cares... But that's life.'

'Why did you have to say goodbye to Marissa?'

Sharon reached forward and tore open the packet of crisps, spreading it out between them so they could share.

'She was going off to America.'

Erika and Moss exchanged a glance.

'When?'

'Tomorrow, it was supposed to be.' Her eyes welled up again and she pulled out the tissue.

'Where in America?' asked Moss.

'New York.'

'Why?'

'She was sick of it here. The weather. The way things work. "I'll always be scum," she used to say. She thought the odds stacked against her, not going to the right school or having money. She had dreams of being the next Dita Von Teese, and the burlesque scene in New York is huge. There's more opportunity in America. Hard work can actually get you somewhere over there. She wanted a new start.'

'Did she have a work permit?' asked Erika.

'No, she got a six-month tourist visa. Obviously, she was planning to work there, but gigs are often cash in hand. And she had Ivan.'

'Ivan Stowalski?'

Sharon nodded.

'What was Ivan going to do?'

'He was going with her. He works in pharmaceuticals, and he'd got a job out there.'

'This is the same Ivan Stowalski who's married and lives in Coniston Road?' asked Moss.

'Their marriage was over years ago. Ezra was living a separate life from him.'

'Did Ezra know?'

'He'd managed to keep a lot of it from her, according to Marissa. He's a bit wet. Spineless. I don't know how he holds down such a well-paid job managing loads of people, because in his personal life he's hopeless. They drove up north, late on Christmas Eve, to see Ezra's parents who now live in the UK. According to Marissa, he was going to tell Ezra when he was there, and then drive back... Well, today.'

Erika frowned.

'I know. Fucked up, isn't it?'

'How long was Marissa involved with Ivan?'

'A year. He'd been paying for lots of stuff for her: costumes, props. A lot of money. He got quite obsessed with her, and was needy.'

'How was he needy and obsessed?' asked Erika.

'He got very jealous about her doing her act. He always wanted to know if any blokes had spoken to her after the shows, and he would go and see her often, and sit on the front row, policing her show... Marissa was going to bin him, and then he told her about the New York thing and she saw it as an opportunity. He paid for everything.'

'What did her mother think?' asked Erika.

'Mandy. I don't know if Marissa even told her. They really don't get on. Didn't. Mandy's a mess. She's never had a proper job, and when Marissa was little she was always shacking up with random guys, getting drunk and doing drugs. Marissa had a pretty horrible childhood. She was taken into care twice, when she was ten and then twelve.'

'Why did Marissa stay living with her as an adult?'

Sharon shrugged.

'It's complicated. They had a bond. And they both claimed all the benefits they could. Mandy claims attendance allowance, disabled; Marissa was paid as her carer, and was signing on and getting housing and council tax...' Sharon furrowed her brow. 'Shit. I've just put Mandy in it.'

Erika waved it away.

'We're not investigating benefit fraud. How did they manage that, though? Living under the same roof, mother and daughter?'

'Marissa has her father's surname. Her mum is Mandy Trent.'

'Yes. Where is Marissa's father?'

'Long gone, when she was little. He was a builder working on something in the local area.' Sharon's eyes started to well up and she pulled out the tissue. 'I'm going to miss her so much.'

She had eaten all the crisps, and now was reduced to picking up the crumbs. Moss went to fetch more drinks and crisps, and Erika waited until she was back for Sharon to compose herself.

'What do you know about Joseph Pitkin?' asked Erika.

Sharon shook her head dismissively. 'He's had life handed to him on a plate, and he's just a waste of space.'

'Why?'

'His parents are minted. They sent him to the best schools and he was expelled. He could be anything, and he chooses to be a creepy little loser. He was obsessed with her, showing up at her gigs.' Sharon shook her head distastefully. 'Skinny little runt, with a weird mother complex. His mum comes in for a haircut every now and again. Her hair is always filthy and she smells of B.O. She's not the type of person we like to encourage, but she's a good tipper.'

'Did Marissa ever ask him to take photos of her?'

'What kind of photos?'

'He was an amateur photographer.'

'Was he now? By that, I take it his parents bought him all the gear. She never mentioned him doing that… Hang on, what do you mean, "was"?'

Erika told her, without going into too much detail.

'Bloody hell,' Sharon said, shoving more crisps in her mouth. 'I'm not surprised. They were a weird family, and he always seemed like a messed-up kid. Rumour is that Elspeth breastfed him until he was nine. Marissa used to joke that the only person his mother wanted him to lose his virginity to was her.'

Moss creased her forehead. 'The boy killed himself.'

'I know. Very sad, but what? You want me to lie and pretend to be upset? I didn't like him.'

'What did he do to you?'

'Nothing, but he wouldn't leave Marissa alone. He was odd and creepy. She told me that a few times she came home late from a gig and he would be waiting to talk to her on her doorstep.'

'Did she ever report him?'

'No. I don't think she felt… like… threatened. I think he weighed less than she did, which wasn't much.'

Erika sat back and ran her hands through her hair. 'Okay. What do you know about Don Walpole?'

Sharon sighed. 'Is this all you want to talk about? The men in her life? This is the year 2017. People screw. She liked him.

She had a thing for older guys. Marissa wouldn't shut up about his big cock, and how he knew how to use it...' She screwed up her face in disdain.

'Did Marissa sleep with other older men? Random men?'

'Yes. She had no qualms about going into detail. Guys she'd picked up on the train home. Classy. A couple of lads from the Fitzwilliam Estate. Don, Ivan. It was just sex. She only used men for sex. Her friendships were much deeper. I was her only true friend. I knew the real Marissa.'

'And what was the real Marissa?'

'Under all that armour, she was kind. We met at school. I was being bullied and she was the only one who would talk to me.'

'Did she stick up for you?' asked Moss.

'Yes, and she gave me tips on how to diet and she offered to give me a makeover, so I wouldn't get bullied. She encouraged me to train as a hairdresser. She also said she would come with me if I got laser eye surgery. You, know, hold my hand and then drive me home from the clinic.'

'Were you planning on getting it done?'

'Yes... Sometime. Although, who will I have to hold my hand now?'

They gave her a moment to compose herself.

'Was Ivan the only man she was serious about?'

'I told you she wasn't in love with him! He had money. He could take her places.'

'What about the old lady Marissa cared for?' asked Erika.

'Elsa Fryatt? That was another case of Marissa landing on her feet. Mrs Fryatt's son was getting funny about her living on her own, she had a fall or something, and he wanted to pack her off into a home. The compromise was that she got a carer. She turned up her nose at all the official carers, you know, the ones who are screened and trained. Mrs Fryatt put up a note in the café on Brockley High Road, the arty one. She paid fifteen quid an hour!

I think she found Marissa interesting. And Marissa would milk it for all it was worth. She got lunch, and they'd go out to garden centres. Mrs Fryatt even insured Marissa on her Porsche. Marissa was going to borrow it for my eye surgery.'

'How many hours a week did she work for Mrs Fryatt?'

'Ten, fifteen. It was a great job. Round the corner. The old girl paid cash.'

'It seems Marissa was quite a complex person,' said Erika. Sharon stared at her. 'Sorry I should frame that more as a question than an observation.'

'No. It's okay. I'm just trying to think of how to comment on that. I don't think she was complex. She had an effect on people around her. She wasn't, like, academic, but she was smart, and so beautiful.'

Sharon burst into tears again, and pulled out a tissue, which she clamped over her face to muffle the sobs. 'She... She pushed people's buttons,' she said, between sobs. 'But who would want to kill her? She was always honest about who she was. And for that I... I liked her very much. Can I see her body? I'm going to ask Mandy if I can be the one who styles her hair. I don't want them to make her look like an old lady at the funeral home...'

'Bloody hell. What do you make of all that?' asked Erika when she and Moss were back in the car. They watched as Sharon walked away from them down Crofton Park Road. She had a slow gait, and she was still clutching tissues to her face.

'She told us a lot,' said Erika. 'Do you think she told us everything?'

'I don't know. She didn't seem to hold back. Although, if Marissa used people, what was she using Sharon for?'

'A free haircut?'

Moss pulled a face. 'Really? London is full of great hairdressers, and you can easily get a trainee to practise on you. No, there's got to be something else.'

Erika's phone rang.

'Oh, this is McGorry,' she said, before answering. 'Yeah?' She listened for a moment, thanked him and hung up. 'Ivan Stowalski drove back to London late last night. Alone. Let's go and find out his side of the story.'

CHAPTER TWENTY-TWO

Ivan Stowalski's house was on the top end of Coniston Road, close to Crofton Park Road. It was sandwiched in the terrace between a house on the left, which was wrapped in plastic and undergoing renovation, and a house on the right, which was crumbling and in need of renovation.

There was no answer at the door, but the curtains were all closed. Erika rang again, and a bell echoed loudly through the house.

'The curtains weren't closed on Christmas Day. In the door-to-door it says that there is a tree in the front room,' said Erika. Moss peered through the letter box.

'Jesus,' she coughed. 'Smell this.'

Erika came to the letter box, put her nose to the gap, and recoiled, coughing.

'Shit. That's gas.'

They came back to the front gate and looked up at the house. All the windows were closed, and the curtains were drawn. It looked like the edges of the windows in one room were stuffed with blankets. She pulled out her radio, and called in the address for backup. Then she went back to the front door, leant down and shouted through the letter box.

'This is the police. Is anyone in there?' She coughed. 'It's really strong.'

'If the concentration of gas is that strong inside, the whole row of terraces could blow. And so many people are home,' said Moss, indicating the lights on in many of the surrounding windows.

Erika nodded. She charged the door, bouncing off it painfully the first time. On the second attempt, it cracked and swung inwards with a crash, and she landed on the carpet in the hallway. The strong smell of gas flooded out, and she covered her nose with her sleeve.

'We need to get the windows and doors open and find the source,' she said, coming back to the doorway to grab fresh air. Moss took a deep breath, covered her mouth and nose, and they rushed into the house. It was smartly furnished inside, but dark. The curtains were drawn in the living room. Erika pulled them open and saw that the double-glazed sash windows looked strong: they were made of thick wood and were all taped shut. At the bottom, along the sill, the windows were packed with blankets. Erika signalled to Moss, feeling her lungs starting to burst. They ran back out onto the front path. Their eyes were streaming and they gasped and coughed.

'We need… to get the windows and doors open inside,' said Erika. Moss nodded. They took deep breaths, then charged back inside, going back into the living room.

Erika picked up a heavy chair by a bookshelf, and Moss looked around the room, finding a pair of scissors on the desk under the window. Her eyes were streaming, and she wiped them with her sleeve, then holding the scissors like a dagger, she stabbed in the corner of one of the double-glazing panes. It took a couple of attempts but she pierced the glass. She then did the same with the other two panes. She stepped back and nodded to Erika, who charged at the windows with the legs of the chair. She bashed all three open. The glass exploded outwards, and fresh air began to flood in.

They came back out to the front path, to get some gulps of fresh air.

'Hey! You! What are you doing?' shouted an older man from across the road. He had glasses around his neck on a chain, and was holding a newspaper.

'Get back inside!' shouted Moss.

'Not until you tell me what you are doing!'

'Police, get back inside!' they both shouted.

'Kitchen, at the back,' said Erika. They took deep breaths and ran back inside, down the hallway, past the stairs, where the smell of gas intensified. A smart modern kitchen looked out over a garden. The oven door was open, and the gas hobs were all hissing. Moss turned everything off. There was a huge glass sliding door, but no key. Erika couldn't see any scissors, but there was a large stone doorstop. She picked it up and flung it at the glass. It bounced off and she had to jump back.

They were now both coughing and choking. Erika picked the doorstop up again and lobbed it at the glass. A sea of cracks burst outwards, almost frosting the glass, but it still didn't break. Erika's lungs were bursting and Moss had now fallen to her knees. On the third attempt, the doorstop smashed through the huge pane of glass. They staggered out to the snow-covered back garden and took more deep breaths, loving the cold, clean air.

'Upstairs; we need to check upstairs,' coughed Erika. They took deep breaths and dived back inside, through the kitchen, feeling that the gas was dispersing.

They heard the sound of a siren as a fire engine pulled up outside. The house upstairs had the same layout as Marissa's, with a bedroom front and back, and a bathroom on the opposite side to the staircase. The small back bedroom and bathroom doors were open. They got the windows open, then ran to the master bedroom door, which was locked. They could feel a breeze as the air was now being sucked out from downstairs, and the toxic air was clearing. They heard feet on the stairs, and voices.

'Up here!' shouted Erika. Three firefighters appeared at the top of the landing. 'We need to get this door open.'

They took an axe to the door, and it splintered and then swung open. Gas flooded out, and the firefighters rushed in and got the curtains and windows open.

On the neatly made bed lay a tall, thin man. He was pale, with thin sandy hair. Erika recognised him as Ivan from the photos they had of him in the incident room. Two paramedics entered the bedroom, carrying medical gear. Erika and Moss stood back as they examined him.

'He's got a faint pulse,' said the female paramedic. Together with the male paramedic, she got him strapped to the stretcher they had brought with them, and once he was on it, they lifted him down to the floor.

'His name's Ivan Stowalski,' said Erika.

'Ivan, can you hear me?' asked the woman. She slapped his face, and he gave a low moan, his eyelids fluttering.

'His blood is flooded with carbon monoxide. Let's get an IV in and oxygenate him.' She opened the first aid box.

Erika then saw what was on the bed. She'd thought, at first, it was a brightly patterned bedspread, but now she saw it was covered with photos of Marissa Lewis, all printed off on paper. There were photos of her performing in her burlesque shows, several of her naked in bed, and wet in the shower. There were scores of snapshots taken of Marissa and Ivan in parks and at famous London landmarks, smiling into the camera. Amongst the pictures, were also a couple of her burlesque outfits, a black corset and a red silk bra.

Erika looked back at the paramedics, who had now hooked up an IV to Ivan's arm and were pumping in air through a large air bag and mask.

'What's that in his hand?' asked one of the firefighters. Erika reached over and gently took it from him.

'Underwear,' she said, seeing it was a small pair of red knickers with a gold embroidered diamond in one corner. 'They belong to Marissa. That's her branding.'

CHAPTER TWENTY-THREE

Ivan Stowalski was stabilised by the paramedics. He was breathing, but hadn't regained consciousness.

Erika and Moss watched from the pavement as the ambulance sped away to hospital.

'There goes another suspect, dying on us,' said Moss.

'He's not dead yet,' replied Erika.

The firefighters then moved through the house, checking the gas connections, and searched the attic. When they gave the all-clear, a forensics team arrived to go through the contents of the house.

Erika ducked under the police tape to join Moss, who was sitting in the car, drinking from a bottle of water.

'You okay?' she asked.

'Yeah. Bit of a sore throat.'

'Me too, and I smoke twenty a day.'

'They've taken Ivan Stowalski to University College Hospital. As soon as he gains consciousness, I've said we want to talk to him. We've got his car leaving the congestion zone and going northbound at 11.30 p.m. on Christmas Eve.'

'Is that late to go and see relations?'

'They would have arrived very late, if they were driving up north.'

'Four or five a.m. Why would you leave so late? We need to find out what time Marissa got back from her burlesque gig. If it was earlier, he could have had time.' Erika coughed, a little of the residue still in her lungs, and she squinted up at the sky, at the bright grey cloud. Several neighbours were looking out of their windows or had come to their front doorsteps, including the man with the glasses who still had his newspaper clutched in his hand. Erika looked back at the mess of glass over the front garden of Ivan's house. Then she looked at Moss, who was downing more water.

'You okay to keep going?'

'You bet.'

'I want to talk to Don Walpole and Marissa's mother.'

Moss got out of the car, and they started up the street. Two doors down from Ivan's house, a large elderly black man with salt and pepper hair was smoking a cigarette.

'Did Ivan try to kill himself?' he asked. He spoke with a warm Jamaican accent, and wore large, billowing grey trousers and a thick orange fleece dotted with cigarette burns. He tilted his head back and squinted at Erika and Moss, as if they were about to do something unexpected. They stopped by his gate.

'We can't talk about a case,' said Erika.

'Bad business, that girl being murdered. I've been watching that Ivan make a fool of himself with that girl for a long time. She was always going to be out of his league. I saw him being stretchered out. Tried to kill himself, didn't he?' He came close and put his hand on Erika's shoulder, the tip of his cigarette glowing. 'You see that car there, opposite?' he said, pointing to a white Alfa Romeo with a huge dent in the bumper. The rear lights on the right-hand side were broken and the plastic littered the filthy snow below. Erika felt the man's hand grip her shoulder. The smell of his breath was a mixture of cough sweets and cigarettes. She delicately unhooked her shoulder and stepped away.

'Yes.'

'That's his car. He arrived back early this morning, drove straight into that car opposite, and crushed the front lights.

Didn't hang about, didn't knock on the door to get insurance details.' He put the cigarette back in his mouth and folded his arms across his chest.

'What time was this?' asked Moss.

'Seven o'clock this morning or thereabouts.'

'Why were you up?'

'I'm old,' he chuckled, with a stream of smoke. 'And my wife doesn't let me smoke in the house.'

'And you're sure it was Ivan Stowalski?'

'I don't know his second name, but I'm not blind! It was the Polish man.' Erika and Moss contemplated that for a moment. The man went on. 'He must have heard she died, the girl he was carrying on with.'

'How do you know he was having an affair with her?' asked Erika.

'You call yourself a detective? I know because I'm out here most of the day. I see a lot, although people don't take no notice of an old man… She used to come and go a lot from his house. After his wife had gone to work.'

'When?'

'Over the summer. Since the weather got cold she hasn't been there as much. Last time I saw her was Christmas Eve…' Abruptly, he walked back up the path and opened his front door.

'Hey!' started Erika, but he only reached inside and returned with an ashtray.

'My wife. She never puts it back out here after she's emptied it,' he said, balancing it on the gate post. He stubbed out the cigarette and lit another.

'What time did you see Marissa?'

'I saw her twice on Christmas Eve. Once in the afternoon. It was just getting dark, so just before four. She came out of Ivan's house with a face like thunder. He came out after her, pleading with her to come back… Oh lordy, he looked pathetic, just in his jeans and T-shirt and no shoes. He got down on his knees, cried and begged, and the ground was covered in snow. That really brought it home, what a knockout she is. Do you know she was a stripper? A stripper with stuff up here,' he said, tapping his head. 'That's a real combination.'

'Did you know what they were arguing about?' asked Moss.

'No. She shouted at him, expletives, to go away and leave her alone. He followed her up the road like a dog, but she told him to keep away from her or she'd call the police.'

'She said that, "call the police"?' said Erika.

'I'm not deaf, woman. It's what I heard.'

'Did he come back to his house?'

'He did, a little while later, tail between his legs.'

'When did you see her for the second time?'

'About 10 p.m., she just walked past on the way to her house.'

'She was alone?'

'Yes.'

'Do you know if Ivan was home?'

The old man thought for a moment.

'The lights were on, I think.'

Erika and Moss chewed that over.

'Has anyone been to talk to you?' asked Erika.

'Like who?'

'The police. There was a door-to-door over Christmas, and I would have expected you to have told one of my officers this.'

The man raised his hand and shook a finger at Erika.

'Hold your horses, Juliet Bravo. I wasn't here at Christmas. We was with my daughter and grandkids – she lives in Brent Cross. We drove over early on Christmas morning.'

'What time?'

'We set off around seven. Terrible, the roads were.'

'Did you see anything else on Christmas morning?'

He shook his head.

'Okay. Thank you. Can I send one of my officers over to take all of this down officially?'

'If I'm here, I'm happy to.' He gave her a broad smile with yellow teeth.

They carried on walking up the road.

'So, she rowed with Ivan the day she was killed,' said Moss. 'He was home when she came back from her gig at 10 p.m.'

'The plot thickens,' said Erika.

CHAPTER TWENTY-FOUR

Don Walpole's house was a few doors further down, six doors up from Marissa's house. It was smart and nondescript. Erika realised just how many terraced houses there were in South London, and how they would all often blend into one. Back in her native Slovakia, there were very few, if any, terraces. Pre-fabricated blocks of flats were the equivalent, which were equally claustrophobic.

The Walpoles's front garden was open, with just a low wall and no hedge. The red hats of a couple of garden gnomes poked up out of the snow, and there wasn't a number on the house. Beside the door, on the brickwork, was a sign which said '*Summerdown*' in curly black iron writing. There was a television on in the living room.

Erika rang the bell, and a moment later the door was opened by a large woman in a grubby red fleece. She had bloodshot eyes.

'Yes?' she said, placing a hand on the wall to steady herself.

'Are you Jeanette Walpole?'

'Who's asking?' she said, tottering a little on her feet. Erika could tell she was drunk.

They introduced themselves and showed their warrant cards.

'Is your husband home?'

She threw back her head and shouted, 'Don! The police want to talk to you about your whore!'

There was a clattering on the stairs and Don appeared, wearing jeans and a polo neck jumper. He looked so much younger and more vital than his wife. He was handsome, in a geeky sort of way.

His wife took pleasure in his embarrassment. 'He's shitting himself, can you see?' She looked him up and down with a sneer. 'He hasn't got the balls to have killed that little bitch… He hasn't got much in the way of balls.' She reached out to grab his crotch, but Don caught her hand in his grip.

'That's enough, Jeanette,' he said.

'Ow! He's hurting me,' she whined. He let go instantly.

'I wasn't hurting her,' he said, apologetically.

'We'd like to talk to you, Mr Walpole,' said Erika. 'Maybe it would be better to meet you somewhere outside the house?'

'It's fine. Go through to the kitchen; I'll join you in a second.'

They walked through the hallway, which was immaculate, past the stairs to the kitchen at the back. It was comfortable, with an ageing wooden fitted kitchen. A television mounted on the wall was on low, showing an old black-and-white film, and there was a mug of coffee on the kitchen table. A copy of the *Guardian* was spread out and opened at the sports page.

There were no photos on the fridge, just a small magnet from Barcelona. In one corner was a flat-screen PC computer on a stand. Erika went over to it and moved the mouse. A screensaver appeared of Don and Jeanette in the gardens at some stately home. He had his arm awkwardly around her shoulders, but she was standing apart from him. Neither of them were smiling.

Beside the fridge were boxes of Pinot Grigio piled high. Moss went to the window overlooking the garden.

'Blimey, look at those empties,' she said. Erika moved to join her and saw them piled up and spilling over a small recycling box.

'You think that's a week's worth?' asked Erika.

'It's just over a week's worth,' said a voice. They turned and saw Don in the doorway. He gently closed the door. 'I managed to get her to lie down.' He said this in the tone of someone who has just managed to get a baby down for its afternoon nap. 'My wife has had problems with alcohol for many years… But I take it that's not why you're here?'

'We're here about your relationship with Marissa Lewis,' said Erika.

Don nodded. He was a large, imposing man, very trim and fit with broad, muscular arms.

'Would you like coffee?'

'No, thank you.'

They sat down at the table and he cleared away the newspaper.

'We've heard that you and Marissa were involved in a relationship?' asked Erika.

'Lots of people knew about it. About six years ago, she knocked on the door asking if we needed any cleaning done. She was going around the street trying to get work. Her mother had just had her benefits stopped, and they were short of money. I gave her work, as I was aware that her mother drank. Jeanette was getting worse with the booze. I thought, at least I'm an adult with a job, and I can deal with it better. She was only just sixteen.'

'How did it start?' asked Moss.

'I don't know, just having her around. She started giving me looks and then one day, we ended up in bed when Jeanette was asleep.'

'How long did it go on for?'

'A couple of years. Jeanette found Marissa's hair in her brush one day, after she'd taken a shower here.'

'And what happened?'

'She went mad, threatened to divorce me. Slapped Marissa about, gave her a bloody nose. Marissa went home and then Mandy comes round, and there's a huge fight between her and Jeanette. Out in the street, shouting, screaming. My nose got broken and I lost a tooth trying to break them up…'

'And did it end then, you and Marissa?'

'Yeah,' he said, sitting back and folding his arms.

'You didn't see her again?'

'No. Well, I saw her, she only lived a few doors down, but I didn't have anything to do with her.'

'You didn't meet her or have sex with her again?' asked Moss.

'No. I told you. No.'

There was a pause. Erika pulled out her phone. She scrolled through and found a video and then placed the phone between them on the table. On the screen, the video from Joseph Pitkin's phone began to play. Marissa in her bedroom, the man who looked like Don coming into the room, looking around shiftily. They kissed by the front window. Marissa began to unbuckle his trousers.

'Stop, I don't need to see any more,' he said. He got up from the table and went to the window, looking out into the garden. Erika stopped the video and tucked the phone back in her pocket. 'Do you ever feel like, jeez, how did I end up here?'

Erika and Moss remained silent.

'I wanted to do so much. I trained with the under-fourteens squad at Millwall. They said I could have gone professional, and I thought I would, but I broke my leg in a car accident.'

'What does this have to do with you lying to us about seeing Marissa?' asked Erika.

'She was exciting. She was… sexy and… she made me feel alive.'

'She flattered you?'

He paused and nodded, wiping tears from his eyes. 'She wanted to hook up again, a few months ago.'

'This video is dated last September.'

He nodded. 'We had sex, as you've probably seen. It was great.'

'Did she initiate it, or you?'

'She did. She sent me a text message, out of the blue one night. Jeanette was out of it. She's been getting worse, drinking all day, getting abusive and then throwing up everywhere. Her health is getting worse. It's like having a kid. I realised a few months ago, I'm pretty much her carer, and when I'm not at work, that's what I do. I take the shit, I cook and clean, I feed her, I clear up the sick. So, when this text message came from a beautiful young woman who wanted to screw my brains out, I went. I'm not ashamed of that.'

'Why was it only the one time?' asked Erika.

'She told me afterwards that when we first slept together she was fifteen…' He put his head in his hands.

'And let me guess, she was going to report you?'

He nodded. 'She told me that historical abuse cases get lots of press attention, and that she would be believed.'

'Did you abuse her?'

'NO! It was consensual, you have to believe me, and I thought she was sixteen. She was a woman. She had the body of a woman. I'm not into… I would never…' He started to sob now; big fat tears rolled down his cheeks. Erika took out a packet of tissues and passed him one. He took it and wiped at his face, embarrassed. 'She told me that she wanted five grand, or she would go to the police and report me.'

'Did you believe her?'

'Yeah.'

'How did you react?' asked Moss.

'She was clever about it. She asked me to meet her in central London, at a coffee place. It was busy and she told me how it was going to go down.'

'Did you give her the money?' asked Erika.

He nodded and rubbed at his face.

'I thought it would be a one-off but she blackmailed me for another five grand.'

'How did you give it to her?'

'Bank transfer.'

'Was she fifteen when you first had sex with her?'

'Is this on record…'

'Was she fifteen?' repeated Erika, raising her voice.

'Yes! Alright. YES! She was two days away from her sixteenth birthday. I didn't know at the time, she told me in September, but it was just two days!' he said, holding up two fingers. 'If it had been after the weekend, it would have been legal. How does that work? On Friday I'm a paedophile, but the following Monday I'm not? If I'm done for sex offences, do you know what they would do? I'd lose my job. We have a mortgage. My wife can't look after herself. You know what things are like right now. It would make headlines.'

Erika rubbed her face, and Moss shook her head.

'When did you last see Marissa, Don?' said Erika.

'Christmas Eve. At the train station.'

'What time?'

'Around 9.45 p.m. Jeanette saw her by the ticket machines and had a few words to say to her.'

'What did she say?'

'Nothing different to all the other times: "you bitch, you whore".'

'Does Jeanette know about the blackmail?'

'No.'

'And where were you for the rest of Christmas Eve?' asked Erika.

'I was here,' he said, looking up at her, staring her directly in the eye. 'Working.'

'What do you do?'

'I'm a graphic designer. I work from home.'

'Do you have a home office?' asked Moss.

'I use the kitchen table.'

'You don't use your spare room?'

He sighed. 'No. That's where I sleep.'

'And Jeanette?'

'She has the front bedroom. Is it necessary to ask these questions? I don't know what it's to do with?'

'Your wife is your alibi for Christmas Eve, but you sleep in separate bedrooms, and she is often drunk in the evenings,' said Erika.

'I didn't kill Marissa,' he said, his hands starting to shake.

'Why weren't you here for the door-to-door to answer questions on Christmas Day?'

'We drove over to see Jeanette's sister on Christmas morning; she lives in Greenwich and she cooked lunch. She can confirm this.'

'What time did you leave?'

'Around eight. We wanted to be there for when they opened presents. She's got kids and grandkids.'

'Do you have any kids?'

'No. We tried, but Jeanette couldn't. She carried two babies to full term, but they didn't make it... I wish people knew that when they saw her. There's a reason why she drinks. I suppose you're going to arrest me?'

'No. I would like to send an officer round to get all of this in an official statement. I also want you to provide us with a DNA sample. This is of course voluntary, but it will be taken into account if you decline.'

'Can I think about it?'

Erika and Moss exchanged a glance.

'You have twenty-four hours. I'd also like to search your house; I will apply for a warrant if needs be.'

'Search it. I don't have much dignity left. I'm honest about who I am. I don't have anything to hide.'

CHAPTER TWENTY-FIVE

'Jesus, Marissa had guts to tap him for money like that,' said Moss as they left Don Walpole's house.

'The police would have taken her accusation seriously,' said Erika. 'I'm also concerned that he doesn't want to give us a DNA sample.'

'What are you going to do about it?'

'We need to look into him a bit more. I don't see how it would serve anyone to prosecute him for having underage sex with Marissa, now she's dead, but we could use the threat of it for leverage if he doesn't agree to give us a DNA sample in connection with our murder enquiry. I also want to check in with Marissa's mother and see if she knew anything about America.'

Erika put in a quick call to Tania, the family liaison officer. 'Mandy is still over at the neighbour's house,' she said when she came off the phone.

They crossed the road diagonally, and went to Joan's front door. She answered the door wearing another brushed velvet tracksuit, this time in royal blue. She looked tired and harassed.

'We've come to check in with Mandy,' said Erika.

Joan made them remove their shoes, then took them through to the living room. Mandy sat in one of the high-backed armchairs, next to Tania, on the sofa. Tania muted the volume on the television, which was showing *This Morning*. There were cups on the vast polished coffee table, and a half-eaten packet of Mr Kipling's French Fancies. Mandy looked up at them from craggy eyes with dark circles underneath.

'Any news?' she asked hopefully.

'We're still working on things,' said Erika. 'Can we sit down with you?'

'Yes,' she said.

'Mandy wanted me to ask when she can arrange the funeral?' asked Tania.

'I can give you more news about that in the next day or so,' said Erika, taking the seat by the window. Moss perched on the sofa beside Tania. 'There are still things we need to do for Marissa.'

'What things?'

'We need to make sure we have all the information regarding cause of death – forensics. Your daughter's remains are being cared for.'

There was a long silence. Joan hovered in the doorway, anxiously.

'Are you finished with those teacups?' she said.

'Yes, thank you,' said Tania.

Joan started to stack the crockery onto the tray, and noticed a mark on the table. 'What's this?' she said accusingly. They all peered at a tiny drop of tea which had landed on the polished table. She scrubbed at it with her finger and then pulled out a tissue, tutting, 'It's a tea stain! This table has only just had a French polish!'

Mandy looked up at Joan.

'It wasn't me. I used a coaster!'

'Sorry, it must have been me,' said Tania. Joan took the tray and stomped off to the kitchen. Moments later, there was a crashing, as it was loaded up in the dishwasher.

'I think she's getting sick of me being here,' said Mandy in a low voice. 'But I can't face going back to the house. I keep seeing her lying out the front on her back. Her eyes wide open.'

'Tania. Would you go and help Joan out in the kitchen?' asked Erika, giving her a nod.

'Of course,' she said, giving Erika an amused look. She left, closing the door.

Mandy seemed to relax now that the angry sound of Joan crashing about in the kitchen was gone. 'She's a nice girl, that Tania,' said Mandy. She took her phone from the pocket of her hoodie. 'I keep looking at the pictures I have of Marissa. I'm worried I'll forget what she looks like.' She scrolled through and found a picture of Marissa, dressed up in full burlesque gear but standing in the dull confines of the kitchen, in front of the pedal bin and a cupboard door where the carpet sweeper was propped up.

'She was very beautiful,' said Moss.

'Yeah. I don't know where she got her looks from. Look at me. I'm no oil painting, and her father, well, he could have eaten an apple through a picket fence.' She laughed and then the laughter turned to tears. 'We'll never be a family again. We weren't much of one in the first place.'

'Mandy, there's something crucial to our investigation. It's the time when Marissa was attacked in the front garden. What time did you say you went to bed?'

'I dunno, what did I say? Just before ten?'

'Okay, well we've got two witnesses who saw Marissa get off the train at Brockley around quarter to ten, and another who saw her walk past his house on Coniston Road around 10 p.m.'

'Who?'

'Don Walpole and his wife Jeanette were on the same train; they saw her by the ticket machines at the station around 9.45, and a man at number 37 was outside having a cigarette when she went past around 10 p.m.'

Mandy half closed her eyes.

'He's not got the best eyesight.'

'This timing would fit with Marissa getting off the train; the station is less than ten minutes' walk away. If you were still up around ten, or getting ready for bed, you may have heard something?'

Mandy went to say something, but was cut off by Joan, who bustled in with a cloth and polish, followed by Tania.

'Please, I'm trying to talk to Mandy,' snapped Erika.

'You need to get to water marks fast or they're a bugger to shift!'

'Joan, please can you do this later,' said Tania.

'This is my house! I can do whatever the bloody hell I like!' shouted Joan. Her lip curled up in anger, reminding Erika of a small, mealy-mouthed dog.

'Sorry, Joan,' said Mandy. 'I think I'm gonna to try and spend the night back over at my place. The officers only want a few minutes, then you can help me?'

Joan's mood changed and she became overly sympathetic.

'Oh, are you sure, dear? You can stay here as long as you like, it's really no trouble…'

'No. I'd best head home.'

'Maybe it's for the best. I'll pack your sponge bag for you,' said Joan, already half out of the living room and up the stairs. Tania left with her, closing the door.

'Mandy, I was asking you about Christmas Eve. Did you hear anything when Marissa arrived home?'

'Officers, you must know, I have a problem with alcohol,' Mandy said, rubbing her hands together in her lap. 'I was embarrassed to say before, but I had a blackout. I drank more than normal on Christmas Eve. It's the time of year, when it's cold and dark and…I can remember making myself some cheese on toast in the early evening, and then nothing until I woke up the next morning.'

'What time?'

'Early. I had to use the loo.'

'And did you sleep downstairs on the sofa?'

'Yeah.'

'You said before that you didn't…'

'I was in a blackout; I think it was downstairs. I just remember being up on the loo, then I heard the cat.'

'You have a cat?'

'Beaker. Well, he was a stray who hit us up for food. I was up on the loo when he was scratching at the door, so I went down, and that's when I found her.' Mandy put a large pudgy hand to her face as she started to cry. 'I'm sorry officers, I really can't remember anything. I really can't.'

'Did you know that Marissa was planning to leave, and go and live in New York?'

'On her own?'

'No, with Ivan. He'd been asked to transfer there with work and he was going to take Marissa with him.'

'Instead of his wife?' asked Mandy.

'Yes.'

Erika and Moss watched as her face creased with confusion.

'She knew I needed her housekeeping money…' She scrubbed at the table with a stubby finger, her eyes filling with tears. 'That sounds about right. She was going to bugger off without telling me.' She wiped her face with the back of her hand. 'I know you shouldn't speak ill of the dead, but she was a selfish little bitch.'

'I'm sorry to have to tell you, but we want to keep you up to date with all the information,' said Erika.

'I still want you to catch who did it, mind. Marissa might have been a bitch, but she was my flesh and blood,' said Mandy, looking Erika straight in the eye, and fixing her with a cold stare.

CHAPTER TWENTY-SIX

Erika and Moss made their way over to Mrs Fryatt's house.

'Bloody hell. We've now spoken to three people who have completely different experiences of Marissa,' said Erika. 'Was she a different person to everyone in her life? Was she nice; was she a bitch? Was she honest; was she a liar? She gave plenty of people reason to want her dead.'

'You think Mandy did it?'

'I think everyone is a suspect. Although, there's no evidence to back it up. No trace evidence of Marissa's blood was found inside the house. Mandy would have had to get back inside, covered in blood, and clean herself off without leaving any trace evidence. And the house is a state, she hadn't done some hurried clean up. It looks like the place hasn't been cleaned in weeks.'

'And what's her motive? The weekly housekeeping she received from Marissa was a lot of money for her. With Marissa dead, that's stopped,' said Moss.

Mrs Fryatt lived on the opposite side of the large Crofton Park cemetery, on Newton Avenue, in Hilly Fields – near where Marsh lived. The houses on the avenue were large and grand and set back from the road, with huge front gardens. The avenue was close to Coniston Road, but at the same time another world away from the grubby, tightly packed terraced houses.

'She must be posh: she's got a boot scraper,' said Moss when they reached the front door, indicating the elaborate iron boot scraper embedded in the white marble step next to the front door. Erika pulled an iron handle, and a bell rang out deep in the house. A few minutes later, the door was opened by a tall, broad older man with thinning, wispy black hair. He eyed them beadily. They showed their ID and introduced themselves.

'We understand that Elsa Fryatt, who lives here, was cared for by Marissa Lewis?' asked Erika.

'We heard the news,' he said, his beady gaze running over Erika and Moss. Sweat glistened on the top of his head. 'I'm Charles Fryatt, Elsa Fryatt's son.'

'Where did you hear the news?' asked Moss.

'Her mother phoned. Said she'd been brutally murdered, so she wouldn't be coming to work any more.'

He seemed old, in his late sixties.

'Could we talk to your mother?'

He stood to one side and invited them in. The hallway opened out to a grand staircase and double height ceiling.

'She's in the drawing room,' he said. They passed a large grandfather clock by the base of the staircase, under a huge crystal chandelier. Charles Fryatt had an odd loping gait, and a hunched-over neck. They passed the front room, which was dominated by bookshelves, and contained a huge Christmas tree, tastefully decorated with white lights. At the back of the house was a large sitting room, which looked over the snow-covered garden. This room looked more lived-in, with a big television, lots of armchairs and a coffee table littered with magazines and books. On the largest sofa sat an old lady. Erika had been expecting a wizened invalid, but instead, a small woman with a strong jaw and steely eyes sat bolt upright on the edge of the sofa. She was dressed in a woollen skirt and a tweed jacket, and her only concession to the cold was a large pair of sheepskin-lined slippers. Her ash-blonde hair was short and fashionably styled. Her face, however, showed her years and was deeply lined.

'Good morning, officers, I'm Elsa Fryatt,' she said, standing and shaking their hands. 'The hearing aid picks up everything,' she added, indicating the two aids in her ears. She moved with fluidity, more so than her son. She also had a faint metallic crispness to her accent, which Erika couldn't quite put her finger on. Erika and Moss introduced themselves again and showed their warrants.

'Would you care for some coffee, and perhaps a mince pie?' Elsa asked. 'Charles, you know how to use the coffee machine?'

'Yes, of course.'

'Warm up the Marks and Spencer mince pies… And throw away the ones we bought at the Christmas Fayre.'

Charles nodded. Erika watched as he left the room and wondered if he was ill. He was sweating profusely.

'I much prefer the bought ones to home-made, don't you?' Elsa said.

'I'm happy with a mince pie, wherever it comes from,' said Moss. There was a fire burning in the grate. They sat down on the sofa opposite the old lady. She clasped her hands in her lap and fixed them with startlingly blue eyes.

'You've asked to speak to us regarding Marissa?' She tutted and shook her head. 'Terrible business. Who would do that, and to someone so young?' She put one of her gnarled hands to her mouth and shook her head, but stopped herself from breaking down in tears.

'Can I just confirm that Marissa was your carer?' asked Erika.

Mrs Fryatt waved the word away.

'She was more of a companion. She did my shopping, she would manage my diary. I trusted her to do the things that one wouldn't ask of a general domestic servant.'

'Can I ask… Do you have a large staff?'

She laughed. 'No, I make myself sound more glamorous than I am. I have a cleaner who comes in every day for a few hours;

she also cooks me a meal. There is a gardener who doubles as a handy man. Charles is in a lot. Marissa was in charge of washing my clothes and helping me with shopping and all the other personal things.'

'How long did she work for you?'

'Just over a year. I had advertised in the local café, as well as on the internet – well, Charles, he did all that. I wanted someone who lived locally.'

'Were you aware that Marissa also worked as a burlesque dancer?' asked Erika.

'Of course. I went to see her perform on several occasions.'

'In the strip clubs?' asked Moss.

Mrs Fryatt turned her attention onto Moss, almost for the first time.

'Strip clubs!? I have never been to a *strip club*. I saw Marissa perform at the *Café De Paris* just off Leicester Square, and she had a regular weekly show in Soho – I forget the name of the club, but it was smaller, and much more fun… Stripping it was not. Burlesque is an art form, and she was very good at it…' She bit her lip and looked as if she was about to break down again. 'I'm sorry. She was just so vital. She made things so much fun here.'

'Can I ask how much Marissa earned in your employment?'

'I don't talk about money,' she said, turning up her nose at the thought. 'I paid her very well, and she worked three or four hours every day during the week.'

'Mrs Fryatt, I'm trying to place your accent,' said Erika.

'Are you now…'

Erika paused, and when Mrs Fryatt wasn't forthcoming, she went on, 'Can I ask where you're from?'

'I'm originally from Austria. How is that relevant?'

Erika looked surprised.

'It's not. I just detected something there. I'm from Slovakia.'

'Yes, I wondered about you, too, but you flatten your vowels. You say "ask" instead of "aaask".'

'I learnt English in Manchester, where I lived when I first came to the UK.'

'Oh dear,' Mrs Fryatt replied. She tipped her head to one side and gave Erika a chilly smile.

'So where did you learn your… charm… with the English language?' asked Erika icily.

'My family came to England when the war broke out; my father was a diplomat.'

Charles came loping back into the room with a large tray covered in an elegant china tea set: cups, saucers and a milk jug and sugar bowl. Mrs Fryatt eyed him as he struggled with where to put the tray, balancing it on his knee, but she didn't help him move the piles of books and magazines on the table. Then the cups and the cafetière of coffee started to slide. Luckily, Moss leapt up and took the tray from him.

'Christ! Put the tray down first, and then move things,' Mrs Fryatt snapped. 'Men are incapable of thinking more than one step ahead…'

Charles eyed her murderously, scooping up a pile of books and magazines to make space for the tray.

'Charles is an expert jeweller, with an encyclopaedic knowledge of gemstones, precious metals and antique jewellery, but he is hopeless at everyday tasks.'

Charles took the tray and set it down on the table.

'There we are, mother.' He sloped off out of the room and Mrs Fryatt sat forward and poured them coffee.

'He doesn't know what to do with himself when the shop is shut.'

'Shop?' asked Erika.

'He's a jeweller, in Hatton Garden,' she said, proudly. 'Married a lovely Jewish girl and they inherited the shop. Of course, he's become the linchpin. His knowledge is so broad. He's become accepted in that community, and it's tough, if you know what I mean.'

They sat back and sipped their coffee.

'Do you have any suspects?' Mrs Fryatt asked.

'We've found that Marissa lived quite a colourful life. Did she tell you much about her private life?'

'Not a great deal. I got the impression she was professional. She seemed to be getting lots of acclaim for her burlesque work, and she wanted to go places. I met a few of the girls she danced with. They seemed to have great camaraderie. I wasn't too impressed with this – what was her name? – dreadful, lumpen creature she was, with thick glasses. She had one of those situation comedy names…'

'Sharon,' said Moss.

'Yes. That was her. Marissa said she was a bit of a pain, always hanging around. She said this Sharon was constantly pestering her to be the "face" of the hairdresser she runs on the high street…' Mrs Fryatt pulled a face.

'I take it you're not a client?' asked Erika.

'No, I am not. I go to Charles and Charles in Chelsea and it's worth every penny to travel that far.'

'So you didn't get the impression Marissa had any enemies?' asked Moss.

'Well, as much as I knew her. Don't forget dear, she was… Well, I know it's not a fashionable way of putting it any more, but she was *the help*. I thought she was a lovely girl, but the chasm of our age difference and our social difference meant we weren't on intimate terms. Well, I wasn't; she seemed to have no qualms in telling me all about her awful mother, however. Alcoholic, obese, and a nasty piece of work by all regards.'

Mrs Fryatt leant forward and offered them a top up, which Erika accepted.

'Marissa did recount something to me, which was upsetting…
This was a few weeks ago. She was coming home from a gig, and
left the train at Crofton Park station. It was late and rather dark.
When she passed the cemetery, she was approached by a very tall
man wearing a gas mask.'

Erika put her cup down.

'What?'

'Yes, she was walking back late from the station on her own –
which was madness in my mind – and he appeared out from the
cemetery, and pulled her into the shadows by the tall iron gates.
Luckily, she fought him off and got free.'

Erika and Moss exchanged a glance.

'Did she tell the police?'

'I don't know. She was almost flippant about it, chalking it
up as another crazy creep. But it seems more serious than that.
I've seen the news reports. The man in a gas mask, attacking
people late at night on their way home from the train stations.
He attacked a woman and a young man a few weeks back, and
then there was that poor woman on Christmas night. Have you
any idea who it can be?'

Erika ignored the question. She thought back to the conversation that morning with the two officers at the station. The case
suddenly moved from her peripheral vision, and it had her full
attention.

'Do you know exactly when and where this was?' asked Erika.

'I don't know the exact date, perhaps early November. She told
me she'd got the last train home, so the station was quiet. It was
after midnight. She walked home from Crofton Park station, and
just by the entrance to the cemetery on Brockley Road a tall, dark
figure appeared from nowhere. He was dressed all in black – a long
black coat, black gloves – and he wore a gas mask. Terrifying, it
was, she said. He tried to pull her into the cemetery.'

'Did he assault her?' asked Moss.

'Yes. He tried to, but she managed to escape. A car came along, and the headlights scared him off. She ran for it, all the way home. She was very, very lucky, but that was Marissa. I always thought she had a guardian angel,' said Mrs Fryatt. 'Well,' she added, her face clouding over. 'Until now.'

CHAPTER TWENTY-SEVEN

Erika and Moss grabbed some lunch on the way back to the station. It had been a morning of revelations: Sharon telling them that Marissa had planned to leave the country, Ivan's suicide attempt, Marissa blackmailing Don, and now Mrs Fryatt saying that Marissa was attacked by a man in a gas mask.

Along with all of these thoughts and questions running through her mind, Erika could feel a headache looming ominously at the back of her head. When they arrived back at Lewisham Row, they went down to the incident room. A large poster of Marissa Lewis in her burlesque gear had been added to the whiteboard. McGorry, Peterson and a couple of other male officers were grouped in front of it next to the desk.

'I really fancy some of that,' Peterson was saying.

'What's going on?' snapped Erika, feeling anger rise in her. Peterson went to speak, but she cut him off: 'I get that Marissa was a sexy burlesque dancer, but she's a murder victim. Do you all need to hang around photos of her dressed provocatively in her underwear?'

There was an awkward silence.

'The reason that's up there is because the poster shows the brand name on her costume, and the embroidery work which has been added,' said Peterson. 'You see the pink corset with the embroidered diamond?'

'Yes. I'm aware of that. Her stage name was Honey Diamond,' said Erika. The bright lights in the incident room had sharpened the dull thumping at the back of her head.

'We've been in touch with the shop where the costume was bought. It's called Stand Up and Tease, and based in Soho. I found out they also offer an alteration and embroidery service, and they've given us the name of the man who did this embroidery work on her costumes…'

'Okay, so why are you standing around making comments?'

'We're standing around because lunch just arrived,' said McGorry, indicating a box of Pret sandwiches on the table in front of the whiteboard.

'I was just saying I really fancy some of that cheese and pickle,' said Peterson. He stared at her. The other officers looked away, and Moss looked uncomfortable.

'Okay. Good work. I'd like a print-out of all the shows Marissa has been performing in over the past month. And send me the contact for this person who does the customisation of the costumes.'

'Of course,' said Peterson.

'Moss, can you fill everyone in on what happened this morning, and update the whiteboard?'

'Sure thing, Boss.'

Erika left the incident room. Moss reached over and grabbed a sandwich.

'What's up with her?' asked McGorry.

'It's been an eventful morning,' she said.

'No need to take it out on us,' said Peterson. Moss gave him a look and then she started to tell them what had happened.

Erika left the incident room feeling foolish. She saw how the other officers had looked at her while she ticked Peterson off. Did they know the two of them used to be together?

She stopped at the coffee machine, seeing it was now fixed, and grabbed herself an espresso. She thought of Peterson being back, and how they would have to work together. He was a good officer, and a valuable part of the team, but if it was going to be like this, perhaps she would have to have him reassigned.

'You should never shit where you eat, stupid idiot,' she muttered as she waited for the machine to fill her cup. She took the stairs up to her office. Sitting at her desk, she booted her computer up and logged into Holmes. She input the phrase 'gas mask attack' and a list of results came up.

In the past three months, there had been four cases – two women and two men – assaulted by a large male wearing a gas mask. The assaults had all taken place around train stations late at night or early in the morning. The first victim was a twenty-year-old woman called Rachel Elder, who had been walking to Gipsy Hill station to work as a nurse at Lewisham Hospital. She was pulled into an alleyway, where a male exposed himself and then grabbed her by the throat. The attack went on for a long time, as she was asphyxiated to the point of passing out, then allowed to breathe for a moment, before being asphyxiated again. She reported passing out, and when she came back to consciousness the attacker was gone.

The second incident happened close to East Dulwich station. This time the victim was a Kelvin Price aged twenty-three – an actor who was appearing in a West End play. He'd been for drinks after work and got the last train home. Just after midnight he had been pulled into an alleyway close to the station by a man wearing a long flowing black coat and a gas mask with glass eye holes. Again, he had been asphyxiated to the point of unconsciousness several times. He said that the man had been masturbating, and had exposed himself.

'Oh my god,' said Erika as she read the words on the screen. The third attack happened to a Jenny Thorndike, close to Penge East station. She had been walking to get the train early one morning, when a person in black wearing a gas mask had 'appeared from nowhere'. She'd attempted to fight him off, but he'd punched her in the face and pulled her into a small area of parkland close to the station, where she was badly beaten and asphyxiated.

The most recently reported case had occurred on Christmas Day in Sydenham. A woman in her late fifties called Diana Crow had been returning home from her friend's house, when she was grabbed in the railway underpass next to the train station. Again, she was asphyxiated and had been punched in the face, resulting in a fractured cheek. She hadn't, however, reported the incident until the following day.

'Marissa, you had a lucky escape, but why didn't you report it?' said Erika, taking a sip of her espresso. She found the name of the SIO on the gas mask attacker case, DCI Peter Farley, and sent him an email, asking for the case file, and informing him that they could have a crossover with their cases. Her inbox beeped with a new email:

Hi Erika, the Cyber Crime Unit recovered this deleted image file from Joseph Pitkin's phone.
KAY

Erika opened the attachment.

I have these photos and the video file locked away. So long as you keep your mouth shut, they'll stay that way.

T.

'Jesus…' she said, sitting back. It was an eerie drawing, done with what looked like a black biro on yellowing paper.

There was a knock at her door, which made her jump.

'What?'

It was Peterson. He poked his head round the door.

'Is this a good time?'

'Why?'

'I just had Isaac Strong on the phone. He's completed the post-mortem on Marissa Lewis. Wants to know if you've got time to meet him?'

'Okay, thanks. I can call him back,' she said, rubbing her temples.

Peterson came into the office and closed the door.

'What the hell is that?' he asked.

'Another image recovered from Joseph Pitkin's phone. He'd deleted it, along with the pornographic photos and video.'

'A gas mask? You think it's this guy's signature, to send notes with a drawing?'

'I don't know. I just got the bloody thing. I need you to circulate this to the guys downstairs, get it up on the whiteboards. See if any of the other victims received anything like this, either through the post or via email. Also see if we can match this gas mask drawing with any of the e-fits from the victims.'

'Yes…' Peterson looked awkward. 'Can I have a word?'

'I've got one minute,' she said, picking up her coat off the back of the chair. 'Why?'

'I just need to talk to you about something.'

'Work-related?'

'Erm, well…'

'Can it wait? Can we catch up when I'm back?'

He nodded. Erika grabbed her phone and car keys and left.

Peterson came back down the stairs and met Moss at the coffee machine.

'That was quick. How did she take it?'

He shook his head.

'She went off to the morgue. I didn't get the chance to tell her.'

'James! You need to let her know.'

'I know I do. It's just bloody hard when we're in the middle of a case.'

'You need to grow a pair, and make time,' Moss said, sipping her coffee and heading back into the incident room.

CHAPTER TWENTY-EIGHT

The car park was busy when Erika arrived at Lewisham Hospital, and she had to wait to take a ticket before the barriers would let her enter. She got lost, twice taking a wrong turn, and she had to ask a hospital porter where the parking was for the morgue. Finally, she found it and parked the car next to a short, squat building, with a huge chimney pumping out black smoke into the grey sky.

She had to sign in at a front desk, then she passed a doorway to the hospital incinerator, before finding the morgue at the end of a long corridor, where Isaac buzzed her in.

'You found us,' he said.

'Yes, it's not as easy as it was in Penge…'

'And we have to pay for the privilege of coming to work.'

Isaac took her into the large post-mortem room, and she blinked at the bright lights. Six steel post-mortem tables lay in a row, with steel guttering.

'Keep your coat on if I were you,' he said. 'I've got a fleece on under my medical scrubs… Sorry that this has taken longer than I would have liked.'

Marissa's body lay on the first post-mortem table. She was covered to the neck with a white sheet. Isaac pulled it back. Her skin had a sallow yellow appearance. A long line of coarse stitches ran from her navel, spreading out in a Y shape between her breasts and across her sternum. Her body was washed clean of blood, and the repeated slashes across her throat made Erika think of fish gills. Her eyes moved down.

'She has a diamond tattoo just above her knicker line,' she said, pointing above the slim line of pubic hair. 'It's also embroidered on all of her clothes – the clothes she wore to perform.'

Isaac nodded. 'She had a small amount of alcohol in her blood when she died, but this should be expected if she was out partying on Christmas Eve. There were no other drugs, illegal or legal, in her bloodstream.'

Erika looked back at the scar running along Marissa's sternum, and then at her face, which, scrubbed of make-up, was so youthful. She didn't look much more than a child herself. Erika took a deep breath and felt her headache come hammering to the front of her skull. She felt strange, as if she was being pressed down and lifted up at the same time.

'She was healthy. All organs in good health.' Isaac moved to her head. 'The blade used was about eight inches. There are three long slits in the throat, one of which severed the main arteries. Which meant she bled out very quickly. The top of the knife had a serrated edge. Some older knives for paring fruit have this feature on the blade.'

'So it could have been a knife that someone has owned for some time?'

He nodded. 'We weren't able to lift any DNA samples from the body.'

'Nothing?'

'No. No bodily fluids, hair samples. She wasn't sexually assaulted.'

One of Isaac's colleagues came in and went to one of the large stainless steel doors along the back wall. He opened it with a click and the drawer slid smoothly out. Erika did a double take. It was the body of Joseph Pitkin.

'What is it?' asked Isaac.

'This young lad, he killed himself in custody on Boxing Day… May I?'

Isaac's colleague nodded and Erika and Isaac moved over to the body. Joseph seemed smaller in death, and his body was so thin. Angry red wheals surrounded his neck, and a deep purple line showed where the noose had cut into the skin under his chin, crushing his Adam's apple.

'I wanted to check his body again,' said the colleague, a small woman with soft grey eyes. 'I wanted to run something by you, Isaac.' He moved round and she lifted up Joseph's hands. 'He has this pigmentation on the skin, very white spots peppering the backs of his hands and moving up the wrists. I've been back over medical records and there is no mention of skin disorders such as vitiligo in the family.'

Isaac peered at it. 'Yes. I don't think this is disease-related. It looks to be chemical bleaching rather than natural pigmentation.'

'He was an amateur photographer, and he had a darkroom,' said Erika.

'Right, that answers my question,' said the woman.

'Dark room chemicals used in processing photographs can often cause pigmentation of the skin, if gloves aren't used. Was there any scarring in the lungs?'

'No,' said the woman. 'Very healthy. Like his organs.'

The woman's words began to echo arounds Erika's head: *'Very healthy. Like his organs.'* She saw the drawing of the gas mask, and then the video of Joseph, the disembodied hand reaching into the shot and gripping his throat. His face turning red, then purple; the tendons on his neck straining... Erika saw the note again in her mind; the blank eyeholes of the gas mask bored into her head.

The dull pain intensified, and blazed through her skull. The room began to spin, and she had to grip the edge of the post-mortem table.

'Erika?' asked Isaac, as she felt the room start to fade out, and her vision fill with stars. Then everything went black.

CHAPTER TWENTY-NINE

When Erika opened her eyes, she was lying on a small sofa in an office. It was warm and filled with packing boxes. Isaac knelt beside her with a look of concern on his face.

'Here, drink some water,' he said. She took the cup from him and drank. It was deliciously cold, and it washed away the nasty dry taste in the back of her mouth. 'Can I take your blood pressure?' he asked, pulling out a blood pressure cuff. She nodded and he pulled up her sleeve, slipping it over her arm.

'What's in the boxes?' she asked.

'Books.'

She watched as he pumped the pressure cuff and it tightened around her arm.

'Did you eat today?'

'I had some cereal this morning.'

He let it go, and placed the end of a stethoscope on her wrist and counted on his watch, listening as she felt her pulse beat through her arm. Then he released the pressure. 'Blood pressure is a little low: a hundred over sixty-five.' He pulled out a tiny torch and shone the light in her eyes. She winced.

'Since when do you have a little torch to do that? Surely all the patients you deal with can't dilate their eyes?'

'I got this in a Christmas cracker. I swapped a pink hair clip for it.'

Erika grinned. Her head was still banging, but the pain had eased a little.

'You were out for several minutes. Can I take some blood?'

'If you must,' she said. Isaac left the room, and returned moments later with a syringe and sample tube wrapped in sterile plastic. He pulled on a fresh pair of latex gloves. Erika turned away whilst he took the blood from her arm, grimacing at the pricking sensation.

'Okay, that's one sample,' he said, removing the little bottle and screwing another onto the end of the needle. 'Have you had any other fainting episodes lately?'

'No.'

'Been to see a doctor?'

'No… I was called out to a house, earlier today… A guy tried to top himself, turned on all the gas and sealed up the doors and windows…' She explained what had happened.

'You didn't hang around to get checked out by the paramedics?'

'No.'

'Jesus, Erika. You were exposed to high levels of natural gas. What have you drunk today?'

'An espresso.'

'You need to flush the toxins out; you should be drinking gallons of water.'

'Okay, okay.'

He went away and came back with a huge pint glass of water and a Mars bar. He watched as she took a drink and a bite of the chocolate.

'Finish what you were telling me about the post-mortem.'

'That was everything. Oh, there was something else. She had paraffin residue on the inside of her mouth. I can't work out why it would be there. I've only ever seen this with people who commit suicide, or truly desperate alcoholics who try to get a high in the strangest places.'

'She did fire-eating in her burlesque act,' said Erika.

'Ah,' said Isaac. 'Mystery solved.'

'I'm going tonight to The Matrix Club where Marissa worked. I want to talk to some of the girls who she performed with. You wouldn't want to come along?'

'That sounds like a very weird date,' he grinned. 'Sadly, I have to work.'

'Ah, okay.'

'Although you need to take it easy.'

'I'm going to chill at home for an hour, and get some food,' she said. She downed the last of the water and got up.

'I'll run your bloods through all the usual tests. Save you a trip to the doctor,' he said.

'Thanks.'

'I'm sorry about that lad, the one who killed himself in custody.'

'I am too,' she said.

Erika left the morgue and came out into the dark. The car park was busy, and there was a long queue waiting to leave at the barriers. She hunted around for her wallet in the folds of her coat and went to validate her parking ticket. As usual, she pushed down all her feelings about Joseph and Marissa and all the dead she had seen during her long career, brushing them under the carpet, just like she'd been doing for years.

CHAPTER THIRTY

Erika came back to her flat, took a shower, and ate a huge portion of fish and chips that she'd picked up on the way home in front of her laptop. Peterson sent over an email with the details of the tailor who had worked on Marissa's costumes, adding that he would be working that evening at the Matrix Club on Wardour Street in Soho.

Erika had just finished getting tastefully dressed up for an evening of burlesque, and was in front of the mirror, debating if she looked too severe, when the doorbell rang.

'Evening,' said Peterson when she opened the door. He was dressed in a fresh black suit with a navy-blue tie, and a long smart black winter coat.

'What are you doing here?' she asked.

'I'm coming with you, to the Matrix Club,' he smiled.

'Why didn't you call me? Or say in your email?'

'Because you'd probably have told me to piss off.'

'I would have said something more professional. As it was work-related.'

They both smiled.

'You look great,' he said.

'I don't look like an undercover copper trying to be glam?' she asked, looking down at the smart blue tailored trousers and white sleeveless blouse. She touched her hair, which was rock solid. She had blow-dried it, then doused it in hairspray, trying to copy what they had done the last time she had been to the hairdresser, but it had ended up a little severe.

'No. You don't,' he said.

'Good. And you look great; I mean, smart.'

'Thank you. Are you happy for me to come along? It is police business, and I did find you the info about this tailor who worked for Marissa.'

'Okay, I could use another pair of eyes.'

Despite the snow, Soho was buzzing, with people surging down Old Compton Street, making good use of the lull between Christmas and New Year. Snow fell lazily, and the white pavements were dappled with coloured light from the surrounding bars. Erika and Peterson joined the crowds walking up the centre of the road. They had talked about the case during the train journey from Forest Hill to Charing Cross. Erika told him about her visit to the morgue, where she'd seen Joseph Pitkin's body. She left out the bit about her collapsing. Peterson updated her on Ivan Stowalski, who was still in hospital, and hadn't regained consciousness. His wife had appeared at his bedside late afternoon.

'They still don't know if he has brain damage, from oxygen deprivation,' said Peterson. 'We also ran a background on Don Walpole. He extended his mortgage by eleven grand in the autumn, and sent ten grand to Marissa's bank account… He doesn't have a record, not even a parking ticket, poor bastard.'

'That doesn't mean he didn't kill her,' said Erika.

They hadn't had much of a chance to talk about anything other than work by the time they got off the train and walked up to Soho, through the crowds in Leicester Square. The Christmas decorations were magical, and Erika felt sad at the way things had turned out between herself and Peterson. She held a little hope that they might be able to salvage their relationship, but she put it to the back of her mind.

The Matrix Club was on the corner of Wardour Street and Old Compton Street. The entrance was a small black door with a neon sign above. A small strip of the pavement was roped off, and a tall, thin black man stood at the door, behind a podium. He was dressed in a long, thick winter coat, wore bright blue eyeshadow and had a tiny pink fascinator stuck to the side of his shaved head.

'Two tickets, please,' said Erika as they approached him.

'What's the name?' he asked, giving them the once-over.

'Erika and James,' she said, looking back at Peterson. Somehow, saying their first names made it feel like a date.

'Your *full* names? I'm not just making conversation,' he said, rolling his eyes and pointing to a clipboard. His nails were painted bright pink.

'I didn't book,' said Erika, feeling stupid.

'Then sorry. You are the Weakest Link, goodbye.' He waved them away, and beckoned to another couple arriving behind them.

'Cheeky fucker,' said Peterson, getting out his warrant card.

'Shit. I wanted us to go in like Joe Public, without them knowing we're coppers.' She pulled out her warrant card, feeling inept. It wasn't like her to make mistakes. The couple who had been behind them were on the guest list, and the rope was unclipped for them with a flourish.

They went back to the podium. The guy on the door eyed Peterson.

'Have you got any Caribbean in you?'

'No.'

'Would you like some?'

Erika had to suppress a smile.

'I don't need this,' muttered Peterson.

'What do you need?' said the guy, suggestively leaning forward and feigning comedy desire. Erika stepped forward.

'I'm Detective Chief Inspector Erika Foster; this is my colleague, Detective Inspector James Peterson. This is an informal visit, but I would appreciate your cooperation. One of the women who worked here, died a few days ago. She worked as...'

'Honey Diamond,' finished the doorman. The bitchy veneer dropped away. 'Terrible tragedy. We're putting together a benefit show. Do you think someone here did it?'

'No, we'd like to speak to some of the people she worked with. I understand Martin Fisher works here?'

'Yes. He's the dresser.'

'He worked for Honey Diamond, Marissa. We'd like to talk to him, just to get some background.'

'Right, okay, follow me.'

He unclipped the rope and ushered them through the door. The club inside was beautiful, with black polished tables and chairs, dotted around a small stage with a red curtain. He took them to a table near the front.

'What's your name?' asked Erika.

'Mistress Ebony. By day, I'm Dwayne Morris,' he said, pulling out a chair for Erika and using a cigarette lighter to light the small candle on the table. 'It's table service, and feel free to vape.'

He went off and a waitress came and took their order. They stuck to orange juice and Coke.

The club soon filled up, and then the show began. Whilst there was no full nudity, Erika felt awkward being there with Peterson. The acts were women and men of all different shapes and sizes. Some did traditional striptease, but there was a stripping Adolf Hitler, a Star Wars stormtrooper, and then there was a woman who came on dressed as a suicide bomber. She slowly stripped off her clothes whilst a ticking noise got louder, to reveal wires and sticks of dynamite covering her modesty. Then the lights went out, there was the sound of a huge explosion and when they came back up again, she was completely naked.

And that was the end of the show.

'Blimey,' said Peterson. 'The last show I saw was *Riverdance* with my mum before Christmas.'

'Yes, that was much more than an Irish jig,' said Erika.

Dwayne appeared through the members of the audience who were moving towards the bar.

'Martin wants to talk to you,' he said. They picked up their coats and followed him up to the stage and through the velvet curtain. It came out into a chaotic little backstage area filled with stacking chairs, racks of costumes, and old takeaway containers. The door to a small office was open, where a large middle-aged man with a balding head and glasses was working behind a sewing machine. There were racks of costumes along one wall and behind him was a desk with a phone and computer. A huge poster of the original Broadway production of *Mame* was up on the wall behind him, and the remaining wall was covered by a huge mirror.

'This is Detective Chief Inspector Erika Foster, and her colleague, Detective Inspector James Peterson,' said Dwayne, and he left, closing the door.

'Did you see the show?' Martin asked, pressing the pedal of the sewing machine and pushing a large panel of blue fabric past the needle.

'Yes,' said Erika.

'What did you think of the suicide bomber?'

'It was very clever.'

He gave a smirk and adjusted his glasses. He lifted the needle off the fabric and examined the seam. 'You want to know about Honey Diamond? AKA Marissa Lewis?'

'You did alterations for her, and you designed the diamond emblem she has sewn on her costumes?' asked Peterson.

'Yes. Although, she was always late paying… I'm not going to sugar-coat it. She was a little bitch. I'm very sorry that she's dead, but that doesn't change things for me.'

'Why didn't you like her?'

Martin put down the piece of fabric and gave them his full attention.

'She was devoid of grace, without warmth, with a hideous drive and ambition. She'd tread on anyone to get where she wanted to go.'

'Where did she want to go?' asked Erika.

'God knows, she just wanted to be famous. She wanted to be the next Dita Von Teese. What she didn't realise is that she also needed to work on her craft. Anyone can go off and be a Kardashian, or at least they can try. We had some American footballer, don't ask me who, come in last summer. She made no bones about trying to bed him; she even said she would try and make a sex tape with him.'

'Did she?' asked Erika.

'No. He went with one of the blonde girls, Jenna Minx, who has a little more class than Marissa. Although, that's not saying much.'

'How long had Marissa performed here?' asked Erika.

'Since January.' He picked up a pair of scissors and started to cut a bright yellow piece of fabric. 'To be fair to her, despite all her failings, she has real stage presence and she became one of the most popular dancers. Although there have been rumours that she's done more than dance for some of the punters.'

'Prostitution?'

He nodded. 'A few times, rich types have taken her out afterwards, and she's had no shame about saying what she did and how much she got for it.'

'She told you?'

'Yes, me, whoever else was in the room, and the kitchen sink.'

'Did she ever talk about neighbours, friends, any relationships close to home?'

'There's a drippy Polish guy, Ivan, who she's been bleeding dry for a long time. Poor bugger. Used to come often to see the show.

Sat on the front row and kept his anorak on. All goggle-eyed, and crossing his legs over his erection. There was a girl here who had a boyfriend who works in TV, commissioning reality shows. Marissa went after him, but he wasn't interested. There was a fight between the two girls just moments before curtain up. I was frantically trying to mend their costumes during the show.'

'Did Marissa go into much detail about her relationship with Ivan?'

'She used to joke that she kept him in the cupboard... on account of how pale he was. And she'd often ring him up to ask for more money, or a new frock, and she'd put him on speakerphone, for us all to laugh at. Poor bastard.'

'Did Marissa ever say if he hit her, or if she was scared of him?' asked Peterson.

'No. Marissa wore the trousers. She was in control of him and his wallet.'

'Did Marissa ever talk about her other work?' asked Erika.

Martin pushed his glasses up his nose and snorted.

'Yes. She was multi-talented, it seems. She was also a carer. Although, to me that's a bit like King Herod getting a job in the antenatal unit... She stole from that old woman. Food and toiletries at first. The old woman...'

'Mrs Fryatt,' said Erika.

'Yes, she came here one night to watch Marissa as Honey Diamond. All dressed up like Joan Collins in furs and diamonds. That's when we realised why Marissa was her carer...'

'What did you mean, "at first", when you said Marissa was stealing from Mrs Fryatt?'

'Marissa stole a pair of diamond earrings from her.'

'When was this?' asked Peterson.

Martin put down the piece of material. 'Must have been a couple of weeks before Christmas. I thought it was bullshit, and that she'd concocted some story to make a pair of costume jewellery earrings into something more than they were – that was a very Marissa thing to do, she liked to lie – but she took one of the girls up to Hatton Garden, and had them valued. They were the real deal, worth ten grand.'

Erika glanced at Peterson. Mrs Fryatt hadn't said anything about a pair of earrings.

'Did Marissa mention anything about an attack?' asked Peterson.

Martin looked surprised. 'Marissa attacked someone?'

'No, she was attacked, about a month ago, on her way back from the train station where she lives. A man grabbed her.'

Martin shook his head. 'Not that I heard. And I used to hear everything about that girl's life, whether I wanted to or not.'

'You do understand that this is a murder investigation, and you aren't speaking about Marissa Lewis in favourable terms?' said Peterson.

'Do want me to lie?'

'No,' said Erika.

'I know it's not right to speak ill of the dead, and no one deserves to be cut down on their own front step. Awful,' he said, taking off his glasses and crossing himself. He let them hang down over his large belly on a gold chain.

'Did you know she was planning to move to New York?'

'Yes. She talked about it.'

'No specifics?'

'No, but I did ask her how she would fund herself. It's not cheap, and there are visa costs and all sorts. She did say something which stuck in my mind. She said the diamond would bring her good fortune and a new start in life.'

'The diamond on her costume?'

'No, she was thinking of changing that, and her burlesque name.'

'Was she going to sell the diamond earrings?' asked Peterson.

'I know she wasn't the brightest star in the firmament, but she knew the difference between singular and plural. She meant one diamond, and this was before the earrings appeared,' said Martin. 'She was either being cryptic, or talking shit. Sadly, with Marissa, it was often the latter.'

'Were you here when she did her last gig on Christmas Eve?'

'Yes. And she wore the diamond earrings on that night.'

'Can you be sure?' asked Peterson.

'Yes, cos she came in here stark naked, asking me to fix her suspender belt. I kept my eyes above her neck. I'm not too keen on the female anatomy,' he said, pursing his lips. 'Especially when it's shoved in my face with no warning.'

'Who is the woman Marissa took with her to the jeweller in Hatton Garden?' asked Peterson.

'She was performing tonight, I'll just give her a tinkle…' He pulled a phone out, removing one of the clip-on earrings he was wearing to make the call.

'Wench! Are you still here? The police want to talk to you… Nothing bad, just a couple of questions.'

A door outside creaked, and a small woman in jeans and a purple woollen jumper appeared at the door. Erika recognised her as the stripping stormtrooper.

'You wanted to see me?'

'Come in Ella, don't skulk by the door jamb,' said Martin, putting his earring back on. 'This is Ella Bartlett.'

She smiled at Erika and ran an appraising glance over Peterson.

'You went with Marissa to have her earrings valued?' asked Erika.

'Yeah. The guy estimated they were worth ten and a half grand. He offered to buy them as they had *exceptional* purity, he said.'

'And Marissa didn't take him up on it?'

'Not when I was with her; she seemed pretty chuffed to have such a shit-hot pair of earrings. Like she didn't want to part with them.'

'When did you go with her?'

'A week or so ago.'

'Were you and Marissa good friends?'

'Not really. I was just as intrigued as everyone else to see if they were real, and I was going up that way to my gym, so I thought I'd go with her.'

'Can you remember which jeweller it was?'

'No. It was close to the Gym Box where I work out, the one in Farringdon, like, two roads away…' Erika looked at Peterson. That only slightly narrowed it down from the hundreds of jewellers in Hatton Garden.

'Can I give you my number, and if you remember, let me know? It's very important,' said Erika, handing over her card. The girl nodded and was about to go.

'Ooh, Ella, that reminds me. I got you some Febreze for your stormtrooper helmet. I know it gets very hot in there,' said Martin, handing her a bottle. Ella looked at Peterson, embarrassed, and grabbed it from Martin. 'And you owe me five ninety-nine,' he shouted after her. 'Officer, are there any more questions? I've got to run up six G-strings from scratch and I can't miss the last train home.'

'Thank you,' said Erika.

CHAPTER THIRTY-ONE

'Oh my lord, this case,' said Erika, as she and Peterson walked back to Charing Cross station. They took the quieter back streets so they could talk over what they had discovered.

'And what is this diamond thing?' said Peterson.

'It was Marissa's trademark. Perhaps she thought that she, Honey Diamond, would be the one to make a fortune from her career. Dita Von Teese has made millions, and she wanted to be the next Dita Von Teese.'

'There just seems to be more and more layers of…'

'Intrigue? Deception?' asked Erika.

'Shit. The word is shit. This case is a quagmire. Everyone hated her.'

Erika nodded. 'Marissa had a big mouth and was indiscreet, but as far as I can tell, she only told Mrs Fryatt about being attacked by the guy in the gas mask.'

'Just because Marissa was a fantasist and not well-liked by people, doesn't mean she didn't have fears and secrets. So many people are too scared to report when they are attacked or assaulted. And the most confident people can often be bluffers, and feign confidence,' said Peterson.

Erika nodded. They had been so deep in discussion that they hadn't noticed where they were walking, and they emerged from a side street out into Regent Street. Sleet had started to fall.

'Do you fancy a coffee?' asked Peterson, seeing a Starbucks still open on the corner. 'At least until this sleet stops.'

'Okay.'

They waited for a couple of red buses and then crossed the street, hurrying out of the snow and into the brightly lit coffee house. Erika found a seat by the window and Peterson returned with two coffees. Erika could see the Christmas displays in the shop windows opposite, and the canopy of Christmas lights strung above Regent Street. They took a sip of the hot coffee and watched the busy street.

'So, we've got Joseph Pitkin, who stalked and photographed Marissa on several occasions and then filmed her, we think at her request, to blackmail Don Walpole?' started Erika.

'We have Ivan Stowalski, who was obsessed with her, willing to leave his wife at Christmas and go off with her to New York, and he tried to kill himself,' said Peterson.

'There's Don Walpole, who she slept with when she was fifteen, and then blackmailed him, saying he would go on the sex offenders register if he told… She also allegedly stole a pair of diamond earrings from Mrs Fryatt, but Mrs Fryatt didn't mention it, and she seemed sharp as a tack when we spoke to her.'

'Do you think her son knew about it? Isn't he a jeweller in Hatton Garden?' asked Peterson.

'Possibly… But Mrs Fryatt was the only person who Marissa told she was attacked,' said Erika.

'By a man in a gas mask, who it seems is somehow linked back to Joseph Pitkin. He topped himself because of those photos you showed him during the interview… Well, what I mean is that he was scared.'

'It pushed him over the edge,' she said, wearily. 'If only we had been able to recover the note with the drawing of the gas mask at the same time. I might have been able to get more out of him before he died… Or, stop him… I don't know.'

'You weren't to know,' said Peterson, putting a hand on her arm. She gave him a weak smile.

'And Mandy is being evasive about the night Marissa died. She must have heard something.'

'Isn't she an alcoholic?'

'Yes. She could have been blotto on the sofa as Marissa was stabbed on the other side of the window. What we need to do tomorrow is to work backwards and establish who has an alibi and who doesn't. I also want to pay Mrs Fryatt another visit, and ask her about those earrings.'

They took a sip of their coffees, and for a moment they were silent. Peterson shifted awkwardly on his stool.

'Erika, there's something I need to talk to you about…' he started. Her phone rang and she pulled it out of her bag.

She checked her watch and saw it was almost eleven-thirty.

'Shit. I'm going to miss the last train, and I need to finish up writing a report tonight.

Erika downed the rest of her coffee, and picked up her phone again.

'I'm going to get an Uber,' she said, swiping the screen. 'Ah, there's a car close by that can be here in one minute. Brill. Do you want to share?'

'Nah, I'm going to get the train,' he said.

'Do you think you'll make it?'

'Yeah. I fancy the walk. The Christmas lights are cool.'

Erika looked at him for a moment.

'Are you okay? What were you going to say before?'

'I don't know if there's time.'

Her phone pinged, and a car pulled up outside.

'No. That's my car. It was close.'

'It was nothing, you go on ahead.'

'Okay. Thanks for the coffee. I'll see you tomorrow, bright and early.' She grabbed her coat and swung it over her shoulder, and with a wave she was out of the door, dashing through the sleet to the car.

*

Peterson watched her get in and it drive away. He took another gulp of his coffee, and a text message came through on his phone. He took it out and quickly made a call.

'I know, I'm sorry. I thought I would be done by now… Yes, I did see her, but we ended up doing some work on a murder case… Yes, it's a twenty-four-hour job… No, I didn't tell her, but I will. I promise… I love you, too.'

He hung up the phone and stared out of the window for a moment. Guilt and regret flooded through him. Guilt that he was happy, and regret that Erika wouldn't be a part of it. He downed the last of his coffee, and started back towards Charing Cross station, walking under the canopy of Christmas lights and reflecting on how life can often take a turn and shock you. In a good way.

CHAPTER THIRTY-TWO

It was hot inside the Uber car as Erika sped through Piccadilly Circus. The driver looked at her in the rear-view mirror.

'You want a copy of the *Evening Standard*?' she asked. Erika said she did, and the driver passed it back.

She settled back and started to read, preferring to concentrate on gossip articles as she flicked through. They were just crossing the river at Vauxhall when Erika turned the page, and let out a loud, 'Fuck.'

'Everything okay?' asked the driver.

'Sorry. I just forgot something,' she lied. There was a huge single-page article about the previous case she'd worked on: the murders, and the kidnap of Marsh's twins by Max Hastings and Nina Hargreaves. The newspaper had run several sensationalised articles about the case, focusing on Nina and Max as a modern-day Bonnie and Clyde, or Myra Hindley and Ian Brady. This article said that no one had claimed the body of Max Hastings, even though it was several weeks since he had died. The *Evening Standard* had contacted his mother, who said she didn't want to have anything to do with him, and was quoted saying, 'Take him to the landfill, he's no son of mine.' This was the same mother who was on bail for perverting the course of justice.

There was a picture of Erika at the bottom of the article. She was used to the papers portraying her as a trouble-making, scrappy senior police detective. What pissed her off now was that they'd used a photo of her coming out of the front entrance of her block of flats. The road sign, 'Manor Mount SE23'was clear in the corner of the photo, and they hadn't pixelated her car number plate.

She pulled out her phone and searched through for a number. It rang a few times, and then a bleary voice answered.

'Hello?' said Colleen Scanlan, the Met's media liaison officer.

'Colleen, this is Erika Foster.'

'Erika. It's very late.'

'I've just seen a piece in the *Evening Standard* about the Max Hastings and Nina Hargreaves case. They've printed a picture of me coming out of my house, next to the road sign, and you can see my number plate.'

There was a long pause.

'I can't control what they run in the press.'

Erika put her hand over the phone, and took several deep breaths. She loathed Colleen, who was, in her opinion, a lazy jobsworth who did just about enough to keep her job, but never wanted to go that extra mile to help.

'I know you can't do anything about the print edition, but what you can do, please, is check if the online edition has this picture, and if so, get it taken down. NOW.'

Colleen sighed. 'I doubt the office is open, but I can leave a word. I can do that for you,' she said stiffly.

'Thank you,' said Erika and she ended the call.

They rode the rest of the journey in silence. Erika kept checking her phone to see if Colleen had messaged or emailed, but there was nothing. Shortly before midnight, they approached Forest Hill, and the Uber dropped her outside her building.

When Erika got indoors, she flicked on the heating, took a shower and then came back into the living room in her pyjamas. She poured herself a large glass of vodka and settled down on the sofa with her laptop, opening the report she had started writing for Melanie. The floorboards upstairs creaked as Allison, her neighbour, moved around. She clicked on Internet Explorer and opened the *Evening Standard* website. The same article was online with her photo.

'Shit,' she said. She got up and closed her curtains, suddenly feeling paranoid, knowing that information about her and where she lived was online. She told herself not to be ridiculous. It wasn't as if they had published her full address. She checked her phone, but there was no email from Colleen. She tried calling her again, but it went to voicemail. She took a large gulp of vodka, and started to work on the report.

Erika woke with a start. Her laptop was upended beside her on the sofa, and the phone was ringing. She turned to the clock in the kitchen. It was shortly before two in the morning. She sat up as the phone continued to ring. She put her laptop on the coffee table and heaved herself up, her first thought being that Colleen was ringing her back. Then the answerphone clicked in. After the recorded message, a breathless, ragged voice said:

'Erika...'

'Erika...'

'Erikaaaaa...'

She stopped in her tracks in the doorway to the hall. Her name faded out into a breath, and then there was a strange scratching sound. The message carried on, with a discordant, ragged breathing.

'Erikaaaaaa... Erikaaaaaa...'

The voice was hoarse and deep, with a malevolent rumble. There was a distorted sound, a ragged wheeze and an almost inhuman retching which made her cry out with fear.

Erika grabbed at the answerphone machine cord and pulled it out of the wall. Then she did the same with the phone. She hurried to the front door and checked that it was locked, and then worked through the flat, turning on all the lights and checking the windows were locked. She sat back on the sofa, shaking, and tried to control her breathing.

For the first time in her long career, she wished she had a gun.

CHAPTER THIRTY-THREE

Jason Bates's alarm woke him at six. Shortly afterwards, there was a soft knock on the door. It was one of the council carers, arriving to take over, so he could go to work.

'How's she been?' asked the kind woman with the lined face. In his bleary state, it took him a moment to remember which one she was... *Dawn...* Her name was Dawn.

'She had a good night,' he said. A good night for his mother meant that he had only been woken three times. Dawn took off her coat and warmed her hands over the radiator, as Jason busied himself making breakfast and getting ready for work.

The plastics factory was a fifteen-minute train journey away. It was still dark when he stepped out of the house. He looked back to where his mother had been put in her chair and wheeled to the window to watch him leave. He waved back at her, and she lifted a hand. The anger and frustration he felt towards her melted away. He wondered if her carers did this every morning, to remind him that she was a person. He could only see this from outside the house, looking in.

The streets were dark with a freezing fog, which made him feel like he was wading through wet sheets. The small coffee shop outside Gipsy Hill train station wasn't open at such an early hour, and he hurried past, through the open barriers, just making it onto the train as the doors closed. The one good thing about working further out of London was that the morning trains going in the opposite direction from the city were less crowded, even less so between Christmas and New Year. The carriage was almost empty, and he sat in a window seat, the heater by his legs pumping out warm air. He slipped on his headphones and put on an audiobook, which he planned on listening to for the rest of the morning while he drove the forklift – just one headphone, the other ear would be free for safety.

He left the train at West Norwood. Again, he was the only one on the platform. It was a fifteen-minute walk to the warehouse, and there was a long industrial slip road leading up from the station, lined with derelict buildings and overgrown hedges. He put up his hood and trudged through the snow, his footsteps crunching through the silence. The streetlights couldn't penetrate the fog, creating a tunnel of light. The sky in the far distance was only just starting to turn from black to a dark blue. As he passed the gates to an old office block, a dark shape bulged out from the shadows, and a tall figure stepped into the light. It was dressed in a long black coat, and stretched over its head was the dark shiny hood of a gas mask. Vapour streamed out from the large breathing drum which hung down to its chest, and there was a line of small white squares on the breathing drum, which gave the impression of wide smiling teeth.

Jason stopped, and at first he didn't feel scared. It was so unexpected. He heard the clack of a train on the tracks as it sped past. The figure watched for a moment and then advanced towards him.

'Hey, hey!' he shouted as the figure steamed towards him, bearing down, then punched him hard in the face.

Jason came to a little while later. He could feel snow under his back. He could see the outline of the sky above, now a palette of light blues. His hands were fastened behind him, and he was lying painfully on his wrists. His legs were cold, and then he realised that he was naked from the waist down. There was something in his mouth, material or cloth. He looked around, moaning, hearing the sound coming out in a feeble murmur. A train whooshed past on the tracks behind a high wall to his left, to his right was the main entrance of the vast decaying edifice of the office block. Rows and rows of broken windows stared down at him, and in a few, birds fluttered. He felt sick when he saw that in the doorway of the building, about five metres away, the figure in the gas mask was watching him. His coat was open and he was masturbating, his black gloved hand working quickly back and forth. Streams of vapour pouring from the breathing drum of the mask.

It felt at once insane and terrifying. Jason could see a few shapes poking up out of the melting snow: a burnt-out car and some disused gas bottles. Suddenly, he heard voices on the slip road from the station, and he looked over to the tall hedges. The road was obscured.

People walking past. Commuters! he thought. He cried out, but it sounded nothing more than a muffled moan. The voices carried on past. The figure abruptly stopped, fastening his trousers, and started towards him. He picked up Jason's feet, and dragged him through the melting snow. Jason tried to kick, but felt stones and sharp pain as he was dragged up three steps, and onto the bare concrete of the doorway. There wasn't much space on the top step leading into the building. The figure stood directly over him, looking down through the blank eye holes. Then he knelt down.

Jason kicked out, and his foot connected with the gas mask, knocking it to the side. The man gave a muffled yell and fell back through the broken glass door. A shard of glass scraped across the side of his neck, and he tottered over, landing on his backside on the other side of the door. The gas mask almost came off, sliding up at a drunken angle to reveal his mouth and nose.

Jason panicked and stared. The figure's loss of control was somehow more terrifying. Jason scrambled to get up, but his trousers were around his ankles, and his feet tangled. The figure slowly sat up and took off his glove, putting a hand to the scrape on the side of his neck, which was bleeding. He turned away and lifted the mask to inspect his hand. Apparently satisfied that it wasn't a deep cut, he pulled the mask back down and turned, pulling on his gloves again.

Then he walked towards Jason, and dragged him back to the top of the steps.

CHAPTER THIRTY-FOUR

Erika had switched on breakfast TV at six, after a sleepless night spent on the sofa. She prided herself on her stoicism, and even though the call had terrified her, she refused to let that terror overtake her. The sound of her neighbours stirring, and water running through the pipes, started to bring her back to normality. At seven-thirty she made coffee and took a shower, and then as it got light she opened the curtains and felt her fears fade with the pale blue dawn.

Just before she left the house, she plugged her phone back in and played back the message of the rasping voice. The person who'd called hadn't withheld their number. It was a mobile number which she didn't recognise, but which she made a note of. She wound up the cable and took the answering machine with her.

Once she was in her car, and driving amongst the busy morning traffic, she felt reality settle over her. There was still nothing from Colleen Scanlan, no voicemail or text on her phone.

She'd thought a lot about the case during her sleepless night, and the question about the diamond earrings kept coming back to her. Why hadn't Mrs Fryatt mentioned them? She checked the time and saw it was just past 8 a.m. She took a detour from her usual route, and went through Honor Oak Park and down to Hilly Fields. As she approached Mrs Fryatt's house, she peered through the window, and saw the old lady was rugged up against the cold, and waiting outside her house, leaning on a walking stick. When Erika pulled into the parking spot by the kerb, Mrs Fryatt started shouting and waving her stick in the air, shouting, 'Go on, you can't park there, I am reserving this space!'

Erika wound down her window,

'Morning. Can I give you a lift anywhere?' she asked.

'I'm waiting for my son; he's taking me to the doctor's surgery. He said he'd be here…' She looked past Erika and up the empty street, leaning painfully on the stick.

'Is everything okay?'

'It's my leg. I've been waiting four days to see someone; you know what it's like trying to get an appointment… Where is he? I'm going to miss my appointment! Please, move your car.'

Her nose was dripping from the cold, and she juggled her stick to pull out a tissue and wipe it.

'I have some more questions,' said Erika.

'More? You asked me a plethora of questions yesterday.'

'Did Marissa steal a pair of diamond earrings from you?'

'No.'

Erika kept her eyes on Mrs Fryatt as she looked past her distractedly.

'Are you sure?'

'Of course I'm sure. I'm in perfect health, both physically and mentally.'

'Yes, you said that yesterday, but now you're off to the doctor.'

'What is this? I've done nothing wrong. I will cooperate with you, but I don't like your tone.'

A car appeared at the top of the road, and Mrs Fryatt looked hopeful, until she saw it wasn't her son and it sped past.

'I spoke to a colleague of Marissa's; he did the alterations for her costumes. He said that Marissa was showing off a pair of diamond earrings, and she boasted that she took them from you.'

Mrs Fryatt turned to Erika. Her composure regained.

'Really? How strange. That's not true.'

'I don't know why he would make it up,' said Erika, searching the old lady's face, but she was still distracted by the top of the road.

'Well, if you don't know, how the heck should I? Did you find a pair of diamond earrings on Marissa's person, or in her house?'

'I can't share that with you.'

'That's a "no" then,' said Mrs Fryatt dismissively.

'Marissa went with another of the girls and had them valued in a jeweller in Hatton Garden.'

'Ah, here he is! About bloody time!' she said, whirling her walking stick around her head. A sleek white car pulled up next to Erika's. 'Officer, is that all? I don't know what Marissa could have been talking about. She was probably winding this person up. She was like that.'

Mrs Fryatt's son, Charles, got out of the car and came up to the pavement.

'You're late!' she shouted. He looked flustered and he eyeballed Erika.

'The traffic was bad,' he said. 'Hello, Officer. Is everything okay?'

'Marissa never said anything to you about stealing a pair of your mother's earrings?' Erika asked him.

Mrs Fryatt rolled her eyes and started to make her way to the car. 'He wouldn't know. I'm the only one who opens my safe, and all my jewellery is accounted for! Now come on! I can't miss this appointment!'

Charles gave Erika an awkward smile. She noticed that he had a large sticking plaster on the side of his neck, and a little blood had soaked through.

'How did you cut yourself?'

'Shaving, the razor slipped… A symptom of not wanting to be late for my mother,' he said, giving her a smile. It was an odd smile, showing wide crooked teeth, but it didn't reach his eyes.

He hurried off to help his mother, who was now at the passenger door. Another car pulled up behind and honked its horn. Mrs Fryatt started to shake her stick at it.

'Can you wait for ONE MINUTE!' she cried. Charles helped her into the passenger seat and did up her belt. He nodded at Erika, the serious expression back on his face, and then he drove away.

There was something that wasn't quite right, but Erika couldn't put her finger on it.

'Well, I did ambush her,' she said as she got back into her car. She took out her phone and dialled McGorry.

'Alright, Boss,' he said. 'I'll be there in a sec, I just got off the DLR at Lewisham.'

'It's okay. Just a question. You've been going over everything in Marissa Lewis's house, all her belongings. There weren't any diamond earrings?'

'Erm, there was jewellery... But I dunno. I don't know if I would know the difference between a real diamond and costume jewellery. I can look back over the photos taken by forensics. Do you remember seeing anything when we looked round her bedroom?'

'No. Can you have a look for me?'

'Sure.'

Erika came off the phone. She thought of all the people who could have taken the earrings. Joseph Pitkin touched Marissa's body before the police arrived... Mandy found her daughter's body. Could Ivan have taken them? When had been the last time Don Walpole saw her alive?

'He saw her on Christmas Eve, at the station!' she said triumphantly. She started the engine and did a U-turn, driving over to Coniston Road.

CHAPTER THIRTY-FIVE

Don Walpole opened his front door, and wasn't pleased to see Erika again.

'Is this a good time?' she asked. He was wearing an apron, and Erika could smell bacon frying, which made her stomach rumble.

'Does it matter if it is?' he said.

'I just need a few minutes of your time.'

He stood to one side and she came indoors. He took her through to the kitchen, and she saw Jeanette staggering down the stairs, wrapped in a huge purple towelling robe with a towel over her wet hair. She looked dreadful.

'Who's that?' Jeanette said, through half-closed eyes. Erika introduced herself, but Jeanette didn't seem to remember her from the day before. They carried on through to the kitchen.

'I need to ask you a question, about Marissa,' said Erika in a low voice. Don rushed back to the hob and quickly flipped the eggs over in the pan. He wore dark jeans and a thick brown knitted polo neck, which came up to his chin. Jeanette shuffled in, oblivious of Erika, and took a large bottle of orange juice from the fridge.

'Do you need me?' she asked.

'No. This is just…' started Erika, but Jeanette was already shuffling off out of the room.

'Do you want eggs?' asked Don.

'No!' she said. Erika watched as she shuffled down the hall and into the living room. She closed the door, and moments later the television came on. Don sighed and stood over the eggs, pushing them around in the oil. Bread popped up in the toaster and he pulled it out, dropping it onto plates.

'Do you want her eggs? I'll only chuck them,' he said.

Erika hesitated. She was suddenly ravenous, but she stopped herself from accepting. 'No, thank you. I just came to ask you a couple of questions…'

'I try to get her to eat, but she gets most of her calories from alcohol. It's given her this huge belly, and these two tiny stick legs.'

'My mother was an alcoholic,' said Erika.

'Is she?'

'No, was. She died, a long time ago. She was never violent, but she was belligerent and she made life difficult.'

Don nodded. His eyes were sad and dark, and he had black circles under them. He started to butter the toast.

'What do you want to ask me?'

'You said you saw Marissa on Christmas Eve, at Brockley station?'

'Yeah. When Jeanette… had words with her, shall we say.'

'Do you remember if Marissa was wearing earrings? They would have stood out, they were real diamond earrings.'

Don scooped the eggs out of the pan and placed two on his toast.

'Real diamonds? Where would she get real diamond earrings from?'

'I can't go into details. Was she wearing earrings on Christmas Eve?'

'She had no shortage of admirers. I'm sure she was able to convince some poor mug to buy her expensive jewellery.'

'Don. Please, really think. What was she wearing when you saw her at the station? Break it down.'

'All I can remember is that she wore a long black coat.'

'What about her hair and make-up?'

'She was done up. Er, she had those false eyelashes on… I can't remember if she wore any earrings.'

'Can I ask Jeanette?'

'I doubt she'll remember.'

'It's important to my case.'

Don put the plate down on the table. Erika followed him into the living room. Jeanette was lying on the sofa. Her wet hair hung limply down, half over her face. She was watching morning TV, with the sound up high.

'Jeanette. She wants to talk to you,' said Don, raising his voice. He went back to the kitchen and left them alone.

Jeanette eyeballed Erika from behind her wet hair. 'What?'

'I need to ask you a question?'

'Go on then.'

'Can you turn down the TV?' Jeanette made a sulky show of muting it. 'Thank you. You and Don saw Marissa Lewis on Christmas Eve.'

'That whore,' she spat.

'Can you remember if she wore any jewellery?'

'I couldn't see her tits – for once – she had a thick coat buttoned up over her cleavage. But she was wearing earrings.'

'What kind?'

She shrugged. 'White gemstones, little studs.'

'Are you sure?'

'Completely sure,' she said, her eyes not leaving the TV.

'How can you be so sure?' asked Erika.

Jeanette turned to her. 'Cos I was thinking about ripping them out of her ears, and how much it would hurt,' she said.

Erika wished she had a photo of the diamond earrings to show her.

'Would you say the earrings were real diamonds?'

'I doubt they were real.'

'But would you know real diamonds if you saw them?'

'Do I look like the kind of woman who knows real diamonds?' she said, bitterly.

Erika didn't need to answer. She looked around the room and noticed a long black coat spread over a clothes airer. It was in front of the lit gas fire, and steaming lightly.

'Is that Don's coat?'

'Who else's coat did you think it was?'

'Has he been out today?'

'I dunno. Probably went to get milk. Are you done with your questions?'

'Yes. Thank you.'

Jeanette unmuted the TV, and the sound boomed out again.

When Erika left the house, she sat in her car for a few minutes, trying to organise the facts of the case. She drove back up the road and came to a stop outside Marissa's house. The front garden was covered in a fresh layer of melting snow. There were two alleyways, one running alongside the house and one on the opposite side of the road. There was also a junction, just past the school, at the end of the road, which led off to a railway bridge, and a housing estate.

The killer had used a car, according to the blood spatter analysis. Whoever did it would have been covered in blood, and carrying a dripping murder weapon, which left blood up the path and onto the pavement, but it stopped there. Erika inched her car up to the alleyway, and very slowly she turned it in and looked at the bonnet. The alleyway was too narrow for it to fit down.

Her phone rang, making her jump. It was McGorry.

'Boss, you need to get to the station fast, we've had a major breakthrough,' he said.

CHAPTER THIRTY-SIX

Erika parked outside the station, grabbed her bag and the answering machine and hurried down to the incident room. Moss, Peterson, Kay and the rest of the team were gathered around McGorry's desk.

'What is it?' asked Erika, seeing the excited faces looking at her.

'I've been working on all the statements with regard to Marissa Lewis's death, and I've been putting together a timeline of the events on Christmas Eve,' said McGorry. 'She was working at the Matrix Club until eight-thirty. They had an early Christmas Eve show. No one hung around afterwards for a drink, and they all headed off for home. She took the 9.10 p.m. train from Charing Cross…' He maximised a window on his computer monitor. 'Here she is, running for the train, and just making it before the doors close.' He played the short clip of Marissa Lewis running along in towering heels, her long coat flowing behind her. 'She was alone when she got on the train.'

'Okay,' said Erika. 'Does all this have a point?'

'Oh yes,' said McGorry with a grin. Peterson grinned and nodded too.

'Well, get on with it!'

'I also got footage from the train, when she changed at London Bridge. It's a newer carriage and equipped with CCTV.' They saw a crowded train carriage from the viewpoint of a camera mounted in the ceiling above the doors, looking down the carriage. 'There she is, crushed in beside these two guys. Gay, I'm guessing, as they don't seem to be paying any attention to her.'

'Okay, okay, less of the personal comments.'

'I'm just saying that there are no creeps who seem to be interested in her,' he clarified, as he ran through the footage on the screen, showing the ten-minute train journey. 'Okay, here we are at 9.42 p.m., and the carriage empties out at Forest Hill.'

'Is there any footage from TFL of the station?' asked Erika.

'No. Nothing apart from the platform, and Marissa getting off with the rest of the crowds,' he said, moving to another short clip.

'Okay, what else do you have for me?'

'This is the best. The school opposite Marissa Lewis's house on Coniston Road has CCTV on two sides of the playground. One of them shows a view of Marissa Lewis's front gate.'

The last video showed half of Marissa's house, from the gate past the alleyway, and a portion of the street leading up to the junction.

'What's the time stamp on this?' asked Erika.

'This video is from 9.40 p.m.'

He scrolled through the black and white video, showing the empty snow-covered street, and the gate.

'What's that?' asked Erika, when there was a flash of black at 8.51 p.m.

'A cat jumping up on the gate,' said McGorry.

'Marissa had a cat,' said Kay. 'Beaker, its name is.'

'Did you interview it?' asked one of the uniformed officers.

'Piss off,' said Kay.

'Quiet!' said Erika.

'Here we go,' said McGorry. A figure in black, wearing a gas mask, walked into shot by the gate, moving carefully and purposefully along in the snow, almost staggering against the slippery surface. It reached the gate and looked up at the house.

Then it carried on walking past the house, and stepped into the shadows of the alleyway.

'Jesus,' said Erika.

'Okay, we run this forward for seven minutes,' said McGorry, as the time stamp on the video whirred past. 'There, you can just see Marissa Lewis arriving home.'

Marissa appeared at the gate. The room fell silent. Most of them had already seen the video, but the impact of it was just as striking the second time. Marissa opened the gate and went through, vanishing in the shadows of the front garden. Ten seconds later, the figure in the gas mask moved out of the shadows and approached the gate, carrying a long knife. It moved quickly through the front gate and was swallowed up by the darkness.

'The camera doesn't pick up anything that happened in the front garden,' said McGorry. 'Four minutes later, he comes back out.'

'Are you sure there's nothing?' asked Erika.

'I've watched it several times, slowed down. There's nothing; the camera doesn't pick up anything.'

He moved the video forward, as the figure came out, carrying the dripping knife. It stopped in the gate and looked back into the shadows.

'He wipes it with a cloth, conveniently taken from his pocket. He stashes the knife in the pocket with the cloth, and then immediately turns to his right, leaving the shot.' The team around Erika was silent. 'I've lost him after that; there's no CCTV in the residential area. He could have got in a car out of shot, or gone into a house; we don't know.'

'Run it back again,' said Erika. She paused the video where the man in the gas mask emerged from the gate, and for a moment there was a clear view of the mask. She got up and went over to her desk, where she had a copy of the note sent to Joseph Pitkin. She held it up against the screen, looking at the hand-drawn gas mask in black biro ink.

'Does this look like a similar kind of gas mask?' she said.

'I don't know, it's perhaps an old military gas mask,' said McGorry.

'We need to go back over the e-fit images given by the people who were attacked. And if there aren't any, we need to go back and get them to work with an e-fit artist. Also, now we have this CCTV with the date and time stamp we could concentrate on a new door-to-door in the houses overlooking Marissa's, in case anyone saw anything. This is great work.'

'I was working with Kay,' he said, grinning at her. One of the phones started ringing in the background and Moss hurried over to answer it.

'This is good work, both of you.'

'Boss,' said Moss, holding her hand over her phone. 'There's been another attack by the man in the gas mask, in West Norwood, early this morning. A young lad on his way to work.'

CHAPTER THIRTY-SEVEN

Jason Bates had been taken by police to the SARC, the Sexual Assault Referral Centre in Camberwell. Erika drove alone to the centre, and arrived there late afternoon. It was a small, nondescript building off the main road. Erika was met by a big burly police officer with a thick beard at an unmarked door at the side of the building.

'Have you managed to take any evidence?' asked Erika.

'Yes, he's already been examined; we've taken swabs and samples.'

'Did you manage to get anything workable?'

'Blood.'

Erika nodded; she couldn't let her enthusiasm show.

'Can I talk to him?'

'The SIO of this case is with him now; he's been through a terrible ordeal. He's deeply traumatised.'

'I know, but the murder case I'm working on has just crossed over with this.'

He nodded. 'Wait here a moment, please.'

Erika took a seat on a small bench in the long corridor. The officer went through a door marked 'Initial Room', which was a forensically safe examination room: a sterile space with wipe-clean plastic surfaces so that there could be no possible contamination of evidence.

Erika looked around the corridor. There were pictures of a sunny meadow and of a few sacks of brightly coloured oriental spices that had been hung in an attempt to dilute the clinical atmosphere. The door opened and the police officer emerged with DCI Peter Farley, a middle-aged man with greying hair. Erika showed her warrant card.

'Hi Erika, good to meet you,' he said. She followed him into the small room, which again had been unsuccessfully disguised with posters and pot plants.

A nurse sat with a young lad who had a blanket wrapped around his shoulders. His bare feet poked out of the bottom of a long paper gown. There was an untouched cup of tea beside him. He was slight, with strawberry-blond hair and pale eyebrows. His left eye bloomed with red where a blood vessel had burst. His lip was cut and his nose was crusted with blood. His eyes had black bruises. He shifted in his seat painfully.

'This is Erika; she's my colleague,' said Peter.

Jason stared ahead and nodded.

'What can you tell me about the person who did this?' asked Erika.

Jason swallowed with difficulty and winced. 'He was tall. I'm five nine. I think he was taller than me. He wore a gas mask.'

'Can you describe it?'

Erika listened, waiting for him to mention the white squares painted on the breathing drum. He did. He went on to describe what had happened, how the attacker's mask had almost come off his head and how he'd cut himself on the glass in the door frame.

'This is where we got the DNA blood swab,' said Peter.

Jason went on, 'He, he forced himself on… He…' A tear formed in his bloodshot eyes and ran down his cheek. Erika went to take his hand but he pulled it away. 'He put his, the mask, close to my face. I saw his eyes, they were dark and small, and the whites… I could really see the whites around his eyes. He then… He raped me.' He started to gag and retch and bent over and gripped his stomach. The nurse pulled out a tissue and gave it to him to wipe his mouth.

'We should stop there,' she said to Erika.

'No,' said Jason, wiping his mouth and scrunching the tissue up into a ball. 'I want to talk to her.'

The nurse nodded.

'Thank you, Jason. I can understand this is hard for you,' said Erika.

'You don't understand… The sick bastard put on a condom.' He wiped his eyes. 'He was well-built, strong.' He looked up at the ceiling and shook his head, not believing that this was happening.

Erika looked over at Peter. She wanted to know if they had been able to get any semen swabs, but he shook his head.

'Is there anything else? Anything, however small?' asked Erika.

'He was dressed all in black. A long winter jacket. He had on black boots, the mask. Thick leather gloves… When he took one of the gloves off, he touched me.'

'Where?'

'My throat. He touched my neck to feel my pulse…'

'What about the gas mask, how would you describe it?' asked Erika.

'It was a gas mask. I dunno, like the ones you see people wore in the war. There were these white squares on the breathing bit, the round bit where his breath was coming out…' Jason shook his head and scrunched up his eyes. 'It was only just getting light. But there was this smell, his breath when he got close. It was like a chemical smell, like industrial, or nail polish. I don't know.'

'It's okay. Thank you, Jason.'

When Erika came back outside, she put in a call to Moss, who was back in the incident room. She relayed the information, and that they had a DNA sample from blood on a piece of glass.

'I want a DNA sample taken from Don Walpole. Send an officer round with a DNA kit to get a mouth swab.'

'You checked out the Matrix club with Peterson last night. How did that go?' asked Moss.

Erika briefly outlined what had happened and that she'd gone to see Mrs Fryatt and Don about the earrings.

'I've just been checking over everything from forensics, and what the police recovered from Marissa Lewis's house, and there are no earrings. I also had Tania ask Mandy Trent, but she wasn't aware of Marissa having a hugely expensive pair of diamond earrings,' said Moss.

'Okay. Oh, if you check out my desk, there's my answering machine.'

'Okay, not sure I understand why you brought that to work?'

Erika explained what had happened with the *Evening Standard* and then the strange message late at night.

'There are more than enough weirdos in the world who probably have my number and want to give me a fright. Can you just run the number? It's from a mobile; I've left it on my desk.'

'Sure. One more thing, Boss. University College Hospital called. Ivan Stowalski is still unconscious. His wife, Ezra, arrived this morning and she's there with him.'

'Okay, I'm halfway there. I'll go over and see what I can get out of her. It will be interesting to hear her side of things. Keep me posted.'

CHAPTER THIRTY-EIGHT

Ezra Stowalski was a small woman with short fair hair, and a kind, careworn face. Ivan had been given a room on the top floor of the hospital, and when Erika arrived, a nurse was taking some blood from his arm. Erika waited until she was finished and then produced her warrant card and introduced herself.

'I'm so sorry for everything that's happened,' said Erika.

'Why didn't you leave him?' Ezra said, becoming angry. 'Why did you have to break the door down and save him?' She had a slight accent, but pronounced every word correctly.

'I'm trained to save lives.'

Ezra looked down at Ivan. His skin was grey, and he was hooked up to so many machines, tubes and wires. His chest rose and fell with a hiss of a ventilator. Ezra looked away from him and closed her eyes, her face registering pain.

'I didn't know anything. About him leaving with her. How stupid am I?'

'You're not stupid.'

'Are you trained to humour people, too?'

'I'm not usually very good at it. Something must be going wrong today.'

Ezra smiled.

'Did you know he was having an affair?'

'Yes.'

'How did things start?'

'She put a leaflet through the letter box, asking if anyone wanted any cleaning or ironing done. Her mother has never looked after her. I felt sorry for her. I thought it was admirable that she wanted to work her way out of her situation. I asked if she'd like to come and do some ironing…' She looked over at Ivan. 'I never thought that he would go for a young girl.'

'When was this?'

'A year ago, maybe more.'

'Did you confront them?'

'No. I was scared to, and I was happy he wasn't… that he didn't want anything from me. We'd been sleeping in separate bedrooms for some time. I just buried my head in the sand. Although, I never thought he would leave me, or plan to leave me so callously. The cheating I could deal with; it was the lies and the lack of respect for our life together that hurts me.'

'Why did you come back?'

'My wedding vows,' she said, looking back at him. Although, she didn't sound too convinced.

'What was your husband doing on Christmas Eve, after 8 p.m.?'

'He was upstairs in his office, going over paperwork. I was packing.'

'Why did you leave so late to drive up north to your parents? You left around 11 p.m.'

'How do you know what time we left?'

'We have your car on CCTV, at 11.30 p.m. leaving the congestion charge zone, and heading up north.'

'You think he killed her?' asked Ezra, her eyes wide. Erika didn't answer.

'Where was Ivan between 8 p.m. and 10.30 p.m.?'

'He told me he had to do some work.'

'On Christmas Eve?'

'His job, his work, it never stops. He's always having to work in the evenings and at weekends.'

'Where were you packing?'

'Upstairs in our bedroom.'

'And where does Ivan work, when he's at home?'

'In the kitchen.'

'Were you up and down the stairs as you were packing?' asked Erika.

'No. I finished what I had to do by nine. I stayed upstairs and watched TV in our bedroom.'

'Did you see Ivan working in the kitchen between nine p.m. and ten thirty p.m.?'

'No. I just waited upstairs… I might have fallen asleep, I was dozing. That's around the time she was killed, isn't it?'

'Yes, we think so.'

'Was there anything out of the ordinary about Ivan that night? And is there anything else you want to tell me. Was he a jealous type? Was he obsessive about who you were friends with, who you spoke to?'

'No. Not with me, anyway…I thought it was just a silly affair. I didn't know he was so serious about her. That he wanted a future with her. That he loved her. Perhaps he did kill her. It just goes to show, you don't really know the people who you share your life with.' She put out her hand and touched the blankets, pulling them up around Ivan's chin. 'He doesn't deserve to wake up. Is that bad, that I think that?' she said. Again, Erika didn't answer.

CHAPTER THIRTY-NINE

McGorry rang the bell of Don Walpole's house just after 5 p.m. He was flanked by two uniformed officers, one of whom carried a portable DNA kit. The road was quiet, and the snow was melting, leaving the road with a grey slush. He leaned up and rang the bell again, hearing it chime from inside the house. He stepped back and went to the window, peering through the curtain.

'No one in,' he said. The two officers shifted on their feet in the cold. McGorry took out his mobile phone and tried the number they had for Don. It went straight to the answer machine. McGorry noticed an old man standing at the end of his front path a few doors down, smoking, with an ashtray balanced on the gatepost. McGorry came out of Don Walpole's front garden and approached him.

'Do you know the person who lives here?' he asked. The old man took a drag of his cigarette, his whispering lips making a small 'O', then he exhaled, nodding.

'That's Don and Jeanette.'

'Have you seen them today?'

'They left this afternoon, about an hour or so ago. In a hurry, they were.'

'How can you tell if someone is in a hurry? What do you mean?'

'They was moving fast… And have you seen Jeanette? She's a big woman. She don't move fast.'

'Did they say when they were coming back?'

'What do you think this is? People don't talk to each other. I saw them leave.'

'Did they drive?'

He nodded.

'Did they have any bags?'

'No.'

'Shit,' said McGorry. 'Thanks.'

As he went off, the old man lit up another cigarette, and McGorry overheard him mutter, 'Useless bloody police; takes three of them to knock on a door.'

CHAPTER FORTY

It was gone six when Erika left the hospital, and she realised, again, that she hadn't eaten or drunk anything all day. She walked to the Starbucks across the road, and joined a long line to grab a sandwich and a cappuccino. It was very busy, and she thought about taking it back to the car, but she felt so exhausted, and it was so cold outside. She just needed ten minutes to sit down and think about the case and all the new developments. Did Ivan have motive to kill Marissa? He certainly felt guilty enough to try and top himself.

The seats were all full, mostly with kids in their twenties sitting and chatting on their phones, or working away at their computers. At the back, she found a small table, with three big easy chairs dotted around it. A young couple in their teens occupied two of the chairs, and they were holding hands and leaning across to nuzzle and kiss. Shopping bags were piled up on the third chair.

'Excuse me,' said Erika. 'Can I sit here?'

The young guy was kissing the girl. He opened an eye to look at her, but carried on.

'Hey. I'm talking to you! Could you please move your bags,' said Erika, showing that her hands were full.

The couple broke apart and the girl said, in an infuriatingly ironic tone, 'Um, sorry, but we've got, like, a friend coming.' She turned back to kiss the young guy.

'When is your friend coming?'

'I don't know. Soon.'

'Well, until he does show up, can I please sit here?'

The girl sat back and her eyes widened in shock.

'Look, lady, I've just told you my friend is coming, okay? You're making me feel uncomfortable.'

Her condescending tone made something snap in Erika. She slammed her coffee cup and sandwich down on the table. She picked up the shopping bags and dropped them on the floor.

'Hey! That's so rude. And there's, like, expensive stuff in those bags. Can't you see they're from the Apple Shop!' said the guy.

Erika sat down, tore into the wrapping on her sandwich and took a bite.

'Excuse me,' said the girl, attracting the attention of a barista carrying a plastic tub filled with used coffee cups. 'This woman has just been rude and abusive and she's damaged my shopping. She threw my bags on the floor!'

The young male barista seemed to be taken in by the girl's doe-eyed stare, and he turned to Erika, who looked dishevelled in her coat and mucky shoes, cramming the sandwich into her mouth.

'I'm sorry, ma'am. If that's the case, I'm going to have to ask you to leave.'

Erika chewed her sandwich and looked up at the young barista, who was bearing down on her with a firm, condescending smile. She chewed the last mouthful and swallowed.

'No.'

'I'm sorry?'

'No. I'm not leaving.'

'He just, like, told you to leave,' said the girl indignantly. 'You do realise that coffee shops invite you to be in them until they say otherwise? It's, like, the law.' The boyfriend nodded solemnly.

Erika took another bite of her sandwich and then a sip of her coffee.

'Do I have to go and get my manager?' asked the barista.

Erika reached in her pocket and pulled out her warrant card. 'I'm Detective Chief Inspector Erika Foster. I suggest you go back to clearing cups. Have you seen what a mess it is in here? And you? You need to learn some bloody manners.'

'What? You can't talk to me like that!' said the girl.

'We can all talk to each other however we want. This is a democracy. Of course, as a police officer, I have the power to stop and search. I can detain you if it really takes my fancy. Now, you could've just given up the spare seat, but no, you're part of this entitled young generation who think you can do exactly what you want. You reap what you sow. You were rude to me, and in turn I could make life very difficult for you. Or you can all fuck off, let me sit in this chair for ten minutes, and leave me to eat my sandwich in peace.'

The young girl and guy got up and picked up their shopping bags, watched by the surrounding tables. The barista eyed her, but he seemed unsure if she was in the right as a police officer. He went off to the cash desk.

Erika ate the rest of her sandwich quickly, under the gaze of the other customers, then grabbed her coffee cup and left, before anyone in charge came to talk to her.

CHAPTER FORTY-ONE

Erika walked back to the NCP car park where she had left her car, her blood still pumping after the encounter in the coffee shop. She started the engine and put the heater on, rubbing her hands to warm up. The snow was whirling past outside the car park, and the warm air and the comfy seat made the tiredness wash over her even more. She sat back and closed her eyes.

It seemed like seconds later that her phone rang. She had fallen asleep, and was soaking with sweat under her coat. It was coming up to 8 p.m. She pulled out her phone and groggily answered.

'Boss, you okay?' asked Moss.

'Yeah,' she said clearing her throat.

'We just got a call from UCL. Ivan Stowalski died half an hour ago.'

'Shit… I was just there.'

'Do you think he was a viable suspect? From everything we've heard he was a bit wet, and was dominated by Marissa.'

'He was obsessed with her,' said Erika. 'And the quiet timid ones can flip out just as much as the hotheads.'

There was silence for a moment.

'You still there?' asked Moss.

'Yeah. It's just been a long day, and hearing one of our suspects has kicked the bucket is never good news.'

'Yeah, it's less satisfying when you have to prove the dead guy did it,' said Moss.

Erika wound down the window and let some fresh air inside the stuffy car.

'Okay. Thanks for letting me know. Let's catch up tomorrow.'

Erika hung up, and was still staring at the phone in her hand when it rang again.

'Hello, is this Erika Foster?' asked a woman's voice.

'Yeah. Who is this?'

'I'm calling from the NHS Health Centre at St. Thomas's Hospital. For data protection, can I just take your date of birth?'

Erika's head was still reeling from hearing that Ivan was dead. 'Hang on, what are you calling about?'

'I need your date of birth before I can talk any more about your medical records.'

'Fourteenth of August, 1972.'

'And your postcode?'

'SE23 3PZ.'

'Thank you. I'm calling with results of your blood tests. Dr Isaac Strong sent samples over yesterday, and asked us to contact you with the results…'

The tone of the nurse's voice induced a mild panic in Erika. She thought back to when she had last had any kind of blood test. There had been an incident when she was working on the Andrea Douglas-Brown murder case, when a young boy had bitten her. She'd had blood tests three months later, which were thankfully negative for anything untoward. She turned off the heater.

'Are you still there, Erika?'

'Yes.'

'You'll be pleased to hear that there's nothing nasty or untoward showing in your blood after you were exposed to the high levels of carbon monoxide. The tests all came back clear. However, the levels of oestrogen in your blood are very low. Can I ask if you are still having regular periods?'

Erika switched off the car engine and racked her brains to think when she'd had her last period.

'Six, eight weeks ago?'

'Right. Have you had sex in the last month?'

'No.'

'Okay. I'd recommend a check-up with your doctor. You may well be pre-menopausal, but all signs are showing that you may have started the menopause.'

'Menopause?'

'Yes,' said the nurse, with a kinder tone. 'You are in the age range. We would expect your oestrogen levels to drop as you advance into your forties. Have you had any other symptoms? Thinning hair, dryness of the skin and the vagina, hot flushes, night sweats, irregular changes in mood… You mentioned irregular periods?'

Erika put a hand to her head and opened the car door a little. Cold air came flooding in.

'Look, I'm at work. Can I call you back?'

'There's no cause for alarm, Erika. I just wanted to inform you of this; everything in your blood shows that you are perfectly healthy. Iron levels good. Unfortunately, the menopause comes to all of us.'

Erika thanked her and put the phone down. The shock of what she had heard hit her hard. She had spent so long working, and focusing on her career, and getting through each day, and now this was full stop, a dead end. Her body would no longer be able to give her children.

She started the engine and drove back to South London. She thought long and hard about her life, and about the evening she'd had with Peterson. She didn't want to have a child with him, but she'd felt happy with him, and despite the fact that their outing last night had been work-related, she'd enjoyed his company. She tried to call him, but his phone rang out and went to voicemail.

Then she tried the station and got Crane, who said that Peterson had headed home for the night. It suddenly felt imperative to Erika that she sort things out with him, to stop this strange limbo – to maybe even rekindle their relationship.

She knocked on Peterson's front door just before 9 p.m. He lived in a small block of flats in Ladywell, a little way from her flat in Forest Hill. A moment later, he opened the door. He was dressed in jeans and a T-shirt and was carrying a little mixed-race boy, who must have been about six or seven.

'Hello,' Erika said, looking confusedly between him and the little boy, who gave her a toothy grin. He was very cute, and wore Spiderman pyjamas.

'Erika, hi,' Peterson said. There was a look of shock on his face, but then his eyes narrowed in concern when he saw how pale and upset she was.

'Daddy, the bath will run over,' said the little boy. A blonde-haired woman in her late thirties appeared behind them.

'James, who is it?' the woman asked, eyeing Erika suspiciously.

'Why did he just call you "Daddy"?' asked Erika, holding on to the doorframe.

'Because he's my daddy,' said the little boy.

There was a horrible pause.

'Fran, can you just take Kyle and turn off the water in the bathroom?' said Peterson.

Fran glanced nervously at him, and took the little boy in her arms. 'Is this…?' she asked.

'"This"? What do you mean, "this"?' started Erika.

'Okay, okay, okay, let's talk about this outside,' said Peterson. He ushered her out into the corridor. Erika stared at him.

'You have a son?'

He nodded.

'How old is he?'

'Six. He'll be seven in April.'

'How? What?' She was lost for words.

'Erika. I only found out two weeks ago.'

'And that woman, that's his mother? Who is she?'

'Fran was my girlfriend; we broke up in 2012, a couple of months before the Olympics.'

'What have the fucking Olympics got to do with it?' she shouted.

'I'm saying that it was a long time ago! We broke up, and she went to work in Germany. She's a graphic designer, and she found out she was pregnant very late.'

'She didn't tell you?'

'No.'

'And now she's in your flat, and you're running baths for her kid? And you've brought me out into the fucking hallway to tell me!'

'Erika, I didn't know how you'd react.'

'This isn't helping!' she cried. She stared at him and her eyes began to fill with tears.

'I've been trying to tell you. I tried at work and then I tried to tell you the other night when I came over, and then we went out and it was for work, and then we had coffee, but you had to go.'

'You should have tried harder, you fucking wimp! And now I have to find out like this, just as I drop by your flat!'

'Who just drops by these days? What do you expect?'

'I called your phone, James.'

'What about my landline?'

'I don't know your landline number.'

'If you didn't bother to learn my bloody landline, that's not my problem.'

Erika slapped him around the face. They both froze. A door further along opened, and a little old lady's face peered through the gap where the chain was on.

'James, is everything alright?'

He turned to her. 'Yes, sorry Doris, everything is fine. We're just...'

He heard the communal door close and saw Erika walking away towards her car. He ran outside after her.

'Erika!'

But she started the engine and drove away, swerving dangerously in the snow. He watched as her car vanished over the top of the hill. 'Shit,' he said, looking down at his bare feet in the snow.

CHAPTER FORTY-TWO

Isaac Strong loved to make bread. There was something deeply soothing about rolling up his sleeves and kneading dough. He loved his kitchen, tastefully decorated all in white: white cupboards, floor, walls, and surfaces. The absolute deal-breaker was the large white Butler sink, which had cost a fortune. He couldn't have dealt with any stainless steel; he saw enough of that at work. As he kneaded, he listened to *Gardeners' Question Time*, and to a very serious young woman who was having a terrible time with her indoor plants, which were suffering from Mealybugs. He was listening to the radio through the BBC iPlayer app on his phone, and the programme abruptly cut out as his phone started to ring. He saw it was Erika and answered with his elbow, carrying on kneading.

'Are you home?' she asked. Her voice sounded bleary and odd.

'Yes, of course.'

'I'm outside.'

When he opened the door, he saw an Erika he had never seen before. Her eyes were red and streaming with tears. She looked broken. He didn't say anything, and reached out and gave her a hug. She came inside and they went through to the kitchen.

'Drink?' he asked, reaching for a bottle of whisky.

'Please.'

She sat down at the table.

'It's James Peterson. He has a son…'

'What?'

She launched into the story. Isaac listened, poured her another drink, and listened some more.

'I never thought we would have children together,' she finished. 'And I knew from him, and from the times I've met his mother that he wanted kids… But there was this selfish part of me that thought we might end up as this childless couple… You know, happy and content.'

Isaac raised an eyebrow. 'For someone as intelligent as you, Erika, that is the stupidest thing I've heard you say.'

She burst out laughing and wiped her eyes. 'When he opened the door, he looked so happy. He was a father. It suited him. And there's a little boy who now has a father. I could never take that away.'

'Nor should you.'

Erika nodded and took another sip of whisky. She grimaced. 'That's disgusting.'

'You didn't say that about the first two glasses. *That* is a twenty-five-year-old Chivas Regal.'

'It tastes like Benadryl.'

'You fancy a beer?'

'Yes, please.'

He went to the fridge and got her one and popped it open.

'Thanks,' she said, as he set it down in front of her. She took a long pull on it and wiped her mouth. 'Oh god, this is such a mess. I have to work with James. He must have told Moss, because she was asking if we'd managed to have a "chat" the other night. God knows how long she's known for? And what about everyone else on the team? Did they know, and I'm the only one, stomping about in the dark?'

'Come on, this is Moss, I don't think she would keep this from you out of malice. She's loyal. Straight down the line… What's Peterson's son called?'

'Kyle. He looked very sweet.'

'And the girlfriend, or mother?'

'I've forgotten her name…' Erika took another deep pull on the beer. 'She's pretty, and she looks sorted.'

'How does someone *look* sorted?'

'She had a pullover slung over her shoulders, catalogue style, and her hair was sleek and straightened.'

'What if she's a catalogue model?'

Erika looked at him.

'What if she was rehearsing for a job?'

'A catalogue bitch,' said Erika darkly, picking at the beer bottle label.

'Don't go down that road, Erika. You're better than that. And the name Catalogue Bitch will stick in your mind, and you'll end up calling her that at the wrong moment.'

Erika stared gloomily ahead and rubbed her eyes. 'You're right.'

Isaac went back to his dough and dumped it in the bin, then he started to wipe down the counter. 'How is the case going?'

'Impenetrable,' she said, draining the last of her beer. Isaac went to the fridge and got her another.

'You're not going to join me?' she said.

'I'm on antibiotics. I had a chest infection.'

'Two cases have merged. The murder case, and now another case concerning a man in a gas mask who attacks his victims close to public transport late at night, or early in the morning. I am clueless on both counts.' Her phone began to ring and she saw it was Crane. 'Sorry, I have to take this. Hello?'

'Boss, sorry to call so late. I got back the information about that number that called your house in the early hours of the morning. It's a pay-as-you-go mobile, registered to an Edward Foster? Is this someone you know?'

Erika felt her blood run cold.

'Oh my god, yes. That's my father-in-law.'

CHAPTER FORTY-THREE

Erika made some calls, and discovered that Edward had been admitted to the Manchester Royal Infirmary Hospital in the early hours of the morning. He'd had a fall, and had to have an emergency hip replacement operation. There had been complications, and he had been placed in intensive care.

It was late, but Isaac offered to drive her up from London to Manchester, reminding her she was far over the limit. He had thrown some things for himself into an overnight bag, but she didn't want to waste any more time driving back her to her flat, so they set off straight away.

The snow was falling steadily, and Erika was quiet in the car. When they reached the top of the M25 motorway, a huge sign appeared up ahead for THE NORTH'. As it passed above them on the dark motorway, she felt fear and trepidation. This would be the first time she'd returned to Manchester since Mark's death.

'What are we going to do when we reach the hospital?' asked Isaac, looking at the GPS on the dashboard.

'I'm going to ask to see Edward, of course.'

'The GPS is saying we'll get there just after three in the morning. They won't let you in to see him.'

'What do you think we should do?'

'Where does Edward live?' asked Isaac, flicking on the windscreen wipers.

'Slaithwaite; it's a small town in Yorkshire, about an hour from Manchester.'

Isaac tapped in the details and waited as the GPS recalculated the route.

'It's saying we can get to Slaithwaite a little earlier than we would get to Manchester...'

'But it's close to the Dales, and Edward talked about snow,' said Erika, peering out as the headlights lit up the whirling snow outside.

'Do you want to stay near the hospital in a hotel, then?'

Erika thought of how close Manchester Royal Infirmary was to the house she owned – the house she'd lived in with Mark, which was now rented out. It was less than three miles away. She hadn't been back there since the day Mark died. Friends of theirs still lived close by, people she hadn't seen since then. The windscreen wipers dragged rhythmically across the windscreen and the leather heated seats in Isaac's Jeep Cherokee made her feel sleepy.

'No, let's head for Slaithwaite,' she said.

Isaac switched on the radio very low, and a news reporter started to murmur. Erika thought of their house. She'd left that morning, the morning of the raid on the drug den in outer Manchester. A mass shoot-out had killed Mark and four other officers in her team – officers she had called friends. She'd known their wives. One of their wives had been a civilian support officer on the same team.

The news report on the radio moved to a story about fighting in the Middle East, and faint gunshots could be heard. Isaac reached over and changed to a music station.

Erika had been shot during the raid: a bullet had passed through her neck, narrowly missing major arteries. She'd been airlifted to hospital, and had spent two weeks recovering in intensive care, only emerging to attend Mark's funeral. She'd never gone back to their house. She'd arranged for a removal company to take out all their things and put them in storage.

It had shocked Erika, how easy it had been to pack up her former life. A few phone calls and a large chunk of cash had meant that she had never had to deal with any of it. The house was now rented to people she had never met.

The car ploughed on through the snow, lulling her into an exhausted sleep.

It had been early when she'd left the house on the day of the drug raid – before seven – but it had been summer, and the sun had been streaming through the windows in the kitchen. She'd grabbed her phone off the kitchen table. There had been fruit in the bowl, an apple and a banana, and there had been two tickets on the kitchen counter for them to go and see a Woody Allen film that night: Magic in the Moonlight.

Erika had had the opportunity to offload the case to another team, but she'd held onto it, like a dog with a bone. She had been tracking the drug dealer Jerome Goodman for the past two years, and she'd wanted to nail the bastard.

But where had that got her? She'd taken the risk and lost her husband, her four colleagues, and nearly lost her life. Although, the life she'd been left with wasn't anything to write home about. And to top it all, Jerome Goodman had vanished. He was still at large. Still out there.

In her fitful sleep, her thoughts moved to Edward. Why hadn't she been more vigilant? Why hadn't she spent more time with him, or made more of an effort to see him? Why didn't she know his mobile phone number? She saw him lying on the floor at the bottom of the stairs. A bone sticking out of his leg, pushing through the material of the old towelling pyjamas he wore… But in her dream, it was snowing inside… And behind the stairs there was no wall… She moved to help Edward, but he had changed. It was Marissa lying there, but there were no stairs, she was lying on the path outside the front of the house, half-covered in snow and frozen blood… Erika crouched down and Marissa opened her eyes;

blood started to pour from her mouth and she reached up to grab at Erika…

'Erika? Erika?'

Her eyes snapped open and the dark interior of the car came back. It was warm, and on the radio, 'Do They Know It's Christmas?' was playing. Isaac was looking over at her. 'You okay?'

'How long was I asleep?'

'A couple of minutes… You were shouting out names: Edward, Mark and Marissa.'

Erika rubbed her eyes.

'Just a dream,' she said.

'Do you want to stay at Edward's place? We'll get some sleep, and then go over to the hospital for visiting?'

'Yeah. Are you still okay to drive?' She peered outside, but there was darkness all around. Only the snow-covered motorway was visible.

Isaac nodded. 'We've got another couple of hours at least. Get some sleep, if you want.'

'No. Let's talk, about anything. Anything but work.'

CHAPTER FORTY-FOUR

Moss and her wife, Celia, were eating their breakfast in the kitchen early the next morning when Moss's phone rang. It was Erika, who started to explain that Edward had been in an accident, and that she would be taking a few days' leave.

'I'm in Manchester,' said Erika. 'Slaithwaite, the village where Edward lives. Isaac is with me.'

'Isaac Strong?' said Moss, swallowing a mouthful of cereal.

'Yeah…' Erika clearly didn't want to elaborate, so Moss didn't press her.

'Are you okay?' she asked.

'I'm fine.'

'What about Edward?'

'He fell and broke his hip. They've operated, but he's on a high-dependency ward.'

Moss and Celia's son, Jacob, came crashing into the room with his toy electric guitar. He skidded across the floor on his knees, the guitar blaring out a tinny squealing. Moss waved her free hand at Celia, who jumped up from the table and grabbed Jacob, switching the guitar off.

'Mummy's on the phone,' she whispered.

Jacob stopped and watched his other mother as her face creased, listening to the call.

'What's the snow like up there?' Moss asked.

'A foot or so,' said Erika, on the end of the phone. 'Luckily, the roads were cleared and we're in Isaac's four-wheel drive. I'm going to be here for at least a couple of days. I've just phoned Superintendent Hudson and made her aware of the situation.'

'Okay, I can brief whoever covers for you…'

'I'd like you to cover for me. I've already discussed it with Melanie, and she's in agreement that you are acting Detective Chief Inspector and SIO on the case.'

For a second, Moss was lost for words. 'But… It's a complex case; we've got so many strands and now we're taking over the assaults from the gas mask attacker…'

'Don't you want to take over?'

'Yes! Of course I do,' she said quickly. Celia was watching her, dying to know what was going on, and what had made Moss's face flush with excitement. 'So this is for a few days?'

'It could be longer. I need some time to make sure that Edward's okay. My life seems a little unbalanced; it has been for some time.'

'Okay,' said Moss, the enormity of the case starting to dawn on her.

'This is now your investigation. I wouldn't trust anyone else to take this on. I'm here if you need me. Melanie is already working on giving you clearance as a DCI. You do know that overtime doesn't exist for my rank. We're always on duty.'

'Sure,' said Moss, looking over at Celia and Jacob.

'Phone me if you need anything,' said Erika, and then she was gone.

'What is it? You look like someone just died!' said Celia. Then, seeing Moss's serious face: 'Did someone die?'

'No. Erika's had a family emergency, her father-in-law is sick. She's promoted me to acting DCI on this case.' Moss sat down heavily. She pushed her bowl of cereal away, no longer hungry.

'But that's great, babe – not the father-in-law part, but that she trusts you,' said Celia.

'Yeah, that's really great, babe,' said Jacob, imitating her voice. Moss grabbed his feet and gave them a good tickle. He screamed and squirmed.

'Stop the tickles; you know I detest the tickles!'

'He *detests* the tickles. Good vocabulary for a five-year-old,' said Celia, with a knowing smile. 'I hope they're paying you more?' She put Jacob down.

'Of course… There's so much to sort out. I'll have to do the briefing this morning. Perhaps I should get everyone on the team a coffee.'

'You'll be great. Everyone likes you,' said Celia, gripping Moss's shoulder and giving her a kiss. 'Just don't become as obsessed as Erika.'

'She's not obsessed; she's bloody good at her job. And it's not about being liked. I now have to lead everyone.'

'I think the two things go hand-in-hand. Be yourself. How's Peterson doing? I take it she didn't put him in charge because of their history. Has he told her yet, about his long-lost son?'

Moss shrugged. 'I don't know. I told him to do it fast, but he chickened out.'

'Do you think it's a bit weird that this woman phones him suddenly, just before Christmas, and announces that he has a son?'

'Yes.'

'What do you think her motivation was?' asked Celia.

'She wanted him to be part of Kyle's life… Maybe she wanted some security. He told me she's been living in Germany, and she was made redundant.'

'But she actively withheld the information from him for six years.'

'He almost died earlier this year. And he's wanted kids for so long.'

'Do you think she wanted kids? Erika?' asked Celia, smoothing a strand of her long blonde hair behind her ear and starting to clear away the breakfast things.

'She probably still wants them.'

'I don't mean to be horrible, but hasn't that boat sailed for her?'

'I don't know, and I don't like talking about this.'

'What? She's not here.'

'It feels disloyal. She's a private person, and a good friend.'

'I know that, but you can talk to me. It's not going to go any further.'

Moss leant in and gave her a kiss. From the corner of her eye, she saw Jacob staring up at them.

'We have a little spy,' she said. 'It seems that he needs another good tickling.'

Jacob shrieked in delight and ran away as Moss and Celia chased him around the kitchen table and into the living room, where they collapsed on the sofa and tickled him until he shrieked again.

*

When Erika came off the phone with Moss, she looked around at the gloom in Edward's upstairs bedroom. It was just getting light outside, and through the window, the view of the snowy Yorkshire Dales was just appearing in the blue haze of dawn. The room was a shocking mess, with filthy sheets on the bed. A cracked sash window was letting in freezing gusts of air. The floor was filthy with dirt, and there were tablets scattered over the carpet beside the bed. The power was also off. She came back out onto the landing, where Isaac was just coming out of the bathroom.

'It's a complete mess,' he said. 'Damp up the walls, black mould, and it hasn't been cleaned in a long time.' He held up a clear plastic bag filled with prescription pills. 'He's got a whole medicine cabinet filled with old antibiotics, heart pills, blood thinners, statins, and there are antidepressants. It looks like he's not been finishing the course, or not taking them regularly, because there are several half-full bottles, all repeat prescriptions.'

Erika pulled her coat around her and tried to block out the musty smell. The cottage had always been so warm and cosy. What had happened?

They had arrived late, in the darkness. They had managed to get the wood-burning stove lit, and took a sofa each for a restless night's sleep.

'The heating is gas-powered,' said Erika. 'I need to find out if the bill hasn't been paid, or if it's the boiler.' They came down the small flight of stairs to the living room. It was a little cleaner here, but there were still dirty dishes over the coffee table. There was a small Christmas tree in the living room, but it was only half-decorated. They went through to the kitchen and found that the sink was overflowing with dirty dishes, and the counter littered with crumbs and scraps of food. The fridge was almost empty, with half a mouldering white loaf, and some blackening carrots in the salad drawer. They jumped as a cockroach crawled out from underneath an upturned saucepan on the draining board and scuttled along the counter.

'Christ almighty!' Erika cried, grabbing an old newspaper and whacking the cockroach. They both stared at the squashed body.

'If there's one, there could be more,' said Isaac softly. His thin eyebrows knitted together with concern. Erika threw the newspaper down, went to the phone on the wall, and lifted the receiver.

'Disconnected,' she said, looking down at the plug. She put her head down and wiped her eyes. 'He phoned me over Christmas; he said he was with neighbours and I presumed they were here. I didn't know he had a mobile phone. I just didn't know. When I spoke to him on Christmas morning he was confused about a few things, but he seemed fine other than that. I should have asked if he was able to look after himself.'

Isaac reached out and squeezed her hand. 'You're here now. We're here now. Focus on that.'

She nodded. 'Are you as cold as me?'

'Colder,' he said. 'Let's get some breakfast and a cup of hot tea. We'll be able to make plans with some hot food inside us…' He checked his watch. 'It's eight o'clock; visiting won't start for a couple of hours. We can make plans.'

'We need to get this place cleaned up, and I need to check his bills… and…'

'Food, and hot tea,' said Isaac. 'Then we'll make a plan.'

CHAPTER FORTY-FIVE

Moss could see through the glass that the incident room was busy, and she took a deep breath before she went inside. Superintendent Hudson was with her, and when the officers saw Hudson enter with Moss, the room fell silent.

'Good morning, everyone,' said Melanie.

'Morning, ma'am,' the officers replied, almost in unison.

'Erika – DCI Foster – has been called away on an urgent family matter. Her father-in-law is ill, and she has had to go to Manchester to be with him. Detective Inspector Moss will be taking over as the Senior Investigating Officer; she will be acting Detective Chief Inspector. I ask you to show her the same respect and courtesy that you show Erika. It's very straightforward, but does anyone have any questions?'

The officers all looked at Moss standing beside Hudson, who looked a little uncomfortable, and no one said anything.

'Good. Then I'll let you take over, Moss.'

The moment Melanie left the room, and was out of earshot, everyone started to ask Moss questions about Erika, and when she would be back.

'I know as much as the Superintendent,' she said, putting her hands up to quiet them down. 'Nothing has changed from yesterday. We are still hunting this bastard.' She went to the whiteboard and pointed at the e-fit of the gas mask, and then moved to the line drawing of the gas mask that had been in the note sent to Joseph Pitkin. 'We need to start finding links and unlocking information. We no longer have the luxury of questioning Joseph Pitkin, but I want to talk to his parents and see if we can find out more about this note. We also need to work on unlocking Marissa's iPhone. She didn't have a laptop or a PC, so all of her online activity on the iPhone could be crucial to this case.'

She moved along the whiteboard, to the photos of the other victims who had been attacked by the man in the gas mask.

'We need to look for a link between the victims, if there is one. Something that the attacker zones in on. Now, the link has to be something deeper than just physical. The victims were different ages and sexes, ranging from twenties to late fifties, men and women. Of the two men who were attacked, one was straight and one was gay. There is only one murder. Marissa Lewis. She was also the victim who was targeted closest to home. All the victims were targeted either close to their homes or close to their place of work, near train stations. Marissa had arrived back on the late train and she got the furthest away from the train station of all the victims. Did the attacker slip up? In the most recent attack, the victim kicked out and dislodged the gas mask on the attacker's face. Was Marissa killed because she saw the identity of the attacker? Or did she know the attacker?'

Moss moved along to the crime scene photos of Marissa. 'In Isaac Strong's post-mortem report, he says that the weapon was a long knife with a serrated edge. We still have no murder weapon, and time is moving fast. Perhaps now is the time for extreme measures. Perhaps we need to knock on every door in Coniston Road and check people's cutlery drawers.'

There were a few smiles and laughter from the team. Moss held up her hand.

'Okay, okay. I know I like a laugh, but I'm being serious here. What is it the boss says? There are no stupid questions. Well, I want to add to that: there are no stupid lines of enquiry.'

'But you're the boss now,' said Kay.

'Yes, I am.'

Moss went on, moving to the photos of the suspects and persons of interest.

'Our list of suspects is dwindling. Joseph Pitkin, now dead – but there was a new gas mask attack yesterday, which seems to rule him out. The same applies to Ivan Stowalski, he died in hospital yesterday evening after being exposed to the gas leak at his house. It was self inflicted, and we are ruling it as suicide. We do, however, have Don Walpole: no record, cares for his alcoholic wife, but cheated on her with Marissa when Marissa was underage. Marissa then tried to blackmail him, saying she would go to the police about the underage sex. We attempted to get a voluntary DNA swab from him yesterday, but he wasn't at home, and he wasn't answering his phone. I am going to attempt this again today. Also, Marissa alleges that she stole a pair of diamond earrings from Mrs Fryatt. Another dancer from the Matrix Club states that she went to Hatton Garden with Marissa, and saw the earrings being valued, but Mrs Fryatt denies any jewellery was stolen from her, and no earrings have been found. Charles Fryatt runs a successful jeweller's in Hatton Garden. There's a bit of a question mark there.'

'Could Marissa have got the earrings from an admirer?' asked McGorry. 'The boss… I mean, the other boss' report, says that the girls in the clubs had a lot of admirers – rich guys, hanging around after shows in the hope that they'd get a bit more than a dance?'

'Yes, but we need to rule all of this out. I want one of you to get back in contact with the girl who went with Marissa to the jeweller, and if needs be, one of us should take her back to Hatton Garden to see if she can remember which jeweller it was.'

There was a pause, and Moss looked around at the despondent faces. She felt the same inside, but was determined not to show it.

'Okay. Let's get to work and we'll reconvene back here at 4 p.m.'

When the team dispersed and started to work, Peterson came over to Moss, and asked if they could speak privately.

'You need to make it quick.'

'Well done, by the way.'

'Thanks. Although I thought she might ask you instead.'

He shook his head, and pulled her over to the back of the incident room, next to the line of photocopiers.

'She found out last night, about Kyle and Fran,' he said in a low voice.

'Found out?'

'She dropped round, late, at bath time. Kyle's bath time, I mean.'

'Obviously…'

'I opened the door holding Kyle; he called me Daddy. Fran was there too.'

'Shit.'

'I tried to talk to her, but she drove off in her car, swerving up the road. I didn't know if I should follow, but I didn't, and now she's gone off sick.'

Moss saw how worried he looked.

'James, it's nothing to do with you. It's true that Mark's dad had a fall and was rushed to hospital. He had to have an emergency hip replacement and there were complications. That's why she's gone.'

'Oh, shit. She didn't say anything to you about me?' he said.

'Her mind was on other things… As is mine.'

He nodded. 'Okay. And well done, I'm made up for you taking over.'

'Thanks. I need you and Crane to keep things moving here.'

'Sure.'

Moss went over to Kay, who was sitting at her computer.

'You're with me today; I want to go and see the Pitkin family and ask some questions about Joseph.'

CHAPTER FORTY-SIX

The snow was melting when Moss and Kay arrived at Coniston Road, and they tried Don Walpole's front door. Kay was ready with the portable DNA kit, but there was no answer.

'Shit,' said Moss. She pulled out her radio, and called into the station. 'Crane, I need you to do a search for Don Walpole…' Moss looked up and saw the old man in his usual spot, smoking a cigarette. 'Hang on, I need to call you back.'

They came out of the front gate and went over to the old man.

'You looking for Don?'

'Yes, we are,' said Moss, showing him her warrant card. 'My colleague said that you saw him and his wife leaving yesterday afternoon. Have you seen them today?'

The man shook his head. 'I'm out here a lot; the wife don't let me smoke indoors. I was out just before six and again at seven-thirty and eight… And again at nine.'

'So, you're quite a heavy smoker?' asked Kay.

'You will go far as a detective,' he said, pointing his cigarette at her and grinning with a set of yellow teeth.

'You didn't see any lights on, any movement?' asked Moss.

'Nope.'

They came back to the car and Moss called back in to Crane at the station, telling him to keep trying Don's phone and to put out a search on his number plate against the national database. They then drove the short way around the corner to David and Elspeth Pitkin's house.

David Pitkin opened the door; he was dressed in black, and had deep, dark circles under his eyes. They showed their ID and asked if they could come inside to talk.

'Haven't you people done enough?' he said imperiously.

'We have some more questions about Joseph, about his friendship with Marissa Lewis,' said Moss, trying to be tactful.

'I'm sorry, no. My wife is in a terrible state. She hasn't left her bed since…'

'I'm so sorry about what happened to your son,' said Kay. 'We just don't want his death to be in vain. We think he may have known things about this case. He may have been able to help us with our investigations.'

David looked down at them from the step, chewing over what they were saying. 'Where is she?'

'Who?' asked Moss.

'That bloody awful detective with the blonde hair.'

'She is on leave. I have taken over the case,' said Moss.

'Is this because of my formal complaint? I wrote to the assistant commissioner, asking for a full enquiry and that she be removed from duty.'

'Yes, that's in process. That's why I am now on the case,' said Moss. She was sure Erika would understand her playing along with David Pitkin.

He took them through to the kitchen. 'Would you like tea?'

Kay looked at Moss for guidance.

'We wouldn't want to impose,' said Moss. 'We just need to ask you a few questions.'

'Have some bloody tea!' he snapped. 'I need to keep busy.'

They nodded and sat at the long table. Moss noticed that all the clocks, of which there were many on the walls, had stopped at 1.25 p.m. The room was silent.

'It's something I wanted to do,' he said, noting her gaze. 'That's the time the doctor pronounced Joseph…' He didn't finish the sentence. They waited in silence as he made three cups of tea and then came to join them.

'How long had Joseph been involved in photography?' asked Moss. David Pitkin looked surprised at the question.

'I don't know, four or five years.'

'And you bought him supplies?'

'At school, his art teacher did a project where students made a pinhole camera out of lavatory rolls, tinfoil and photo paper. He found it fascinating, and pestered me to buy supplies so he could make his own pinhole camera.'

'And he needed a dark room to process the photos?'

'Yes.'

'Where did you buy the chemicals?'

'I got them locally from a camera shop in Greenwich. Detectives, I'm not sure how relevant this line of questioning is, unless you are planning to start doing photography as a hobby?'

'We are trying to establish where Joseph went in connection with his hobby.'

'It's wasn't a hobby. He wanted to do it as a career.'

'When did Joseph graduate to having his own camera, buying his own materials?'

'I don't know. As I said, a few years. I was still practising as a barrister back then and I rather neglected my home life. I wouldn't see my family for days on end…' David looked wistfully out of the window and sipped his tea. 'Makes me think it wasn't all worth it, my job. The law… It's just a huge chess game.'

Moss didn't press him.

'Was Joseph a member of any camera or photography clubs?'

'Again. I don't know.'

'Could we speak to your wife?' asked Kay.

'No, you may not. The doctor had to come early this morning to give her something to sleep.'

'Did Joseph get paid for any of his photos?'

David gave a bemused smile.

'No. He was signing on, for a long period. You must know this, officers.'

'Did Marissa Lewis ever come to your house?' said Moss. 'I'm asking in particular about the past year?'

'No. Not that I know of. We were always rather worried about him; he never seemed to have any interest in either sex.'

Moss looked at Kay. They had exhausted all of their questions, and there was just one other thing they had to ask about.

'Mr Pitkin. I need to show you some photos we found on Joseph's mobile phone. They may be upsetting, but I only ask you to look at them because they are vital to our investigation.'

David's eyes narrowed as Moss pulled out a cardboard file. She opened it on the table and took out the photos of Joseph tied up in the restraints. She also took out the note with the gas mask drawing.

David looked through the photos, attempting to stop his emotions from showing. Finally, he looked up, and his eyes were full of anger.

'Who the hell do you think you are, to come into my house and show me these?'

'Mr Pitkin. Did Joseph ever mention a friend, or that he was scared for his life?'

'Did anyone mention to you that Joseph looked at risk of taking his own life?' he shot back.

'No.'

'But you must have seen that he was distressed when he was being interviewed? Did no one at your station think to call a doctor, or think that he shouldn't have been put back in that cell, BY HIMSELF!?' David swept the photos off the table. 'NOW GET OUT OF MY HOUSE!'

Kay hurriedly picked up the photos from the floor and stuffed them back in the file.

'Mr Pitkin, please, do you have any idea who might have sent Joseph a note like this?'

'DID YOU HEAR ME?' he bellowed. He grabbed Moss by the back of her coat and dragged her up out of her chair and into the hallway.

'Sir. Please, stop this,' said Kay, moving after them as David dragged Moss to the front door.

David let go of Moss, leaned across, turned the handle and pulled it open. Moss put up her hand when he tried to grab her again.

'That's enough,' she said, stepping outside. Kay was no sooner out of the door behind her than it was slammed shut. They walked out onto the pavement.

'You okay, ma'am?'

'Yes, and please don't call me "ma'am". I'm not a member of the royal family,' said Moss. She straightened her jumper under her jacket. 'What else were we expecting? I just thought it was worth a shot, in case he knew something.'

'Do you think he knows anything?' asked Kay.

'No, I don't. But I'm not much good with my gut instinct. That's Erika's speciality.'

CHAPTER FORTY-SEVEN

McGorry had been tasked with following up on Ella Bartlett, the burlesque dancer who had been to the jeweller with Marissa. Earlier in the morning, he'd spoken to an extremely camp man called Martin, who had given him Ella's number. She had agreed to meet him after her workout, but she was now late. He had been waiting for her outside the Gym Box in Farringdon for twenty minutes. It had stopped snowing, but the air was damp, and his feet were starting to go numb. The Gym Box was on a busy road on the edge of the Hatton Garden jewellery district in central London, and as he'd drunk his coffee next to an old-fashioned red phone box, he'd seen six security vans move past.

'Hi, are you John?' said a voice. He turned to see a petite blonde woman in her early twenties. She was breathtakingly beautiful, with long honey-coloured hair, and big blue eyes.

'Yes, I'm Detective Inspector John McGorry. I take it you're Ms Bartlett?' He realised how ridiculously formal he sounded.

'Call me Ella. Can I call you John?' she said. 'And can I see your ID? You know you can't be too sure, these days.'

He pulled out his warrant card and passed it to her.

'You're much cuter in real life,' she said, handing it back.

'Let's get started,' said McGorry.

'Do you have a gun?'

'No. Detectives don't carry guns.'

'Cuffs? Pepper spray?' she asked, her eyes wide and innocent.

'Sometimes. In my car.'

'How did you get here?' she asked, looking around.

'I came on the tube; I travelled on the tube…' McGorry suddenly felt flustered and stupid.

'So you're unarmed? Vulnerable? Sorry, I'm kidding.'

'I need you to help me find this jeweller's shop. It's very important to our investigation. It's not a big laugh.'

'Sorry… I thought she was alright, Marissa. I've thought about jacking it all in and going to L.A or New York. I haven't got the guts. She had guts.'

They started walking down the road, and then turned right onto Hatton Garden, where the first jeweller's windows looked out over the street. They glowed brightly against the cold grey day, showing fabulous displays of gold and silver. The two of them walked for a few minutes. Ella kept stopping at intervals to peer into windows and look down the street.

'We were talking loads, and we were coming from the other direction; I wasn't paying attention,' she said. 'They all look quite similar after a while.'

They went a little further, and then she stopped at a red post box.

'I think it was here,' she said, pointing at a door opposite.

'What makes you think it's this one?' asked McGorry.

'The post box. It's a really old one.'

McGorry looked up at the frontage. It said: 'R.D. LITMAN & SONS FINE JEWELLERS EST. 1884.'

They went inside, where a comfortingly old-fashioned bell rang above the door. There was a hushed elegance to the interior, and a long glass counter, which gleamed. An elderly balding man with a slightly hunched back came out from a door at the rear of the shop. He sized them up with a practised glance, but waited for them to speak first.

McGorry showed his warrant card and explained why they were there. Ella didn't seem to recognise the man, but he recognised her.

'Yes. You came in with another young lady with dark hair. Diamond earrings, princess cut: 1.62 carats of exceptional purity, set in 24 karat gold.'

'You can be sure of all that?' asked McGorry.

'It's my job to remember,' said the man, sniffily. 'And of course, I always remember a pair of beautiful ladies. Did your friend reconsider selling? What was her name?'

'Marissa? No. She died,' said Ella.

'I see. I'm sorry,' he said. 'Do you wish to sell?'

'No, we don't want to sell,' said McGorry. 'I need to verify that they existed. Is there any chance you could be mistaken about their value?'

The look on the old man's face told him in the negative.

'I valued them at… The exact figure escapes me… Ten…'

'Ten and a half thousand,' finished Ella.

'Yes.'

'What's your name?' asked McGorry.

'Peter Litman.'

'Do you have much contact with the other jeweller's shops around?'

'Contact?'

'Yes.'

'This is a tight-knit community of traders which goes back a long way. Family businesses – but we remain businesses. With business relationships.'

'Can I give you my card, in case you remember anything else?' said McGorry.

'Yes.' He took the offered card. McGorry thanked him, and they left.

*

Peter Litman watched McGorry and Ella from the window, with his hands neatly behind his back. When they had receded from view, he went out back to an office, where there was a huge walk-in safe.

'Charles, that was a police officer, Detective Inspector McGorry. He was asking about the princess-cut earrings belonging to the dead girl.'

Charles Fryatt looked up from where he was working at a computer and a desk piled high with paperwork.

'I heard everything.'

'You would have also *heard* that I told them the truth. I won't lie to the police. I'll ask you again. Are you involved with the death of that young woman?'

'No,' said Charles, shifting in the seat. 'It's to do with the earrings. Nothing more.'

'They were your mother's earrings?'

'Yes.' Charles kept working at the computer and didn't look up.

'Charles, as your father-in-law, you have my loyalty, but only to a point. If anything comes back to me that embarrasses me or my daughter…'

'It's nothing!' said Charles, raising his voice. 'And you didn't lie, and it's fine.'

Peter looked at his son-in-law for a long moment, and then went back out to the shop front to rearrange the displays, a deep feeling of unease rolling over him.

CHAPTER FORTY-EIGHT

It was early afternoon when the man who called himself 'T' left work. The shop he worked in had been quiet all day, apart from a man and woman who had come in with some enquiries.

He felt lucky that he worked for a private family business; he was able to come and go as he pleased when business was quiet. He took the short train journey into central London.

As he walked up Rupert Street and into Soho, the derelict facade of the Raymond Revue Bar rose up in front of him. His heart began to hammer in his chest, and he felt his penis grow hard. There was always a frisson of excitement when he entered the sex district, with its garishly lit bars and sex shops. It was a place where one could be both anonymous and coveted, and in this small quadrant of streets, all vestiges of polite British upper-class reserve fell away. The gays felt they could hold hands; people could express themselves. As he passed the Prowler store a couple of young guys emerged and did a double take, admiring his height. He waited for a council road sweeping machine to rumble past, the brushes working frantically on the filthy street. He crossed the road, heading past the sex shop on the corner and along Walker's Court. It was a narrow, pedestrianised street made dingy by the tall buildings rising up either side. Sex shops and lap dancing clubs packed each side, with gaudy neon lights illuminating the gloom.

Meltwater from the rooftops ran into a broken gutter and then spattered the floor next to a sex shop with blacked-out windows.

A neon teacher's cane with the word 'SPANKING' repeated in flashing rows, advertised the shop's specialist sex gear and porno vids. T felt his excitement grow, and almost without noticing, put his hand down to his groin, feeling the leather through the thin material of his dark trousers. He always imagined that the street had looked pretty much the same two hundred years ago, just without the garish lights and blacked-out windows. Back then, young men or women could go missing, and little would be said about it. Life was cheap.

A small girl in a thick silver puffy jacket hung around outside one of the small lap dancing clubs, where music blared out. T felt the booming bass fizzing on his teeth and rumbling through his chest. He slowed as the girl made eye contact, and she opened her coat. Underneath she wore a skin-tight mini skirt and a cut-off black top which showed her emaciated ribcage. Her eyes were a piercing green, but dead, and her plump lips were dotted with cold sores.

'You want some fun?' she said, raising her voice enough to be heard at close range.

'I want someone to model for me,' said T, leaning down to her, his lips almost touching her ear. She moved back, looking from side to side, green eyes scanning the narrow street for police. A short, dark-skinned man with heavy stubble glanced over from his spot by the sex shop at the end.

'Yeah? How much?' she said.

'Private work. Very private.'

'A hundred quid for an hour. You have a hotel?' said the girl, her eyes remaining dead throughout. Like an animated corpse. The loud music cut out, and then another track started, trance music, starting off with a low beat. The short man at the end was tilting his head towards the girl. T felt nerves growl in his stomach: this was both thrilling and worrying. This girl would give him consent, but he wanted to go far, and he didn't want too many people to see her with him. The short guy at the end was her pimp, he was sure.

'I'm going shopping,' said T, tipping his head towards a sex shop further down. 'I need a girl who's not afraid to bleed, but I would make it worth your while. You also need to travel. My place is a little far out.'

'It's a hundred and fifty an hour if I have to travel, minimum three hours up front…' The girl was so nonchalant. There was no fear or trepidation. She had the look of someone who was deep in drugs, perhaps in hock to a dealer or the short pimp.

She suddenly bolted away and down towards Rupert Street. T looked for the pimp, but he was gone. A couple of community support officers had entered Walker's Court at the other end. They were deep in conversation, as community support officers always seemed to be, but their eyes scanned the street, which was clearing out. Shadows vanished into doorways.

T felt relief and picked up the pace, moving like a commuter, fast and in a rush. He breezed past the two community support officers and out into the fresh air at the other end, into a fruit market and away from temptation and excitement.

CHAPTER FORTY-NINE

Erika and Isaac couldn't get in and see Edward until early afternoon. Isaac said he would wait for her to go and see him first, and he hung back and grabbed a cup of coffee in the cafeteria downstairs.

The ward was on the fifth floor. Erika was buzzed in through a set of double doors and directed to a row of beds at the end. As she approached the row of beds, she couldn't work out which old man was Edward. So many of them were asleep, lying on their sides, with identical grey hair.

She found him at the end of the ward, by a window overlooking the car park. He was tucked up under blankets. His face lit up when he saw her.

'Erika, love,' he said, lifting a bruised hand with a drip coming from it. The cabinet beside him was empty. She saw lots of the other old men had cards and fruit, and she wished she'd brought him something.

'Hello,' she said, reaching out and taking his hand. It was very dry. She pulled up a chair and sat close to the bed. 'What happened?'

'I had a fall. I got up in the night, and I don't remember much else. The postman heard me shouting the next morning.'

'You tried to call me, didn't you?'

'I can't remember.'

'I didn't know you had a mobile phone.'

'I don't usually use it, but me phone was cut off a couple of days after Christmas, and I couldn't find out why. I always pay my bills…' He sat up, agitated.

'I know you do.'

'And then the heating broke. I tried to get by with the fire. The 'lectric went. I always pay the bills, Erika. You know that, don't you?'

She nodded.

'I'm here now, and I'm going to make sure that everything is fixed,' she said.

'You're a good lass.'

She shook her head. 'You've had a hip replacement?'

'Yes. They put some pins in there too, the doctor said…' He swallowed and started to cough. Erika took a cup from the cupboard by the bed and poured him some water from a jug. 'Thanks, love.' He drank the whole cup and passed it back to her. 'I'll be on the mend before you know it. Although, I'm not sure if I'll have a bit of a problem in the shops.'

'Why the shops?'

'Won't the pins beep when I go through the security barriers? It's right embarrassing when it happens in Tesco.'

'No, it's not a metal detector in the shops, that's only in airports.'

'Oh,' he chuckled. 'I'm not planning on going anywhere, so that doesn't matter. It's so lovely to see you. Are you staying long?'

'I'll stay as long as you need me.'

He waved it away. Isaac appeared at the top of the ward, and Erika nodded and beckoned him over.

'This is my friend – colleague – Isaac Strong,' said Erika. Edward looked up and took his hand, and they shook.

'Very nice to meet you, Mr Foster. Erika's told me a lot about you.'

'Bet you think I'm a right fool though.'

Isaac shook his head and smiled.

'You're a big lad… Tall.'

'Er, yes. No good at sports though.'

Edward squinted up at him. 'Shame, I bet you would have made a cracking high jumper.'

'Isaac is a doctor, a forensic pathologist.'

'Is that dead people?'

Isaac smiled. 'Yes.'

Edward chuckled. 'I nearly needed your services. Thankfully the postman saw me.'

'No!' said Isaac, his eyebrows shooting up in alarm.

'I'm just kidding, lad, nice to meet you. Any friend of Erika's is a friend of mine.'

A doctor appeared at the top of the ward and asked to speak to Erika. She left Isaac with Edward, and followed the doctor to the nurses' station.

'It was a fairly straightforward operation,' he said. 'We've already had him up and about. Recovery time is fast.'

'Good.'

The doctor's face clouded over. 'We are, however, concerned by the situation at home. Edward is underweight, and has a vitamin deficiency. He also came in with a nasty urinary tract infection. Normally we wouldn't risk operating on a man in his condition, but the break was very bad. Luckily, the infection is starting to respond to antibiotics. We can't discharge him until we know he has a care plan in place. Are you local?'

Erika explained that she lived in London. She recounted the conversation she'd had with Edward on Christmas Day, and how he had been confused. The doctor nodded and listened.

'Often, one of the symptoms of a urinary tract infection is con-fusion – or even hallucinations,' he said, regarding Erika gravely. 'This doesn't solve our problem with him living on his own and being vulnerable, though. I'm going to recommend social services pay his house a visit, to see what his living situation is like.'

He left Erika and went off on his rounds, and she stood for a moment in the corridor. Trying to work out how it had come to this. How fast the time had gone. It had come too soon for her to be facing middle age with an elderly father-in-law to look after.

This was why she buried herself in work. Work made her feel alive, and young. Work was constant. There were always bad guys out there to catch. Evil had no age limit. She shook the thought away.

'That's fucked up,' she said to herself. She smoothed down her hair and went back into the ward.

CHAPTER FIFTY

Moss felt the Marissa Lewis murder case, complicated by the gas mask attacks, was spinning out of her control – and as the acting SIO, she was still playing catch up. She was used to being a cog; in fact, she prided herself on being a cog in the overall machine: keeping things oiled, providing support and cracking jokes when things seemed to get tense.

Now she was the boss, she felt the pressure of scrutiny, and despite only being the temporary SIO, she felt the shift in the team and the way they behaved towards her. She was called 'ma'am'. The first time Sergeant Crane had called her 'ma'am', she'd thought of a joke –something along the lines of it rhyming with 'Spam'. But she'd stopped herself, realising she needed to be serious.

The other thing that was hampering her progress was the way Erika worked as an SIO. She didn't write much down, preferring to work in her head, so Moss had spent most of the day playing catch up. The superintendent had asked her if anyone had re-interviewed Marissa's mother, Mandy about her sleeping arrangements, and Moss had been clueless, racking her brains and trying to think back to the reports she'd read: did the superintendent mean Mandy's sleeping arrangements as in the men she shared her bed with, or where she slept? Moss remembered at the last minute Mandy had been sleeping downstairs when Marissa was murdered, but drawing a blank had shaken her up. She couldn't bear the thought of being demoted back to a Detective

Inspector before the case was solved, but she had no clue as to how she was going to solve it, and even whether she could. Erika solved the cases, and she was always there ready to execute orders. Moss realised now how much she enjoyed following orders.

After talking to the superintendent, Moss had gone to the rarely-used toilets on the top floor by the conference rooms, locked herself in a cubicle and phoned Celia, biting back tears as she poured out her woes.

'This is the first time you've been given a case,' said Celia. 'You have to be kind on yourself… And you're taking over in the middle of a complex case. You're a popular member of the team. You should crack some jokes to lighten the mood; is there anyone new who doesn't know your first name is Kate?'

Moss laughed and blotted her cheeks with a scrunched-up ball of loo roll.

'I'm now the boss; I can't make Kate Moss jokes, people are looking up to me to provide them with guidance and wisdom and strategy. And I have to solve the bloody thing whilst jugging case files and…' Her voice tailed off.

'Lists,' said Celia. 'You're bloody good at lists. You've always got a pile of Post-its by the fridge, and we work through them and we always solve problems, and we get things done. You should always break problems and tasks down, instead of trying to tackle them head on in one.'

'You're right,' Moss said. 'It's not a murder case, it's a series of to-do lists.'

It was now late afternoon, and Moss was back in the incident room, working at her cluttered desk in the corner. She had been offered the use of an office, but there hadn't been any time to move her computer access and the vast amount of paperwork on her desk. On Celia's advice, she now had a terrifyingly long to-do list, but she felt better about it. One good thing about being the boss was that you got to delegate.

'Any news on Don Walpole's location?' she shouted.

'We're still waiting on the national ANPR data centre,' said Crane. ANPR stood for the Automatic Number Plate Recognition database. 'If he crossed the congestion charge zone, that will be the bullseye.'

'Can you chivvy them along, and tell them we're not asking for our health!' she said, scanning her list. 'We should also put out a check on his passports and his credit cards at this stage. He is the closest we have to a suspect.'

Crane nodded and picked up his phone.

'What about the diamond earrings? Where is McGorry?' Just as Moss asked, McGorry came back into the incident room. 'You went this morning to find the jeweller in Hatton Garden, yes?'

'Yes, Moss, I mean, boss.'

'Stick with Moss.'

'Okay. The guy in the jeweller, Mr Litman, remembered Ella coming in with Marissa to have the earrings valued. He said they were genuine and worth ten and a half grand. I then went back to see Mrs Fryatt at her house, to ask her again about the earrings… I even had a description. They were princess-cut diamonds in twenty-four karat gold.' He blew his cheeks out. 'She's a nasty old cow, she accused me of being in the wrong, saying that all her jewellery is accounted for and up in her safe.'

'Did you ask to see the safe?'

'I did, and she said it was in her bedroom, and that she didn't invite young men into her bedroom without a warrant.'

Peterson and Crane laughed, and Moss had to keep a straight face. It was on the tip of her tongue to crack a joke that no one ever needed a warrant to get in her knickers, that all it usually took was a slap-up meal at Nando's, but she reminded herself she was now acting SIO.

'Did you think Mrs Fryatt was lying?'

'I'm confused, because I also asked her to confirm the name of the jeweller where her son works,' said McGorry. 'It's the same jeweller, R.D. Litman & Sons. Charles Fryatt is married to Mr Litman's daughter, Lara… She's a retired schoolteacher and they have three children who are all grown up. It's quite a big family business. Mr Litman's other two sons also work there.' He paused for everyone to take in the link. 'Charles Fryatt wasn't at work when I went in. We only saw Mr Litman. I asked Ella if there had been anyone else in the jeweller when she and Marissa went in to have the earrings valued, and she said they had only seen Mr Litman.'

'There's a chance that Charles Fryatt *didn't* know?' asked Crane.

'That's one hell of a fishy chance, but you say Mrs Fryatt offered up the information about where Charles worked?' said Moss.

'Yeah, with no qualms, she didn't seem worried. She seemed proud that he had such a good job,' said McGorry.

'Have you spoken to Charles Fryatt?'

'No. I couldn't get hold of him. When I called the shop back, Mr Litman said that Charles wasn't at work. He wasn't answering his phone either, and his wife didn't know where he was.'

'What if Marissa was lying about where she got the earrings?' said Peterson.

'Why lie that you stole them from someone? Wouldn't it be easier to say that she got them from an admirer who came to see her dance at the club?' said Moss.

'What if it was something more sinister?' said McGorry. 'I don't know what, but Marissa Lewis was a woman with a million secrets.'

'That's all this case needs, is to get more sinister,' said Moss, looking down her list, and once again, feeling overwhelmed.

CHAPTER FIFTY-ONE

Erika and Isaac stayed at the hospital until late in the afternoon.

'He seems very stoic,' said Isaac, as they drove back to Slaithwaite.

'It's a northern thing. People are much nicer than in London, and they have a much more sensible way of looking at life.'

'What did the doctor say?'

'They won't let Edward back home until they can see he's able to look after himself, or it's a nursing home.'

'Shit.'

'I need to clean his house, and try and get things working again. I can't have him being discharged to the place in that state, and what would social services say about it?'

They stopped at the supermarket on the way home, and stocked up on food and cleaning products. The sun was going down when they approached the village, and it looked cosy, with the golden light twinkling off the snow.

'I'll see if I can get the fire going,' said Isaac when they came inside. 'I think it's warmer outdoors.' He started working on the stove, emptying it out and cleaning the grate.

'Mystery solved about the gas,' said Erika, finding and opening a pile of mail. 'Looks like Edward changed over his provider, and they don't have the right bank details…'

Isaac was holding a match to a pile of paper and logs, but nothing was happening.

'And the same with his phone. It looks like one of those comparison companies persuaded him to switch over *all* of his utilities, but they've got the wrong address, the wrong bank details… Bastards,' she said, picking up her phone. Isaac watched in amusement as Erika tore into the utilities companies, registering a complaint and getting Edward reconnected.

They spent the rest of the evening scrubbing and cleaning Edward's house. An engineer came out very quickly, and the gas supply was back on around 8 p.m., so they were able to get the central heating working, and more importantly they were able to wash. Isaac took a shower, and then Erika ran a bath in the newly clean bathroom. As she eased into the hot water, she felt her aching body relax, and the cold which had dogged her for the last few days started to ease away. She'd lit candles, and they gave the bathroom a homely, cave-like feel. Edward's bathroom had been the same for years, with its lavender-coloured tiles. There was a set of shelves above the toilet, with a stack of boxed Pears soap, a knitted Spanish señorita toilet roll holder, boxes of talcum powder, and hair dye in 'conker', the shade Mark's mother used to use. Erika hadn't dared throw anything away on the shelves when she'd cleaned. They seemed sacred; they were the remnants of Edward's life with Mark's mother, Kath. Erika thought back to Mark's mother, and how kind and innocent she had been. She'd lived in her own little world, wrapped in the protection of Edward and Mark, in this cosy little Dales village.

As she shifted in the hot water, there was something about that shelf – a memory that niggled at the back of her mind, but she couldn't quite access it. The steam floated up to the ceiling and made the candle flames flicker and fizz. She tipped her head back against the cool tiles, and her eyes began to lull shut in the warm water.

Erika found herself back in Forest Hill, on Foxberry Road. It was late at night, and the road, which was usually busy with rows of parked cars, was empty. Snow was falling, but it felt hot, like she was

breathing in steam. She crouched down, and scraped away the snow:
there wasn't tarmac underneath the snow, there were tiles. Lavender
bathroom tiles with white grouting. She scraped more of the snow
away and saw the road was laid with tiles as far as she could see.
The silence was broken by a crunching sound, footsteps on snow. She
turned. A tall man dressed in black was walking towards her. He
was wearing a gas mask. The slick, shiny leather of the hood reflected
the streetlights above. He slowed and stopped a few feet from her. He
lifted his head and sniffed the air, the long breathing drum of the gas
mask reminding her of a dog's snout. He seemed to stare around her,
but not see her, like she was invisible. She moved closer, so close that
she could hear his breathing, and see the reflection of the streetlight
on the hood as his head moved. She looked into the glass eyeholes,
but couldn't make out a face, it was a swirl of black. As the vapour
streamed out from the breathing drum, she caught a strong chemical
smell, intoxicating and metallic…

Erika jolted awake as her mouth and nose hit the cool water. The
steam had cleared, and her fingers had started to prune. She got
out of the bath, and wrapped a thin towel around her. Standing
on the mat, she stared at the shelf above the toilet. The Pears soap
and the hair dye… Just after she and Mark had got married, they'd
come to visit Edward and Kath, and Mark had gone up to use the
bathroom. The rest of them were having tea in the front room,
when Mark had come back down holding a small black bottle,
with the words RELAX-FUN' written on it in red.

'Mum, why have you got poppers in the bathroom?' Mark
said. Kath looked up from rearranging Eccles cakes on her best
cake plate.

'What's that, love?'

'You've got an open bottle of poppers in the bathroom. I
started to get high just having a wee.'

'That's a room deodoriser,' said Kath. 'I got it down the market. It's for keeping rooms nice and deodorised. Only cost a quid. There were quite a few young lads there. One of them mentioned he was having a party… I suppose he wanted his house to smell nice for his guests. Although, I'm not sure about the smell.'

Erika had choked on her tea, laughing.

'Mum, this isn't a room deodoriser. It's amyl nitrate,' said Mark.

'What?' she said, putting on her reading glasses and going over to him. 'No, look. It says on the label that it's a room deodoriser.'

Mark had explained to his mother that people inhaled poppers for the 'high' or 'rush' that the drug could create.

'Is this true, Erika, love?' Kath had asked, turning to her.

Erika had tried to keep a straight face. 'Yes. It's classed as a drug, though not illegal… Some people do use it for a high. It's popular in the gay community, as it relaxes…'

Mark had shot her a look to make her stop.

'Oh my word, what must they have thought of me?' Kath had exclaimed, clutching at her chest.

'You weren't to know,' said Erika.

'But I told them I was getting it for my husband, for when he visits the bathroom,' she said in horror.

Erika smiled at the memory, but it then hit her. She rushed downstairs in her towel and grabbed her phone. She called Moss, but it went to her machine.

'Moss, it's me. I told the team to focus in on the guy in the gas mask, and look for someone who could be a collector of old masks from the war. Go back and look at the statements from all the people who were attacked. Jason said he smelt something weird and metallic, see if any of the other victims mentioned this.

Whoever it is could have had the breathing apparatus packed with tissue or cotton soaked in amyl nitrate, for a sexual high. You should also be looking at S&M gear. If you can get a clear idea of the exact design of the mask then you can start working on suppliers... I don't know how it fits in with Marissa Lewis, but it could unlock who this person is... Anyway... I hope things are going well.'

Erika hung up her phone, feeling very far away from the investigation.

CHAPTER FIFTY-TWO

Moss sat bleary-eyed at the kitchen table the next morning, eating her cereal. Jacob came in with his guitar and started to play a new song he'd made up. As he strummed at the guitar and started to sing, Moss shouted at him to cut it out. Jacob looked up at her with shock on his little face, and his eyes started to run. She never shouted.

'Mummy's got a headache this morning. Why don't you go and put the guitar away, get dressed, and then I'll make you some hot chocolate,' said Celia.

'I thought you wanted me to make up a song for you. That's what you said yesterday, you said for me to make up a song and now I've made one up…'

'I just need some peace and quiet this morning,' snapped Moss. Celia took Jacob out of the kitchen and returned a few minutes later. 'You don't want to get him into the habit of having hot chocolate every morning,' Moss added.

'He's only having it over Christmas…' said Celia.

'Yeah, well tomorrow is New Year's Eve; he's been having it every morning for the past ten days!'

'Is this really about Jacob having hot chocolate? Or are you taking stuff out on him, and me, because things are bad at work?'

'Things are not bad at work!' said Moss, getting up and dumping her half-full bowl of cereal in the sink. 'I just need time to think! You have no idea how complicated this case is… And there's all this noise here.'

'That's called having a five-year-old. You made a big deal last night about him writing you a song, when what you were really doing was fobbing him off!'

Moss's phone started to ring, and she pulled it out. It was Peterson.

'We've tracked down Don Walpole. His wife was taken ill the other day, and he's been staying at her bedside in hospital. University College London. The ANPR came back with details of his car crossing the congestion charge zone.'

'Good work. Can you get me there?'

She hung up and left the kitchen. Seconds later, Celia heard the front door slam.

'Charming. She becomes an acting DCI and I'm just the help… No goodbye or kiss on the cheek.'

'I'll kiss you on the cheek, Mummy,' said Jacob, appearing at the door, still holding his little guitar.

Moss and Peterson arrived at UCL hospital just after nine. Jeanette Walpole had been admitted to the renal department, and they had to get directions from the front desk.

'Renal is kidneys, yeah?' said Peterson as they travelled up in the lift.

Moss nodded. 'You've got everything ready. The paperwork? Spit kit?'

He nodded, holding up a thick folder. The 'spit kit' was shorthand for the Forensic DNA Evidence Collection Kit. 'You okay?' he asked, seeing her tense face.

'Had a row with Celia this morning, and I shouted at Jacob for being noisy.'

'I'm liking the noise, having a kid around…' Peterson got out his phone and swiped through, holding up the screen to Moss. It was a video of Kyle playing on pots and pans. He was crouched on the kitchen floor with a sheet around his shoulders like a superhero cape, and he was banging on a line of upturned pots with a wooden spoon.

'Very tuneful,' Moss said, her eyes flicking to the digital display. The lift stopped and a porter wheeled in a long metal box, which both she and Peterson knew to contain a dead body. 'How is it all going?'

'Good, really good. They're living with me on a temporary basis, until we work out what we're going to do,' he said.

'I can see that you want them to stay.'

'Yeah.'

'Did you talk to Erika?'

'I figured she's got a lot going on with her father-in-law, and I'd rather do it face-to-face, when she's back.'

'Don't let it fester. Although, I think she's the one who'll be doing the festering.'

'I've got another video of Kyle singing,' said Peterson, swiping through his phone, his face beaming with pride.

'James, later. We need to concentrate.'

The lift doors opened, and they inched past the long box destined for the morgue. They came to a set of double doors for the renal ward, but they were locked. Moss peered through the glass windows.

'Can't see anybody. And there's no buzzer or bell.' She hammered on the glass with the flat of her hand. 'Hey… HEY!'

'Jeez, Moss, take it easy,' said Peterson.

'We could be here for bloody hours.'

A nurse appeared at the top of the corridor and came towards them.

'Or, we chill out and everything is going to be okay,' he said.

She took deep breaths and nodded. 'I'll be happier if his DNA is a match. Don Walpole is our man. I can close this case and move back to a happier pay grade.'

The nurse opened the door and they showed her their warrant cards. She took them to a side room at the end of the corridor.

'Mrs Walpole is in here,' she said, opening the door. Jeanette was sitting up in bed, hooked up to a dialysis machine. Her skin was bright yellow, and her breathing laboured.

Don was sitting beside her, and he eyed Moss and Peterson. 'Yes?'

'Can we have a word, please? Best outside,' said Moss. Don kissed the back of Jeanette's hand and came outside. Moss and Peterson showed him their warrant cards.

'We've been trying to get in contact with you, Mr Walpole,' said Moss.

'You can see, my wife is very sick.'

'We need to take a DNA swab from you,' said Peterson. Don looked him up and down.

'Are you arresting me?'

'No.'

'Then I have to volunteer my DNA, and I'm not prepared to do that.'

'Mr Walpole. Legally, we are able to take a DNA sample if we have grounds to suspect you have been involved in a crime. Now, we can find a place and do this here, or we can go to the station,' said Moss.

Don looked between them.

'I have here a document detailing your rights,' said Peterson. 'We can give you time to read it.'

Don stared through the strip of glass in the window at Jeanette, who now lay back on the bed with her eyes closed. 'Okay,' he said.

Peterson saw there was a small kitchen next to Jeanette's room. They went inside and closed the door. Don sat at a small table. Peterson pulled on a pair of gloves and then took out a plastic tube with a long cotton wool swab.

'I need a sample of your cells from the back of your throat,' he said. Don opened his mouth and Peterson swabbed the back of his throat and the inside of his cheek. Then he placed it back in the tube and sealed it up.

'Thank you,' said Moss, handing Don a form to fill in. He scanned down the page and then signed.

'She's dying,' he said. 'Her body is giving up on her.'

'I'm sorry to hear that,' said Moss. 'We expect the DNA results in the next twenty-four hours.'

The sun was fighting to come out from behind the clouds when they left the hospital.

'I'm going to head over to the lab in Vauxhall with the sample,' said Peterson.

'Good. I'm going over to speak to Mrs Fryatt. I need to solve the mystery around the earrings. I want to get a DNA sample from Charles Fryatt, too.'

'You want me to swing by Hatton Garden? I have another kit.'

'No. Get that in for testing. I need to ask her a few more questions, I want more than just a suspicious coincidence before we go after her son.'

CHAPTER FIFTY-THREE

There was no answer at Mrs Fryatt's house. Moss rang the bell several times, and peered in through the window. She came back out onto the pavement and looked up at the large house. The polished windows reflected the grey sky and stared back blankly.

Moss leaned on the railing and felt a wave of fear and anxiety roll over her. This was not an emotion she was used to. She thought of how she'd left that morning, forgetting to say goodbye to Celia and Jacob. As she took out her phone to call them, it started to ring. She didn't recognise the number.

'Hi, this is Lisa Hawthorne. I'm an advisor at Jobcentre Plus in Forest Hill. One of your police officers asked me to come back to you with details of Joseph Pitkin's past employment.'

'Oh, yes, but…'

'Sorry for the delay, we're snowed under here with work. Joseph Pitkin was claiming benefits for the past four years. He's only been claiming Jobseeker's Allowance off and on. He's had four periods of employment. On three occasions, he was working in a pub in Honor Oak Park – seasonal work over December in 2014, 2015 and 2016.'

'I'm sorry, could you call one of my colleagues at…' said Moss, trying to get her off the phone, but she went on:

'The fourth period of work was for a photographic studio in New Cross, called Camera Obscura. He was there for six weeks during early 2016…' There was something about the photography link which made Moss listen. She put the phone under her chin and pulled out her notebook and pen. Lisa went on, 'It's run by a man called Taro Williams. It's an old-fashioned photographic portrait studio.'

'Do you know why the job ended?'

'No. Joseph's records show that this was meant to be a full-time position as a photographic assistant, but after six weeks he unexpectedly quit. Which was odd, as we worked hard to get him into the job, and he was very enthusiastic about it.'

'There was nothing else? No complaint from the employer?'

'No. It's such a shame Joseph didn't get the chance to pursue his passion for photography.'

'How well did you know Joseph?'

'I worked on his case, and used to see him twice a week when he signed on, that for three years.'

'I'm afraid to say that Joseph recently took his own life.'

'I'm sorry to hear that,' she said, wearily. It sounded like she often heard this kind of news about her claimants. Moss thanked the woman, and came off the phone. She looked back at Mrs Fryatt's dark house, weighing up her options. New Cross was only a short drive away.

CHAPTER FIFTY-FOUR

Taro Williams was a tall, broad man in his late thirties, with a thick wide forehead and large features. He'd inherited Camera Obscura, and the living quarters above it, from his father, who had started the business during the 1960s. It was on Amersham Road, a residential street of large crumbling terraced houses, a few minutes' walk from New Cross station. In years gone by, these grand four-storey structures had been built by merchants who had found their fortune during the industrial revolution. They'd boasted well-to-do families and quarters for live-in staff. As well as three storeys rising above the street, each house had a large basement. The shop front of Camera Obscura, with a plate glass picture window, was set back from the road, and partly shrouded by a huge hawthorn bush by the front wall.

The photography shop had functioned for many years as a studio, but over the past few years, with the advent of digital cameras and smartphones, business had slowed. This didn't worry Taro. He was independently wealthy, and he liked to have time to himself. When it took his fancy, he worked as a wedding photographer. He only opened the shop a couple of times a week to take portraits, mostly of young couples who'd got engaged, and couples with small children who wanted to document their little darlings in an official capacity.

It depressed him that most of the parents with small children shunned the solid silver-gilt frames he had on offer, and instead wanted their photos printed on cushions or jigsaws, or even worse, baseball caps and mugs.

Taro was just breaking down the lights and backdrop from a photoshoot that morning. A young Japanese couple had been to have pictures produced for their engagement invitations. It always struck him how tiny the Japanese were. They'd seemed quite intimidated by his huge frame and his serious face, but he'd broken the atmosphere with a joke and a broad smile, which transformed him into a jovial bear of a man. They had both giggled along with him during the shoot, but hadn't noticed that the smile never quite reached his eyes.

He was just packing away the last lighting softbox when a short red-haired woman came up the path to the front door. She tried to open it, and when she found it locked she knocked on the glass.

He strode over and pointed at the sign propped up at the bottom of the window: PLEASE RING FOR ASSISTANCE

His face broke into a smile and he indicated that she should ring. She rolled her eyes and pressed the bell by the door. He smiled and gave her the thumbs up, then unbolted the door.

'Hello, I'm Detective Chief Inspector Moss,' she said, holding up her warrant card. 'Can I have a few minutes of your time?'

'Of course.' He smiled. He stood to one side and she came through the doorway.

CHAPTER FIFTY-FIVE

'How can I help you?' asked Taro, as he invited Moss to sit down in one of the oversized chairs he used for photo shoots. There was a camera on a tripod, a huge sheet of white reflective paper hanging along a square of the wall, and several lights dotted around on stands.

Moss sat down and pulled out a file from her bag. 'I'm here to ask a few questions about a former employee of yours. Joseph Pitkin. He worked here for six weeks in early 2016.'

'Yes, that's correct.'

'Can I ask why he left?'

Taro nodded regretfully. 'I'm afraid I had to fire him.'

'Why?'

'He was… dishonest. He stole from me…'

Moss nodded. 'How much did he steal?'

'Nothing vast. I think it was fifty pounds.'

Moss looked around at the cash register, which was alongside the wall, towards the plate glass window.

'Did you inform the police?'

'No.'

'What about the Jobcentre?'

'I can't say I remember. It was almost two years ago.'

'He was signing on, and his advisor found him the job. Did anyone get in contact with you to find out why the job had ended so fast?'

'Yes, I think someone did…' His voice trailed off. He smiled again, and came closer, perching on the arm of the chair in front of her. He wore a tailored chocolate brown three-piece suit. A gold watch chain hung from one of the pockets.

'Can I ask what kind of photography you do?'

'Portraits, mainly. Young couples, bouncing bundles of joy…' He indicated a display of portraits on the back wall. 'Nine times out of ten, you put a baby in front of a camera and it screams its head off. Although, I do tend to scare children.'

'Do you take any other kinds of photos?'

'Weddings, but I tend to go along on the day.'

'Any erotic work?'

'Are you asking on a personal level?' he said, grinning the wide grin again.

'No,' she said. He was a handsome man, but there was something about him that made Moss uncomfortable.

'Sorry, bad joke.'

She waved it away.

'How would you rate Joseph as a photographer?'

'I can't say I got much of a chance, he was here for such a short time.'

'Did he take photos for you?'

'Yes.'

'Photos of what?'

'I let him do a session with a young couple who'd got engaged.'

'Did he show an interest in photographing nudes, or anything more… I don't know how to put it.'

'Explicit? No. I'm not that kind of business… Look, I'm parched after a long morning, are you sure I can't get you a cup? I can also look out my employment records to check if I made any other notes about Joseph and the contact I had with the Jobcentre.'

'Okay, thank you,' said Moss. Taro got up and went off through a door in the back, closing it behind him.

Moss had a look around the photographic studio. There was a large machine at the back used for processing pictures.

It was covered in dust and junk, and had a 'one-hour photo' sticker on the front. Above it was a cabinet, displaying all of the options for having your photos produced: cups, jigsaws, magnets, hats and cushions. Each one had a stock image of a young girl holding a yellow balloon. On another wall were the examples of past shoots that Taro had indicated earlier: mostly baby photos.

Moss went over to the counter with the till. Behind it were shelves containing a trophy, and several plaques from 1991, when Camera Obscura won South London's Business of the Year. An older version of Taro, presumably his father, was pictured with his wife and children, out the front of the shop.

'You've found the embarrassing family photos,' said a voice behind her.

Moss jumped, and turned to see Taro standing directly behind her. She forced herself to smile.

'I've just put the kettle on,' he said. She could see there was a storm coming: the cloud outside was heavy and dark. The lights inside reflected the interior of the studio back at them from the shop window. 'I've found my records about Joseph.'

Moss came back to her chair, and Taro took the one opposite. He took a pair of glasses from his top pocket and put them on, then opened a folder. 'I don't have many people who come to work for me, but there have been a couple of assistants over the years. This is Joseph? I knew him as Joe,' he said, holding up a passport photo of Joseph, taken in an instant photo booth.

'Yes, that's him,' said Moss. Joseph stared up blankly, as most people do in ID photos, going through the motions. 'I wanted to ask about your experience of employing him. Did he borrow any equipment? Did you meet anyone he was friends with or associated with?'

'Is he under investigation?' asked Taro, looking up from the folder, his face amiable and placid.

'I'm afraid he's dead.'

'Oh, how awful. How?'

'Suicide.'

Taro took off his glasses and chewed one arm.

'That really is terrible. When?'

'Boxing Day.'

'So recent… And over Christmas, too.' Taro started to leaf through the folder. He found another photo, this time printed in 10 x 8 format.

'I did take photos of him.'

'I thought he worked for you?'

'He did. Joseph posed for me when I decided to transfer over to digital, and I needed to test the new cameras. I think I hung on for too long to the old technology and processing methods.'

The photograph was a full-length shot of Joseph, standing against the pale backdrop, wearing just a pair of jeans. He looked uncomfortable.

'Why is he shirtless?'

'He wanted some photos to give to a girl he was interested in,' chuckled Taro. 'Here's another.' He handed her a photo of Joseph standing in a crinkled pair of briefs. He was flexing his puny arms in what was supposed to be a macho pose, but it was the blank look in his eyes which bothered Moss. She'd seen that look before, a long time ago when she'd been fresh out of training college and had been assigned to work on sexual abuse cases. She'd seen that look on victims who had zoned out, and taken themselves to another place.

'You say he asked for these photos to be taken?' said Moss. She jumped as a kettle began to whistle out the back.

'Yes. This is a photographic studio,' said Taro, getting up. 'I'm often asked to take strange pictures, although I always draw the line at photographing nudity.' He looked at her for a moment, as the kettle continued to scream. 'I won't be a moment.'

As soon as he'd vanished through the door. Moss took her phone out of her coat pocket. She had dialled Peterson's number when Taro popped his head around the door.

'Milk and sugar?'

'Yes.'

'This road has a bit of a black spot when it comes to mobile phone coverage. Perhaps it's the trees.'

Moss had the phone against her head as she heard the no signal tone. Taro smiled at her again, so amiably, and disappeared off to the screaming kettle. Moss was completely thrown by his behaviour. She moved to see through the door and noted that behind it was a long corridor. She heard the clank of the kettle and a spoon in a saucer at the end of the hall. She moved to the till and picked up the landline. It was dead. She then moved to the door and found it was locked. There was no key. Had Taro locked it when she came in? Hadn't she noticed?

This is ridiculous, she thought, trying to calm herself. She had been so concerned about doing her best, about being in charge of the investigation. She moved around the room with her phone held high, trying to get a signal.

As she crossed behind the two chairs where they'd been sitting, she noticed that Taro's folder lay open on his seat. There was a form inside from the Jobcentre, neatly filled in with spidery blue handwriting. Then there was a blank page of handwritten notes, and rows of figures. In the bottom right hand corner, in the same ink, there was a drawing. With shaking hands, Moss picked up the folder. It was a sketch of a face wearing a gas mask, intricately done and shaded using a black biro.

Moss had her phone in her other hand, and she scrolled through to the image of the gas mask, drawn above the note to Joseph. Both the handwriting and the image matched: they had been drawn by the same hand.

There was a faint rattle. Moss turned. Taro was standing behind her, holding two china tea cups.

'Did you draw this?' asked Moss, turning and taking a step back. The folder shook in her hand.

'Yes. Yes, I did,' Taro said softly. The tea cups rattled again as he gently placed them down on the small table.

Moss opened her mouth to speak, but Taro moved swiftly to the door and flicked off the lights, plunging the room into a murky gloom. Moss hurried towards the front door, where a dim light came through the huge plate glass window, but she felt something hard hit her on the back of her head, and then everything went black.

CHAPTER FIFTY-SIX

Erika and Isaac had been to visit Edward again, and he had shown great signs of improvement. The nurse had got him up and walking, and he said his leg felt brand new, after years of having dealt with a twinge of pain in his hip. He'd said goodbye to Isaac, who had to return to London for work the next morning.

On the way back to Slaithwaite, Erika asked Isaac to take a detour through a series of pleasant avenues with detached houses.

'Can you stop just here,' she said. He pulled the car to a halt outside a detached two-storey house. The front lawn was covered in snow, and a snowman sat close to the front door with a carrot nose, two black eyes and a red scarf. Christmas lights were strung around the eaves, and through the front window they could see a Christmas tree.

'This is nice,' said Isaac. 'Why have we stopped here?'

'It's my house,' Erika said, staring up at it sadly. 'It's the house Mark and I lived in for fifteen years.'

'Oh.'

Erika stared at it. A tear formed in her eye and she wiped it away.

'I haven't been back since the day he died. I had all my stuff packed up and put in storage, and I had an agency rent it out.'

'Do you know the people renting it? Do you want to get out and knock on the door?'

'No.'

Isaac nodded. 'How long are you planning to stay up here?'

'I need to get Edward settled back in at his home. Find him a carer.'

Her phone rang. She didn't recognise the London number, but answered.

'Erika?' asked a woman's voice, sounding worried.

'Yes.'

'It's Celia, Kate's wife. Moss's wife.'

'Hi Celia, sorry. I don't have your number in my phone, I didn't recognise it.'

'Have you heard from Kate?'

'No. I left her a message a while back but she hasn't replied.'

'It's just that she usually calls me in the day. We had a silly row this morning, nothing serious, but she's the kind of person who'll ring and smooth things over. I phoned James and John McGorry, but they don't know where she is. I've left her six messages.'

'She's now running a huge case. Believe me, it can make you lose track of everything.'

'I know. Kate's been very stressed out about taking over this case from you…'

'She's probably picked up bad habits from me. I tend to lose track of time working on an investigation…' Erika's voice tailed off. She only lost track of time because she never had anyone waiting for her to call. 'She's probably been called into a briefing meeting. She'll have to be attending them now she's acting DCI, and they can go on and on.'

'Okay,' said Celia. 'Sorry, you must think I'm weird.'

'No. I think Moss is very lucky. When I have rows with people, they often never speak to me again! If she calls, I'll tell her to ring you.'

'Yes.'

'And here's the direct number for Superintendent Hudson,' said Erika. She gave Celia the number and then rang off.

'Everything okay?' asked Isaac. Erika dialled Moss's number, but it went straight to answerphone.

'Celia says Moss hasn't been in contact since this morning.'

'And that's unusual?'

'For them, yes.'

'I miss having someone who expects me to ring them,' said Isaac.

'Me too,' said Erika, staring up at the house. 'The wisteria, it's grown so fast,' she added, pointing at the high, thick branch which curled up the side of the house and snaked its way along the eaves at the top. 'I bought that in a tiny pot, the day we moved in. We'd stopped to get some paint at B&Q and it was on this discount table. It was 70p. Mark said, don't waste money on that little stick, it looks dead.'

'I bet it's pretty when it flowers,' said Isaac.

Erika nodded and wiped her eyes. 'Come on. Let's go. I just wanted to see it, but it's just a place, a house. What made it a home was the people inside it, and we're not there any more. There's another family in there now.'

CHAPTER FIFTY-SEVEN

Taro, or 'T' as he liked to call himself for short, hit Moss hard over the back of the head with a leather sap. He kept it in the kitchen drawer, and he'd pushed it into his back pocket as he was making the tea in the kitchen. His mind was whirring, but he wasn't scared and he wasn't panicking. She hit the floor hard, but it was away from the window and in the shadows, with the lights out.

He listened to the clock ticking. A car trundled past on the road. He crouched down, holding the sap in his right hand in case she still had some fight left in her. He took her wrist with his free hand, and felt her pulse. It was beating slowly, rhythmically. He held his finger there. Feeling the life beating through her, moving it over the firm, pulsing nodule deep in her skin. He moved his hand around to the back of her head. Her hair was slick with blood. He stood and placed the sap back in his pocket. He stepped over her and moved to the window. The road outside was quiet. Retreating back into the shadows, he rolled her over.

'Big girl,' he muttered as he patted her down, kneading her breasts and running his hands between her legs. He held them there for a moment, savouring the warmth, then he switched his attention to her pockets. He took out her car keys, phone, wallet and warrant card. He placed them on the counter, by the till, then came back to her. With considerable strength, he bent down and picked her up in one fluid move, throwing her over his shoulder.

He carried her limp body through the doorway, disappearing for a few minutes, then came back.

He flicked on the lights. The carpet where she had fallen was clean and there was no sign of blood. He would be thorough, though, and give it a clean. He came back to the counter and retrieved her phone and car keys. Unbolting the front door, he came outside and walked down to the pavement. A smattering of cars was parked up in the permit spaces. He pointed the key fob to the right, and nothing happened, then he pointed it to the left, and the lights flashed on a dark Rover fifty yards away.

T stopped for a moment. Thinking. He was surprised how calm he was. His heart was beating faster, and he could feel the blood pumping through his legs and wrists, but he was in control. He wasn't panicking.

He didn't know if she'd told anyone she was coming. It was early afternoon. Police officers weren't always the most sociable creatures; Moss might not be missed until the next morning, but when the alarm was raised, someone would eventually come and question him. He would need to acknowledge that she had dropped by, but he would tell anyone who asked that she'd left. He looked down at the keys and wallet. How would he make it look as if she'd left?

A van from Lewisham Council's gardening department rounded the corner up ahead. It was one of the ones with an open flat-back truck, used to transport grass cuttings and plants. He moved round to the driver's side of Moss's car and fiddled with the door, then quickly wiped the phone on his jacket. As the van drove past, he dropped Moss's mobile phone onto the flat bed, amongst a pile of branches and dead leaves. He climbed into her car, and watched as the van paused at the traffic lights at the end, then drove on. Hopefully to the South Circular.

Taro started the engine and drove the car two miles away, working rhythmically up and down the residential streets to avoid any CCTV cameras. He parked the car up at the end of Tresillian Road, a quiet residential street. He locked the car, then, after wiping the key off, he dropped it down a drain.

He walked back to the photography studio, the light fading as he passed, unhurried, through the streets. The lull between Christmas and New Year was the perfect cover for his movements. He didn't see anyone. He almost wished he'd brought his gas mask with him, to have some fun. But he knew he had to get back to his studio and deal with the policewoman.

CHAPTER FIFTY-EIGHT

Mrs Fryatt was sitting by the fire, drinking tea from her favourite bone china tea set, when the doorbell rang. It took her a moment to remember that there was no one else in the house to answer, so she heaved herself up out of her favourite armchair.

It took her a while to get there, the size of the house and the stiffness of her legs from sitting for several hours impeding her speed. She opened the first door and went into the cold porch. Through the glass in the door she could see a black man in a suit, flanked by five police officers in uniform.

A black man, she thought disapprovingly as she unlocked the door and opened it. He held up his warrant card.

'Mrs Elsa Fryatt? I'm Detective Inspector James Peterson.'

'What do you want?' she answered imperiously. Despite her small height, the front door was raised up, so she was able to see most of them at eye level.

'We have a warrant to search these premises in connection with the murder of Marissa Lewis,' he said, handing it over.

'This is no use to me; I haven't got my glasses,' she said, handing it back.

'I'm not waiting for you to read it,' said Peterson. He stepped up into the porch, suddenly towering above her. She put out her arms to stop him, and he gently lifted them away, and moved into the house.

'You get your black hands off me!' she cried. The police officers surged around her and into the house, and started pulling on latex gloves. 'What are you doing? Why are you coming into my home?'

A young policewoman started opening the small drawers in one of the occasional tables in the hall, and Mrs Fryatt tried to close them.

'Ma'am, you need to step back, or we will arrest you.'

'On what grounds?'

'Obstructing a police officer with a warrant.'

She moved to the banister and watched as the police fanned out and started searching through her house. She went to the phone, and with shaking hands, she dialled her son's mobile phone.

'Charles? The police are here!' she shrilled, her voice climbing a register. 'They say they've got a search warrant… They're going through everything…' She listened as her son fired questions at her, watching through the doorway to the front room where books were being taken down from the shelves, upended, shaken and dumped on the floor. 'I don't know. I haven't got my reading glasses. They won't tell me what they are doing. One of them manhandled me on the front doorstep… Okay, come quickly!'

She put the phone down and tried to find a spot in the house where she could wait, but the police seemed to be everywhere. There seemed to be more than the six officers who had initially been on the front doorstep. She went back out to the freezing porch and sat on the small chair she used for putting on her shoes. Her hands were shaking, and it wasn't just from the cold.

An hour later, Charles Fryatt appeared through the glass outside the front door.

'Why the hell did it take you so bloody long!' she hissed when she opened the front door.

'Where's the warrant?' Charles said. He took it from her, scanning the writing on the page and the signature. They moved into the hallway as Peterson was just coming down the stairs.

'Are you Charles Fryatt?' he asked.

'Yes. I think this is quite ridiculous, what could my mother have to do with the murder of Marissa?' Charles said. 'Look at her, she's ninety-seven years old!'

Peterson ignored him. 'Is the front bedroom yours, Mrs Fryatt?'

'Yes! You've been in there? You?' she cried.

'Yes.'

'I would expect a *lady* police officer to have been assigned to do that. No doubt you've had those hands all over my personal items!'

Charles shot his mother a look. 'Mum. You need to watch it,' he warned.

'I can say whatever the hell I like in my house. There's freedom of speech for a reason!'

'We need you to open the safe in the wardrobe,' said Peterson. Charles looked at his mother; his eyes were wide and fearful.

'I take it I don't have a choice?' she said.

'No, you don't. Either you open it, or we drill it open.'

They followed him up two flights of stairs to the front bedroom, which held her huge four poster bed, a heavy wooden dressing table in front of the bay window, and a large fitted wardrobe lining one wall. The middle door was open, showing a heavy metal safe with a combination dial.

'I'm the only person who knows the combination,' said Mrs Fryatt imperiously.

'What if you can't remember it?' asked Charles. There was something about the way he said this that suggested to Mrs Fryatt that her son was giving her some kind of cue to forget, but she tottered over to the safe and slowly knelt down.

'I need you all to turn away,' she said. Peterson, Charles and two of the uniformed officers also in the room looked away. There were some soft clicks and then the safe's lock opened. Charles tried to catch his mother's eye, but she refused to look at him. 'There,' she said.

Peterson went to the safe, and crouched down to peer inside. There were three shelves. The first had a stack of twenty-pound notes and some old-fashioned bank bonds. The second was packed with velvet-lined jewellery boxes. The two uniformed officers joined him, and pulled on fresh latex gloves to take these out, placing them on the carpet. The first box was wide and flat and contained a dazzling diamond necklace; the second and third contained a Cartier diamond watch and two bracelets. Peterson sorted through the other boxes laid out on the carpet, which contained a diamond brooch, gold earrings, and another necklace with a six-ounce block of gold pendant. The final two boxes contained a pair of huge round-cut diamonds in gold, and the second a pair of square princess-cut diamonds.

The bottom shelf of the safe was empty.

'Do you own any other princess-cut diamonds?' asked Peterson.

'No,' said Mrs Fryatt. 'You will see underneath the bond certificates on the top shelf that I have all the insurance paperwork for my jewellery. It was made up at the end of last August. You will find everything there, present and correct.'

Peterson spent several minutes checking through it all. Then he got up and went to Charles, who was watching from in front of the window. His grey skin glistened with sweat, despite the cool temperature.

'Can you confirm that Marissa Lewis came to the jeweller where you work, with a pair of princess-cut diamond earrings, exactly the same as these?' he asked, holding up the box.

'Er. Yes… apparently, she did,' Charles said. Mrs Fryatt stared at her son coldly.

'Why didn't you tell my colleagues this when they visited you before to talk about Marissa's murder?'

'Because I didn't know she had been in to the shop, until one of your colleagues came in and spoke to my father-in-law. I'm one of four in the family who work there,' said Charles. His eyes darting between Peterson and his mother's steely gaze.

'This is your wife's family business?'

'Yes, I work there along with two of her brothers.'

'I need to take these earrings away for testing,' said Peterson.

'What do you propose you test for?' asked Mrs Fryatt.

'DNA.'

'Well, you'll find my DNA, and no doubt there might even be some from my daughter-in-law, who's borrowed them on a couple of occasions. And of course, you'll find Marissa's DNA on them.'

Peterson stared at her. 'Why do you say that?'

'Because I let her try them on, officer. If you care to wait, I could even dig out a picture of her wearing them. She did a photoshoot here for her burlesque portfolio. Her friend Sharon came and helped out.' She held out her hand for the earrings.

'I would still like to take these earrings for testing and analysis.'

'Is that all you'd like to take? Do you want a blood or urine sample? Or perhaps you want to dust every surface for prints?'

'Just the earrings,' said Peterson, locking eyes with her, refusing to look away.

'Fine. Test them, but you're wasting your time, and I warn you, if there is any damage to them, however minor, I will sue you, and the police force. I have the money to do it.'

Peterson bagged up the earrings. He left the room, followed by the five officers. No one spoke until they came out onto the street to the waiting cars.

'Shit,' said Peterson, banging his fist on the bonnet. 'Fuck!'

CHAPTER FIFTY-NINE

Moss slowly regained consciousness, but everything was black. She could see nothing. She lay on her back, on a hard surface, and her head was throbbing. She breathed in. There was a strong goaty smell of body odour, and sour sweat. Strong feelings of nausea flooded over her; she thought she was going to throw up. Panic shot through her as she realised that her mouth was taped up. As she came fully awake, she felt that her hands were fastened tightly in front of her, bound at the wrists, and her ankles were bound too. She swallowed and tried to stay calm. She listened. There was a faint hiss, and then a *whoomph* and a tiny blue square appeared in the corner of her vision. It stayed on for a few seconds and then vanished.

Moss swallowed again. Her throat was so dry and sticky. She slid from side to side, feeling around on the floor. She moved her bound arms to the right and felt a metal grille, and the same on the left. She shuffled up and down, feeling bars above her head and below her feet. Her heart began to beat again and panic rose in her. It threatened to overwhelm her. She was in some kind of cage.

Keep calm, keep calm, calm, calm, came the voice in her head. She thought of the mindfulness techniques that Celia had started to do, to try and control her worry. She'd taken the piss out of Celia for carrying the mindfulness book around with her. Now she wished she'd read it. She tried to remember what it was about, what Celia had said. It was about concentrating on what was actually happening, and not letting your emotions get the better of you. She concentrated on the cold floor underneath her back. She felt around and was pretty sure it was wood.

What was that blue light? It was a flame; the little flame behind the square hole in a central heating boiler. She had to see if she could sit up, and see what it illuminated, if it came back on again.

Moss slowly breathed in and out. Her nose didn't seem to pull in enough air. She started to sit up, but she had to stop halfway, because the blood beating through her veins seemed to push the pain up to her head, like it was going to explode. She felt nausea roll over her. If she threw up, she would choke.

She slowly lay back down, and took deep breaths, tilting her head to put her cheek against the cold floor. She thought back to what had happened. She thought of the gas mask drawing, the moment when it had all fallen into place – and of course, he'd seen it too.

Panic rose in her again. He was going to kill her. The flame was from a boiler, which probably meant she was in the basement. Tied up. Gagged. In a cage. Fear and hopelessness came over her again. Then Jacob's face came into her mind. His beautiful eyes and his innocent smile. How good he smelt. How he loved to put his arms around her ever-expanding waist, and stand on her feet as she walked around the room, giving him a ride. And Celia, with her honey-blonde hair and her beautiful kind face. Why hadn't she hugged them and told them she loved them before she'd left the house?

Tears filled her eyes, and this gave her energy to fight. She took deep breaths and slowly inched herself up to a sitting position, trying to remember which side of her the blue flame had appeared. She put her head against the bars on the left, and inched herself up. The pain beat through her head, almost overwhelming her. She sucked in more air, deep breaths. He had taken off her jacket, and her hands were bound in front of her from above the wrist and forearm, down to her knuckles. She could feel it was duct tape, by the way it stuck to the fine hairs on her arms.

Something clicked in a far corner on the right, and the blue flame appeared again. Her vision was blurred, but she managed to adjust her eyes and see the outline of a few shapes. The box shape of the boiler high up on the wall. There were several shapes between it and her, and she could see that the cage was on the floor. The flame went out and she was plunged into darkness again.

She felt the nausea return and her back muscles started to cramp painfully, as well as the muscles in the back of her legs. Having her legs bound was bad enough, but the way her arms were bound in front of her, with her hands pointing forward, made it impossible to sit up straight. The cramp got worse and she winced in pain.

Breathe, breathe, breathe. The pain will pass. She gave a muffled cry as the cramps became unbearable. Her shoulders were hunched over, her elbows locked together. She remembered a video she had seen online, some American self-defence dude who had explained what to do if your hands were bound with duct tape. This was another of Celia's hobbies, going to self-defence classes. She'd wanted Moss to go with her, but it always seemed to clash with work. Celia had shown her this YouTube video… A guy had raised his bound arms above his head, and brought them down so that they hit his stomach, snapping them apart. It was something to do with the tensile strength of duct tape; if you try and pull it one way it just stretches like the strongest chewing gum, but if you use force on it another way it will break cleanly along the ridges.

Moss took a deep breath and went to lift her arms up, but in the darkness, she misjudged the angle and her tightly bound wrists bashed her on the bridge of the nose. She gave a muffled sob, and then began to panic as her nose was flooded with blood. She bent forward, but her wrists were still tightly bound, and she couldn't breathe. In the darkness, she started to choke on her own blood.

CHAPTER SIXTY

T enjoyed the slow walk back through the houses. It gave him time to think. He thought of his life as light and dark. His work with the family portraits was so quaint and down to earth, that he thought of this as the light. Then when he closed the shop and he was alone, he would move through to the darkness.

He had been introduced to the darkness by a girl he'd met fifteen years ago – no, that wasn't quite right. The darkness had always been there, but Tabitha had teased it out of him, brought it to the fore. He had always thought he was the only person in the world who had violent fantasies, but Tabitha, a young, precocious student had encouraged him to experiment with sex toys and role play. She had encouraged him to tell her his secrets in the darkness.

Tabitha loved being tied up, and they would act out a fantasy where he kidnapped and raped her. At the time, it had felt shocking and daring, but looking back now he knew it was kids' stuff. Tabitha had been acting. It was only role play. And her acting wasn't quite good enough. Her fear was wooden and hollow. She was a stepping stone to darker places.

One night, they'd gone to an underground bondage club in Soho. This was where he'd discovered hoods, and breath control, and it also saw the end of his relationship with Tabitha. That night, he'd almost suffocated her. He'd seen real fear in her eyes and he hadn't been able to stop. He'd managed to dissuade her from going to the police.

Over the next few years, he'd indulged in visits to Amsterdam, where he would go to bondage clubs and buy extreme porn, but he'd quickly found that even the hardest type of porn wouldn't satisfy him. Then he discovered gas masks, and in particular engaging in sex acts whilst wearing a gas mask, with the breathing drum closed for breath control, or packed with cotton wool soaked in amyl nitrate.

He couldn't quite remember when the idea came to him to stalk the streets late at night. He'd got high with a guy who he'd invited round to the sex dungeon he had built in his basement. They had somehow ended up in the garden, and then he'd staggered out through the back gate and into the street, where he'd crouched in a dark corner, watching people, hidden from view. The power it had given him was bigger than anything that had come before. He'd got bolder, at first exposing himself to men and women, and then, his first attack.

T slowed as he approached Camera Obscura. He needed time to think. The fact it was a policewoman gave it an extra frisson. After all of the attacks over the years, he had never been caught. He had no police record, they didn't have his DNA, and he had never even had a parking ticket or points on his licence.

She was there in the basement. She had seen him. If he let her go, it would all be over.

He was a risk-taker. He had already thrown them off the scent. He would have to think about how to dispose of her body. She was a big girl. He doubled back and decided to circle the block again. He needed to think and plan.

CHAPTER SIXTY-ONE

Moss raised her arms in the darkness and brought them down, her wrists hitting her chest. She repeated it again. Her nose was pouring with blood and she was fighting to breathe. On the third attempt, her wrists snapped apart and her elbows slammed into the bars. She didn't care about the pain and reached up with her numb fingers, ripping off the piece of duct tape covering her mouth. She gagged and spat and managed to pull huge gulps of air into her lungs.

'Oh my god, oh my god!' she cried, relieved by the sensation of being able to use her hands and breathe through her mouth. She started to work quickly, ripping and pulling at the tape around her ankles until they were free. She rolled her shoulders, and shifted around in the cage into a crouching position. She started to feel around inside the cage. Above her head were thick bars, and she couldn't stand and straighten her legs. There was a padlock on one side of the cage, and it was fastened securely.

'Shit,' she said. It was like a cage for a large dog. There was a click, and the flame lit up the small room. Her eyes had adjusted to the dark now and she could see there was a series of posts mounted on the back wall. She could see shapes and outlines: something long and thin coiled up, and there was a hood with eye holes, and a breathing drum. It was a gas mask. She felt around again. The cage bars were solid, thick metal, but underneath, the base of the cage was wood. Now she had taken off the duct tape, she was able to move more freely around. She swallowed and wiped her nose, feeling the blood starting to clot. She braced herself in the crouching position and put her back against the top of the cage. She rocked from side to side and felt it shift across the floor a couple of centimetres. It wasn't fixed to the floor. She started to rock it harder, so that it skidded along, away from the brick wall. It took a huge amount of effort and she had to stop a couple of times to catch her breath. She reached through the bars and couldn't feel the brick wall any more, so she was satisfied she had enough room either side. Moss braced her back against the bars, and rocked the cage from side to side, exploiting its low centre of gravity. The sides of the base started to lift off the floor as she rocked harder. Suddenly, it tipped over and landed with a loud clattering crash which echoed around the basement. Moss cried out as she landed painfully on the left side bars, which now were the floor of the cage.

She took a moment to catch her breath and then she started to kick at the base board of the cage.

'You. Should. Have. Taken. My. Boots. Off. You. Dumb. Fuck!' she hissed, punctuating each word with a kick, rhythmically slamming her boots into the base. With each kick, pain jangled in her bones and the metal bars dug into her back and shoulders, but she kept on. Finally, as her feet felt like they were going to explode, the wood cracked – and then her leg went through it. The splinters scraped at her leg and she cried out with pain, but nothing would stop her. She pulled out her leg and started to work on the hole, kicking and pushing and peeling the thick chip board away. It seemed to take forever, but she finally tore her way through, hands and legs filled with splinters. She was free. She scrabbled around in the darkness, managed to find a light switch, and turned it on.

CHAPTER SIXTY-TWO

Moss had barely caught her breath, when she saw the full horror of where she was. There was another, taller cage in one corner of the room, a set of stocks, and table with leather restraints. There were blood stains soaked into the concrete floor. Pornography was pinned up all over the walls: extreme images of nudity and torture. And there was a large-screen TV with rows and rows of DVDs neatly stacked up on a shelf.

Hung on pegs along the wall were whips and chains, a harness, two full-body latex suits, and at the end was a black gas mask with large glass eye holes and an elongated breathing drum; a series of white squares made it look like a face with teeth.

Moss froze when she heard footsteps outside the door. A bolt shot back in the door, and it opened.

Taro stood in the doorway, shaking and white-faced. In one hand, he held a large syringe filled with a dark blue liquid, and in the other he had a pile of black plastic sheeting. He had come to kill her in the neatest and cleanest way possible, but she had complicated things. She was sure he had wanted to poke the syringe though the bars and inject her. It made her think of a terrible film she had seen, about animals being tested on. The way they shrank away from the bars as a needle was poked through and into their skin.

'How did you get out?' he said. His voice was low and even.

'You can see how I got out,' she said. He kept his eyes on her and stepped into the room, closing the door behind him with one of his feet. He took another step towards her.

'Stay back,' she said.

'You shouldn't have come here. I was going to stop. I was going to stop and just melt away… Now I have to deal with you. NOW I HAVE TO DEAL WITH YOU!'

Moss tried not to show her fear. She moved back, putting the cage, lying on its side, between them. He moved closer. She grabbed the top of the cage and tried to slide it towards him as a battering ram, but it didn't slide smoothly on the floor, inching forward, and she lost her footing and fell forward.

Instantly he was on her, moving quickly around the cage, and grabbing her from behind. She fought and struggled, and saw him switch the grip on the syringe, so he had it in his fist with his thumb on the plunger. He held it up, preparing to bring it down on her.

She bent forward and then threw her head back. The back of her skull struck his mouth, shattering his top teeth and breaking his nose. He cried out and staggered back. Moss ran for the door, but it wouldn't open. She yanked at the handle, but it wouldn't budge.

She turned to see Taro staggering around, blood pouring from his nose. He spat out two of his teeth onto the floor, and looked up at her. His face was now crazed. She looked around for something and she saw a table by the door with a large open padlock, next to a chain. Quick as lightning, she grabbed the padlock, and using everything she had, she hurled it at him, aiming high. Time seemed to slow down and it turned in the air, once, twice, before striking him on the temple. He gave her a look of shock and surprise and then crumpled to the floor, his head hitting the concrete with a nasty crack.

Moss made for the door again. It was stiff, but she managed to turn the handle and get it open. She came out into a brightly lit hallway, and slammed the door behind her.

She could see the hallway had old-fashioned wooden panelling, and that she had exited through a secret door. When it was closed, it blended into the wall. There was an old Singer sewing machine table in the hall, covered in books, plants, plus a bowl for keys. Moss dragged it, squealing, across the stone floor, keeping her eye on the door, thinking that it would open. She pulled it across the door, hoping that it would do for now.

Then she ran for it, down the corridor and into the front of the photographic studio. It was now dark outside and the door was still locked, but she picked up one of the tripods for the photography lights, and with almost hysterical fear, hurled it through the plate glass window. The window exploded outwards. She kicked aside the glass with her foot, climbed through and ran for it, down the path and out into the street.

Her car was gone, and she didn't have a phone. She staggered down the street, the adrenalin pumping, feeling the blood pouring from the back of her head. She tried to find a phone box, but there was nothing on the road.

Moss ran to the end of the road, where it curved around to New Cross station. The road was busy with young teenagers piling out of the station, all dressed up for a night out. The noise was deafening. She pushed her way through the crowds, and saw an old phone box next to the station. She grabbed the receiver and her first impulse was to speak to Celia. She dialled 100, for the operator, and then she asked to make a reverse-charge call.

CHAPTER SIXTY-THREE

Erika was sad to see Isaac leave. He set off back to London late in the day, and she hoped that he wouldn't hit any more snow storms. She lit a fresh fire in the stove and checked her phone, but there was nothing about Moss. She felt restless, and so far away from everything. She thought back to her visit to the old house. In the past few years, she had thought of London as temporary, a place she was exiled to after what had happened in Manchester, but she realised now that London was now home to her. Life up north was in the past. She no longer belonged here.

She flicked through the TV channels, but there was nothing she fancied watching. She pulled on her coat, an old hat and a pair of gloves, and set off to the graveyard, which was a short walk across the fields. It was a clear, starry night, and as she climbed the hill, she could see the houses in the village spread out below, their lights glowing in the windows. The moon sailed out from behind the clouds as she reached the entrance to the graveyard, meaning she was able to see as she picked her way through the rows of graves to find Mark's.

His headstone was made of polished black granite, and it glittered in the moonlight:

IN MEMORY OF
MARK FOSTER
1ST AUGUST 1970 – 8TH JULY 2014
LOVED AND REMEMBERED ALWAYS

Erika took a Jack Daniel's whisky miniature from her pocket, undid the cap, took a small sip, and then poured the rest into the soil.

'I never thought this was how we'd end up,' she said. 'I miss you every day…' She wiped a tear away with her gloved hand. 'I've told you this so many times before, but I have to live my life, and go on living my life. If it were me, I wouldn't want you to stay here on earth and be miserable… I've decided I'm going to sell the house. I went back today, and it's not the place I remember any more. It's not our home. I'm going to buy a new place, and make it my home…' Erika swallowed back the tears. 'Because you're not here, and I can't carry on living my life with a space beside me that needs to be filled. You're never going to be forgotten, and I will always love you, but I can't carry on being half a person.'

Clouds slid across the moon, plunging her into darkness.

'I sometimes check on Jerome Goodman. I wonder where he is. If he even thinks about all of us. I run his name through the computers at work, but he's vanished. If I ever got the chance to spend time in a room alone with him… I'd kill him, slowly, for what he did to you, and me, and…'

A freezing cold chill blew along the path, and she felt the cold seeping into her shoes and gloves, and on the small of her back. 'I'm going to look after your dad. I'm getting a carer to come in, and I'm going to keep more of an eye on things, and visit more.' She pressed her fingers to her lips and put them against the gold letters spelling out his name.

When Erika arrived back at the cottage, the fire had died down. She raked the ash in the stove and put another couple of logs on. Just as she closed the stove, her phone rang. It was Melanie.

'Erika, there's been an incident with Moss,' she said, without preamble. Erika listened as Melanie explained what had happened with Moss, and that she had been found, barely conscious, in a phone box in New Cross.

'Is she okay?'

'I hope so. She's just in the A&E, having a scan. She has bad concussion. We've arrested a thirty-five-year-old man called Taro Williams, who runs a photography studio in New Cross. Moss had been to talk to him, based on a lead she'd got from the Forest Hill Jobcentre. Apparently, Joseph Pitkin worked as his assistant in early 2016.'

Erika felt exhilarated, and then frustrated that she wasn't there. 'I'm up north; I can't leave my father-in-law.'

'I know, and please, stay. Everything is in hand here. Williams is a man of means and he has already hired a top-notch solicitor, so we're going to have to move very carefully and make sure we do everything by the book.'

'Moss should have called in where she was going; she put herself in danger,' said Erika.

'Are you kidding me? How many times have you put yourself in danger? You've been beaten up more times than Jackie Chan. You're like the bionic woman!'

'Very funny.'

'Sorry. I'm just delighted we could have this case sewn up so quickly.'

'Pending DNA tests,' said Erika.

'Of course… Now, take as long as you need with your father-in-law.'

Erika went to say something else, but Melanie had hung up.

Erika sat up for a long time, watching the fire burn down through the window of the stove, feeling a long way away from it all.

CHAPTER SIXTY-FOUR

It was three o'clock in the morning, but the atmosphere at Lewisham Row station was one of intense excitement. Peterson, McGorry, Crane, and Superintendent Hudson had all been called back to work when the news had come in about Moss. After calling Celia, she'd phoned for police backup, and then, finally, about to lose consciousness, she had phoned Peterson.

Uniformed officers had sped round to Camera Obscura, where they found Taro Williams in the basement. He had regained consciousness, and after being checked over by a paramedic, he had been arrested and brought to Lewisham Row. His fingerprints and a sample of his DNA had been taken, and rushed over to the lab.

McGorry and Crane were with Superintendent Hudson in the observation suite at Lewisham Row. They watched as Taro Williams was being questioned by Peterson.

'He's not saying a word,' said McGorry, as they stared at the screen showing the live feed.

'He's a big bastard, isn't he?' said Crane.

'A big hairy bastard. His eyes creeped me out,' said McGorry. 'When they brought him in and booked him, took his fingerprints and DNA, he was completely impassive. Like none of it bothered him.'

On the screen, Peterson asked Taro to confirm that he was the owner of Camera Obscura and the building, and if he worked full-time as a photographer.

Taro leaned forward amiably. 'Yes. I inherited the business from my father when he died twelve years ago,' he said. His voice was soft and he was well-spoken.

Superintendent Hudson's phone rang.

'This is forensics,' she said. The guys watched as she answered the phone, and McGorry crossed his fingers.

'It's a match! The DNA sample taken from blood on the broken glass at the office block doors in West Norwood matches the sample we took from him in the custody suite. We've got him!' cried Melanie. They punched the air with their fists.

'What a sicko,' said McGorry.

'It's enough to charge him for all six of the sexual assaults, and the murder of Marissa Lewis?' asked Crane.

'Yes, especially the murder of Marissa. I don't want him back out on the streets. He has no record, and I don't want to give his slimy solicitor the opportunity to wangle him bail by not making a murder charge,' said Melanie. She leaned over to the microphone. 'Peterson, I need you to suspend the interview for a sec. We have the DNA results back.'

Peterson came out. Melanie gave him the results and the go-ahead to charge Taro Williams.

They watched from the observation suite as Peterson went back in and formally arrested Williams for the sexual assault of Rachel Elder, Kelvin Price, Jenny Thorndike, Diana Crow and Jason Bates, and the murder of Marissa Lewis.

Taro remained impassive, going so far as to pick a speck of lint from his jacket as the charges were read out. He then looked up at the camera, and the officers in the observation suite felt a chill run through them. It was as if he could see them. He smiled. It was a broad toothy grin, but it didn't reach his eyes.

CHAPTER SIXTY-FIVE

Erika stayed up north for two weeks. In between visiting Edward every day, she had had a stair lift put into his cottage. She'd also done some decorating, and registered all his utilities online so that she could check that his bills were being paid.

During one of the last hospital visits, before he was due to be discharged, Edward had been enthusiastic about these ideas and changes. That is until she told him she had hired a carer to come in and visit him three times a week.

'I'm not having some stranger let themselves in to wipe my backside!' he'd said. By now he was sitting up in bed, and well on the road to recovery.

'Edward. It won't be like that. She'll be there to help with whatever you need doing.'

'She?' he'd said, narrowing his eyes.

'Do you want a bloke?'

'Good Lord, no.'

'She'll help with the washing, cleaning, making a meal, or she can ring up about something, like a doctor's appointment. She'll be company. I promise you there will be no backsides being wiped.'

'I'm too young for a carer!'

'Okay. How about we call her your PA?'

He'd laughed. 'Who is she? I can't have a Tory in the house. And I don't want some youngster, glued to their mobile phone the whole time.'

'Of course not.'

'And I want a northerner. I don't mind southerners, but having one in the house three times a week would be too much.'

'She's sort of a northerner... North Slovakia. Her name's Lydia. She's twenty-five, speaks excellent English and she's been caring, sorry, working part-time as a PA, for a lady in the next village.'

'Do you have a photo of her?'

'No. You'll meet her when you come home, which I hope, is tomorrow.'

Edward was discharged from hospital the next day, and Erika was waiting at home with Lydia. He liked her, and they instantly struck up a rapport, and Erika felt like the last piece in the puzzle had been slotted into place.

Erika spent the rest of the day and the next with Edward. On Sunday January 14th, she left to drive back to London. He came to the taxi with her, now walking with the aid of one stick, and they hugged.

'Now, you'll keep doing your exercises,' said Erika.

'Yes, love.'

'And keep eating well. Lydia is bringing over goulash tomorrow.'

'I'm looking forward to it.'

'And use the stair lift. No showing off to her that you can climb them on your own.'

He nodded.

'I've told Lydia to make sure you keep those compression stockings on for another two weeks. They prevent...'

'Yes, blood clots,' he said, lifting up the bottom of his trousers to show the green support stockings. 'And you won't be a stranger?'

'No, of course not,' she said.

Erika felt she was going to cry, so she hugged him again, and got into the taxi. The journey down to London by train was smooth and fast. The snow had all melted, and despite having been busy for the past two and a half weeks, she felt rested. The break had done her good.

When she got into the flat, it was freezing cold and there was a huge pile of post on the mat.

The next morning, she woke early and drove into work at Lewisham Row. She went through the reception, and greeted Desk Sergeant Woolf, a large, red-faced officer who was a few weeks away from retirement.

'Happy New Year,' she said.

'Bloody hell, you're a bit late,' he replied. 'New Year seems in the mists of time. There's already Easter Eggs in the shops!'

Erika grabbed some coffee and went up to her office on the fourth floor, starting to work through all the post and emails which had banked up over the past couple of weeks. Around mid-morning, there was a knock on her door, and Superintendent Hudson poked her head around.

'Alright stranger, welcome back. How's the father-in-law?'

'Well on the way to recovery… I'm just catching up on everything,' she replied, indicating a pile of folders on the desk beside her.

'I sent you an email yesterday, and I didn't want it to get lost amongst everything else in your inbox. We've been putting together the evidence and casefiles to go over to the CPS and defence team involved in the Taro Williams case. We've got the official DNA match, linking him to two of the attacks, with enough circumstantial evidence to implicate him in the other attacks. The CCTV footage will be submitted along with a statement from Mrs Fryatt with regards to the murder of Marissa Lewis.'

'Statement from Mrs Fryatt?'

'Yes, she's gone on record to say that Taro Williams attacked Marissa a few weeks before he killed her.'

'Surely that's a bit vague, she said that Marissa said…'

'The case is a slam dunk. We have him on CCTV following Marissa into her front garden. I want you to check through everything and submit your report before we sign off. Moss and Peterson have been working on it whilst you've been away, as I'm sure you know.'

'Are you confident of a conviction for Marissa's murder?'

'Confident as you can be with CCTV evidence, a DNA sample, a past history of violence… You're not going to tell me that you think there's a copycat killer out there?'

'No. Just asking the questions. No stupid questions when it comes to a murder investigation,' said Erika. Melanie nodded.

'Taro Williams has money, and he has the best of the best working on his behalf, and you know how good they can be at sniffing out a minor error in procedure. The hard copy file is there on top.'

'I'll look at it now.'

Melanie's phone rang and she excused herself. Erika pulled the file off the pile, and started to look through it. There were statements from all the attack victims, from Marissa's mother, Mrs Fryatt, and some of Marissa's colleagues. What upset Erika was seeing Moss's statement, where she described her ordeal of having been captured against her will.

Erika pored over the custody photos taken of Taro Williams. He was a big man, with a wide face and large features. He seemed so impassive in the shots, with dead eyes. She logged in to Holmes, and accessed the police interviews which were being submitted on a disc to the prosecution. He had been interviewed three times in the space of two days. In the first interview, Taro Williams sat impassive opposite Peterson, and in the other interviews, Peterson was joined by McGorry. Taro remained in handcuffs throughout all three interviews, despite his solicitor requesting that they be removed.

Taro was gangly, and sat hunched over the table. The t-shirt and tracksuit bottoms he wore looked too small. Like he had been stuffed into his clothes. Erika ran the second interview forward to the end, and then watched as Taro stood to leave. He towered over the solicitor, McGorry, and Peterson, who was himself six foot tall.

Erika then went back to the CCTV footage taken from the school opposite Marissa Lewis's house on the night she was killed. She watched as Taro Williams arrived at the house ahead of Marissa. The figure dressed in black, wearing a gas mask, walked into shot by the gate, moving carefully and purposefully along in the snow, almost staggering against the slippery surface. He reached the front gate and looked through into the front garden, and up at the house. Then he moved into the alleyway beside the house, to wait in the shadows.

She glanced down at the attached notes with the time stamp, and she ran the footage forward. Marissa appeared at the gate. She was such a beautiful girl, thought Erika, as she watched her move gracefully in her long coat, with her vanity case hooked over her arm. Marissa opened the gate and went through, vanishing in the shadows of the front garden. Ten seconds later, the figure in black, wearing the gas mask, moved out of the shadows in the alleyway and approached the gate, carrying a long knife.

'There you are, Taro,' murmured Erika. On the screen, he moved through the front gate and was swallowed up by the darkness.

Erika peered at the footage and felt panic rise in her chest. She ran it back to when the figure in the gas mask reached the gate post, and played it again, and then again. With shaking hands she went back to the footage from the third custody interview with Taro Williams, when Peterson led him into the interview room. She paused it, and compared it with the figure standing by the gate post. She picked up her phone and called Melanie.

'You need to get up here, now,' she said.

CHAPTER SIXTY-SIX

'How tall is Taro Williams?' asked Erika. Melanie was sitting beside her, as she played back the CCTV footage from outside Marissa's house on Christmas Eve.

'I don't know. He's tall …' Melanie started.

'He's six foot four, or 193 cm,' said Erika, holding up the report from the custody suite when Taro had been arrested and brought to the station. 'Look at the footage again.' She dragged the time stamp underneath the video window to just before Marissa Lewis appeared in shot, arriving back at her house. Erika paused the video as she reached the gate post. 'Marissa Lewis was five foot two, that's about 157 cm. You can see she is only a little taller than the gate post.'

'Okay,' said Melanie, sounding uneasy at where this was going. Erika took a small sticker and where the video was paused, she placed the sticker so it touched the top of Marissa's head. 'OK, moving the CCTV footage on,' said Erika. 'Bearing in mind the marker on the screen…' The figure in the gas mask came moving through the snow with difficulty, head bent down. Erika paused the video when he reached gate post. 'You can see here that the person in the gas mask…'

'Taro Williams,' insisted Melanie.

'The person in the gas mask is only fractionally taller than Marissa.' She placed another sticker on the screen, which was only slightly higher than the first. 'Taro Williams is thirty-five centimetres taller than Marissa Lewis. That person in the gas mask is not Taro Williams. Unless he's the incredible shrinking man.' Melanie leaned in and ran the footage back and then forward, her face clouding over. 'We have two people here to compare against one fixed object, the gate post,' said Erika.

'Shit.'

'And this would be leapt on by the defence team. I've seen cases where it's come down to a height difference on CCTV of a few centimetres. They would ask for the footage to be examined, and they would apply more rigorous tests than a couple of stickers on the screen.'

'Fuck!' said Melanie, slamming her hand down on the desk. 'Our case is screwed. We have no case.'

'Yes, we do have a case!' said Erika. 'Taro Williams assaulted five people, and we can link him with DNA, but I'm more concerned as to who the hell killed Marissa wearing the gas mask. It's not Taro Williams.'

CHAPTER SIXTY-SEVEN

Early next morning, Erika pulled up outside Moss's house in Ladywell. She was going to get out, but Moss appeared at the gate and got in the car.

'Morning. It's good to see you're in one piece,' she said, giving Moss an unexpected hug.

'Oh, you know me. I don't fall down, I bounce,' Moss said, her cheeks flushing red. Erika started the engine, and they rode in silence for a minute. She gave Moss a sideways glance. Her silence was unusual. She was always upbeat and chatty.

'Are you crying?' asked Erika.

'No,' said Moss, wiping tears away angrily.

'It's too early for allergies.'

'I missed the height thing on the CCTV. It's such a rookie mistake. I'm fucking embarrassed…'

'Whose fault is it?'

'Mine.'

Erika nodded.

'You win brownie points for taking responsibility. I'd be annoyed if you tried to blame someone else.'

'Not my style, Boss.'

'I know.'

'When we caught Taro Williams we went into evidence gathering mode. Most of the team was re-assigned so I lost manpower. Again, that's not an excuse. I'm not cut out to be SIO. I've realised I prefer playing second fiddle.'

'But you caught Taro Williams.'

Moss shook her head. 'I feel like I just blundered into it. And then nearly got myself killed in the process.'

'But you didn't,' said Erika. 'And he would have carried on attacking people, and now he's off the streets.'

'Off the streets, and still refusing to talk.'

'That's nothing new. He can talk or he can keep his mouth shut. Either way, we've got DNA.'

'You're a poet, and you don't even know it.'

Erika grinned. 'As I said. You did a great job.'

Moss waved it away, her cheeks flushing again. 'Enough about me. How were things up north?'

'Edward is doing good. For so many years he's been the responsible adult, and me the youngster. It made me aware of how old I am, now I'm caring for him.'

'You're not old! What's the saying? You're only as old as the man or woman you feel.'

'There's nothing happening in that department, unless I count the old geezer in Sainsbury's who rubbed up against me at the till.'

Moss grinned. 'Good to have you back, Erika.'

'Thanks,' she said, smiling in return. 'It's good to be back. Now, onwards and upwards. Let's hope today gives us a breakthrough.'

Erika indicated and they turned into Coniston Road, and drove towards Mandy Trent's house.

They parked a few doors down from Mandy's house. The snow was long melted, and it was break time at the school opposite. The playground was full of kids, their loud playing and chatter filling the street. Erika and Moss got out of the car, and joined a small team of four forensic height analysts who were setting up their equipment outside the front gate of the house. Half of the playground opposite had been cordoned off, giving a clear view to conduct the test using the CCTV camera mounted on the wall at the end of the school building. One of the guys was positioning an oblong of plastic, like a giant ruler, next to the gate post outside the house. It reached up to two metres tall, and 5 cm increments were marked out on it with red lines. Another woman was unpacking a tripod and camera, and setting it up at the same height and angle further along the pavement towards the top of Coniston Road. Some of the more curious children who weren't running around and playing were lined up at the railings, watching.

Erika and Moss introduced themselves to the team, and then went through the front gate. The hedge had been chopped down, leaving just the low wall surrounding the tiny garden, which without snow was just a patch of flattened earth. Marissa's mother, Mandy, was also watching the proceedings from her front doorstep. She was dishevelled, and smoking a cigarette. They said hello, and asked how she was doing. She said she was making the preparations for Marissa's funeral, which would be taking place in a few days.

'I want to have 'All Things Bright and Beautiful' play, cos I loved singing that hymn when I was at school,' she said, sucking on the butt of her cigarette. 'Do you think that's nice?'

'Yes, I love that hymn,' said Moss.

'And with all the flowers. I'm gonna have lilies. Marissa liked lilies. Joan's ex-husband runs the florist down in Honor Oak Park... He's gonna do me a good deal, get some nice ones which are open. I hate lilies on bunches when they're closed,' she said. 'I went to Joseph Pitkin's funeral the other day, I sat at the back, mind. They got lilies for the top of his coffin, and they was all closed up. It was a burial, and all I could think was that they would never open, what with the cold weather we've been having. They would just die, before they had the chance to bloom... And then it made me think of Marissa. She was killed before she got the chance to bloom. What do you call it?'

A look passed between Erika and Moss,

'It was a tragedy,' said Erika.

'No,' said Mandy, impatiently flicking the cigarette butt into the hedge. 'It's what you call it? A metaphor. The lily not opening, that's a metaphor for Marissa, and for Joseph.'

Erika and Moss nodded in agreement.

'So why are you all measuring my gatepost?' she added.

'It's for the CCTV evidence. Standard procedure. It helps give us more detail in court.'

'Does it matter that I had the hedge cut down? I just didn't feel safe with it there. There's nowhere for anyone to hide.'

'It's fine,' said Erika. They could now see up and down the street, and Don Walpole emerged from his front door with a bag of rubbish. He noticed them, and nodded his head, and then went back indoors. Mandy lit another cigarette.

'Jeanette's home from hospital. They put an implant in her stomach, to stop her drinking. One sip of anything alcoholic and she pukes it back up… I just hope he's stocked up on carpet cleaner.'

'Have you packed away any of Marissa's belongings yet?' asked Erika.

'No. I can't bring myself to do it. Not until she's buried. Joan's good with cleaning; she said she'd come and help me, we can work out what to keep and what to give to charity. A lot of her costumes can go on eBay,' said Mandy.

'You take your time, there's never any rush with these things.'

'I'm glad you've got the bastard who done this to her… I'd seen the stuff on the news about him, skulking around the streets at night. I know this is a rough area, but you never expect this kind of thing to happen, literally on your own doorstep.'

'Would you mind if we took one last look in Marissa's bedroom, just to make absolutely sure we have everything for the court case?' asked Erika.

'Yes, go on up. Of course, you know where it is,' said Mandy. The sun came out, and she rested her head against the brick wall, closing her eyes and tilting her pale lined face upwards.

They came inside and went up the stairs to the front bedroom. It looked just as it had when Erika had come to look at it with McGorry. The same posters were on the wall, and all of the burlesque gear was untouched. She went to the window and looked down at the street below. Several of the neighbours had come out to gawp at the team of forensic height analysts. A bell rang opposite, signalling the end of break time, and the children all started to run to line up at the top end of the playground. Mandy had crossed the road, still in her slippers, nightie and thick winter coat, and she was talking to Joan, who was smoking a cigarette on her front step.

'The diamond earrings are still bugging me,' said Erika. 'They feel like they are the key to this. Why did Marissa go to the jeweller where Charles Fryatt worked? And did he know she was there? I've read the reports, and he says he only knew when McGorry went back with Marissa's friend, Ella. And they deny that the earrings were even the same ones belonging to Mrs Fryatt.'

'Charles Fryatt has an alibi, his wife, and he's also a very tall man,' said Moss, picking up a fire-eating rod from in front of the tiny fireplace and examining the tip.

'According to Martin, the costume guy at the Matrix Club, and Ella, one of the dancers, Marissa said she took the diamond earrings from Mrs Fryatt, but who is telling the truth? We don't know where those earrings came from, or where they are now.'

'Could Mandy have taken them off the dead body?' asked Moss, joining her at the window. Joan and Mandy were lighting up fresh cigarettes.

'There's still a question mark where Mandy was sleeping on the night Marissa died. She told us that she was sleeping upstairs in the back bedroom, but there was evidence that she slept downstairs on the sofa.'

'There was a duvet on the downstairs sofa,' said Erika. 'But that's hardly evidence. She could have just been napping.'

'Erika. This case comes down to the height of whoever did it. It's not all about diamonds, or should I say, the diamond earrings.'

'What did you just say?'

'This case is about the height of the person who killed her, we know it's not Taro Williams…'

'No, after that.'

'It's not all about the earrings. At least, I don't think it is.'

Erika was now pacing up and down the room.

'When me and Peterson went to the Matrix Club, the guy who does the costumes told us Marissa kept saying it was all about "the diamond" not "diamonds". That it would be "the diamond" that would make her fortune… He said something along the lines, like, "I know Marissa was stupid, but she did know the difference between the singular and plural". If she wasn't talking about the diamond earrings, then what was she talking about?'

'Now I'm getting confused,' said Moss. 'There's a diamond embroidered on her costumes.' She went over to the three mannequins, which were lined up along the wall and wearing some of Marissa's costumes, embroidered with the diamond logo. 'She was planning to go off to New York, and perform as Honey Diamond. Maybe she thought she was going to make her fortune there?'

Erika shook her head, and looked out of the window. Mandy and Joan were still deep in conversation. Joan said something out of the corner of her mouth, and Mandy hooted with laughter, expelling a long stream of cigarette smoke. The last of the kids were filing back into the school building, and one of the forensic guys was shouting at a group of the neighbours.

'Please get back!' he said, waving his gloved hands at them. They were walking backwards – two old ladies, and a young lad, much like sheep do when they are being herded.

Erika looked back at the bedroom, and spied a large framed photo on the wall, amongst the framed publicity shots of Marissa. It was of a huge diamond, mounted on a ring, sparkling with clarity. She crossed to the picture and carefully lifted it off the wall. She started to examine it. There was a thin paper backing on the frame.

'Do you have any latex gloves?' she said. Moss rummaged in her pockets and handed her a pair.

CHAPTER SIXTY-EIGHT

Erika placed the framed print face-down on the bed, and they stared at the thick backing paper.

'The frame is pretty old and crappy,' said Erika. 'And the diamond image is faded, like it's been on the wall and caught the sun, but this backing paper looks brand new.'

Erika took a pair of nail scissors from a pot on the desk by the window, and Moss held the frame as she neatly scored the thin backing paper, and then carefully peeled it away. They stood back and stared. There was nothing inside but the print, which was on a piece of card. Erika lifted it gently away from the frame. It felt thick, and she held it up to the light.

'It's faded yellow on one side, but the back is white,' said Moss. 'But then again, only the side facing the window would fade.'

Erika examined the edges of the card. 'There's a slight overlap here, look, with this white side, and the other which has the yellower shade.'

'It's two pieces, they've been stuck together,' said Moss. Erika gently moved her gloved fingers over the diamond print. Her fingers stopped in the centre.

'There's a slight ridge, here; it feels like there's something inside. Oblong: could be folded paper, or an envelope which has been glued in between the two pieces of card.'

Erika and Moss bagged up the print and rushed it over to Lewisham Row station, where they took it into one of the sterile medical examining rooms. They donned gloves and masks, and using a scalpel Erika carefully cut between the two sheets of glued-together card.

'Careful,' said Moss, watching as Erika slowly pushed the knife up through the seam between the two pieces of card. Erika finally got the two pieces to part.

Inside lay a small brown envelope.

'We should take this to forensics,' said Moss.

'I know,' said Erika. 'I won't touch where the envelope is stuck down. Forensics will have to test for saliva… If it is anything that needs testing.'

She carefully slit along the top of the envelope with the scalpel, and she pulled out two pieces of folded paper. The first was a scanned image of a set of German identity papers, dating back to October 1942. They were of a young woman called Elsa Neubukov. The woman in the sepia photo was twenty-two, having been born in January 1920. There were three fingerprints in the identity papers: a thumb, and a right and left index finger. What chilled Erika was the stamp of the Third Reich, Nazi Germany: the eagle with wings spread, and underneath, the swastika. The woman in the sepia photo had short fair hair, a high forehead and a handsome face, staring almost defiantly at the camera.

'This Elsa was born in 1920. She would be ninety-seven, almost ninety-eight, now,' said Moss quietly. They turned their attention to the second piece of paper. It was another scanned-in image, this time of an Austrian passport. It was dated six years later, three years after the end of the Second World War. The photo was different, but it was the same woman. This time the name said Elsa Becher. It had the same date of birth and a set of fingerprints.

Moss and Erika looked at each other.

'What is Elsa Fryatt's date of birth and maiden name?'

'We can soon find out,' said Erika. She took out her phone and called up Elsa Fryatt's address, and the council tax records. 'Date of birth is the same. We'll need to check out her maiden name.'

'Elsa Fryatt has been living under another identity?' started Moss.

'But these are scans, where are the originals?' asked Erika. She turned over the first German identity papers scan, and she saw that on the back was a phone number written in pen. It was long, and Erika didn't recognise the code. There was also an obscure web address ending in the .de German domain.

'You think this is Marissa's handwriting?' said Moss.

'We'll soon find out,' said Erika, already dialling the number.

CHAPTER SIXTY-NINE

Two days later, after following up several leads, Erika and Moss arrived at Elsa Fryatt's house. It was a grey morning, and the street outside was empty and quiet. Moss glanced nervously at Erika as they opened the gate and started up the path to the front door. They were about to ring the bell when Mrs Fryatt appeared at the gate behind them, carrying bags of shopping.

'Good morning, officers. Can I help you?' she asked, taking a key from her coat pocket. As she walked toward them, Erika thought how sprightly she was for a woman of ninety-seven.

'Morning, Mrs Fryatt. We've come to return the diamond earrings my colleague took away for forensic examination,' said Erika, holding up a small evidence bag containing the small velvet box.

'And it takes two of you to do this?' said Mrs Fryatt, putting the bags of shopping down and opening the front door.

Erika gave her a disarming smile. 'We understand they are very valuable, and we just need you to sign a couple of forms to confirm that we are returning your property, and everything is in order.' There was a moment when she thought Mrs Fryatt wouldn't invite them in, but she relented.

'Very well,' she said. Moss went to pick up the shopping bags for her, but Mrs Fryatt batted her away. 'I can manage.'

They followed her into the house and down the long hallway to the kitchen. Charles was filling the kettle, and he went very pale when he saw Erika and Moss.

'Charles, would you make these officers some tea? They are here to return my earrings.' She gave him a look and he nodded. She took off her coat and hung it over a chair. 'And put my shopping away.'

They left Charles in the kitchen and followed her through to the large living room. Mrs Fryatt showed them to a sofa, and took the armchair opposite.

'Okay. Here are your earrings,' said Erika, placing the small clear evidence bag on the polished coffee table in front of her. 'Please can you check them over.'

Mrs Fryatt put on a pair of glasses, took the box from the bag and opened it. The earrings nestled, sparkling on the small blue cushion.

'Yes, my babies,' she said, peering at them and holding them up to the light.

'We also need you to sign a form, which states that your property has been returned to you,' said Erika. 'If you could make sure everything is in order and that they are in fact your earrings.'

There was a rattling sound as Charles brought in a stack of teacups on a tray. His hands shook as he took them off and placed them on the table.

'Charles, I need you to cast your expert eye over these,' said Mrs Fryatt, handing him the earrings in the box. 'I have to sign that they are mine. I can tell the difference between a diamond and a zircon, but I need to be sure these officers aren't taking me for a ride.' She smiled across at Erika and Moss, but the smile didn't quite make it to her eyes. Charles took a jeweller's eyepiece from his pocket, and peered through it at the earrings.

'He always comes prepared.' Mrs Fryatt grinned indulgently. Charles peered at them, breathing heavily, and then went to the window to catch them in the light. The clock ticked.

'Everything okay?' asked Erika.

'Yes,' he said coming back and placing the box on the table. Moss opened the folder she was carrying and took out a pre-filled form, and put it in front of Mrs Fryatt.

'Check we have your name and address correct, and sign underneath,' she said.

Mrs Fryatt took a pen from a corner of the table and scanned the form, then signed her name at the bottom.

Erika leaned over and placed the scanned identity papers for Elsa Neubukov on top of the form. Mrs Fryatt stared at the sepia photograph and the swastika stamp of the Third Reich for a long moment, frozen in shock. Then she looked up at Erika. Her eyes moved to Moss, and then to Charles, whose mouth was also agape. She sat back and put a shaking hand to her mouth.

'We found these papers concealed in a print on the wall of Marissa Lewis's bedroom,' said Erika. 'Along with these…' She placed a copy of the Austrian passport for Elsa Becher, dated six years later, beside the identity papers. Then she produced a copy of a marriage certificate, for Elsa Becher and Arnold Fryatt, and placed it beside the Austrian passport. 'You can see we have a paper trail from Elsa Neubukov, to Elsa Becher and then Elsa Fryatt. All of them are you.'

'This is absurd,' Mrs Fryatt said. All the colour had drained from her face, and her hands shook. She leant forward and took the scan of the German identity papers. 'This isn't an original. This is a sick joke. That girl was a liar, and you can do all sorts of things on computers these days…'

'You'll see there's a phone number written on the back,' said Erika. 'Marissa's mother has confirmed that is Marissa's handwriting. It's the phone number for a Dr Arnold Schmidt, who works in Hamburg at an office responsible for investigating historical Nazi war crimes.'

Charles had slumped against the wall by the door, and he looked pale and ill.

'You should sit down, Charles,' said Erika. He moved to the sofa and sat at the opposite end to his mother. 'Dr Schmidt wasn't aware of your identity, Mrs Fryatt, but Marissa was. Or she put two and two together when she found these identity papers. She called him a few weeks before Christmas, making some vague enquiries. She said she had seen an article in one of the tabloid newspapers that these so-called Nazi hunters were offering a reward for information about anyone who worked in concentrations camps during the war. He says he told her that the reward was two thousand euros… I think Marissa realised that she could make much more money from blackmailing you.'

'Lies!' she hissed. 'That little bitch; she made this up. Where are the originals? Tell me? Where?'

Moss opened the file again and gave Erika a sheet of paper.

'Mrs Fryatt, or can I call you Elsa Neubukov? Elsa, you worked at the Mauthausen–Gusen concentration camp in upper Austria.'

'Lies! Austria was *never* a willing participant in the war. We were annexed into the German Third Reich. The people didn't have a choice, we just became part of it all, on the whims of politicians.'

'Dr Schmidt was able, very quickly, to access records from the Mauthausen-Gusen camp. You worked there, Elsa,' said Erika.

'Don't call me that,' she cried, putting her hands to her ears.

'You took part in the extermination of people. based purely on the race they were born. They were used for slave labour, experimented on, tortured.'

Elsa slammed a hand down on the coffee table. 'You think we were responsible for this? You think the Austrian people wanted this? We had no choice!' she cried, her eyes blazing.

'Mauthausen was one of the biggest concentration camp complexes in the German-controlled part of Europe,' said Erika.

'I don't need a fucking history lesson!' cried Elsa. Charles was staring blankly at the paperwork on the table.

Erika went on, 'Prisoners at Mauthausen–Gusen were forced to work building arms, quarrying stone. The conditions were horrific. What did you do, exactly? The records state that you were a guard, which is very broad, but it was your job to control the prisoners, yes? To move them from place to place, to dole out discipline and order, to carry out orders. And what were those orders? They were from Hitler and the Third Reich. Orders to reshape Europe to their Aryan ideals. Do you see yourself as part of a superior race? What do you think of me, Elsa? I'm Slavic, and we were thought of by the Third Reich as a subhuman inferior race.'

'Officers, this is too much. My mother is an old lady, look at her!' said Charles.

'Too much?' said Erika, starting to lose it. 'Just because she's an old lady, we should just forget? Or perhaps I'm being too political? Or am I trying to force my liberal agenda onto you?' Charles was shaking his head. 'It makes me sick that people think anything to do with the Holocaust and concentration camps is somehow diminished by time. The systematic slaughter of millions of people based on their genetic makeup or the colour of their skin is something which should never be forgotten or excused. It's still going on today. Your mother is as guilty today as she was all those years ago.' She stared at Elsa, and looked around at the opulent house, at Elsa's fine clothes and at the diamond earrings lying in their open box next to the tea cups.

'Dr Schmidt, Dr Schmidt,' muttered Elsa. 'How old is he?'

'I don't know,' said Erika.

'Is he the same age as me?' she said, thumping her chest with her fingers.

'He's of working age. In his fifties.'

'Then how can he possibly know what it was like?' Elsa spat.

'You were a guard at a concentration camp, Elsa. It wasn't a holiday camp!' said Moss.

'And if I had refused the job, they would have put me in that camp!' insisted Elsa, her voice low, her eyes blazing. 'The German soldiers, they came knocking around the farms… Where we lived it was farmland, we had a farm. My father was one of the best farmers for miles around, and they went to the farms, demanding that the young adults came to work at the camps. They told us if we didn't, then we'd be put there with our families. You people never lived through it; you can't imagine what it was like!'

'And yet you lived through it, and you must have watched hundreds die, even thousands,' said Erika.

'Do you have family?' snapped Elsa.

'No.'

'You?' She pointed at Moss.

'Yes,' said Moss.

'You have children?'

'I have a small son.'

'Then if the Germany army knocked on your door and told you that if you didn't go and work in the camp, your little boy would be gassed? What would you do?'

'I would fight. I would fight for my boy, and I would fight them,' said Moss, red-faced and shaking.

'Everyone has morals until it matters.'

Erika resisted the urge to punch the old woman in the face, and when she looked across, she could see Moss fighting the same impulse.

'So, you trotted off every day to work and brutalised prisoners, sent people to their death, and played your part in the extermination of millions. Did you whistle on your way to work, thinking that you were safe?'

'Of course not!'

'The concentration camp where you were a guard was labelled grade three, which were the toughest camps for the "incorrigible political enemies of the Reich." It was also one of the most profitable.'

'How many times do I have to tell you. I didn't agree with Hitler! I worked there because I had to!'

They were silent for a moment, and Erika could hear the clock ticking again.

'Elsa. Your son married a Jewish woman,' said Erika. 'I just don't understand.'

'We didn't know,' said Charles, speaking for the first time. 'My father went to his grave not knowing. My mother, she changed her details when she immigrated to England. She forged her papers. Dad knew she was Austrian, and that she was the daughter of a farmer. He knew that Austria had been occupied, but none of us knew...' He buried his head in his hands.

'When did Marissa find out your identity?' asked Erika.

'A few weeks before Christmas. I have kept this secret for years, and all it took was for the safe to not be locked properly.' Elsa shook her head. 'One mistake, one small mistake and it all... It all comes crashing down.'

'You kept the paperwork in that safe, and your husband didn't know?'

'I had a safety deposit box in a bank in London... I opened it when I first came to the UK in the 1950s. I kept hold of that paperwork, because that was who I was. My family name wasn't anything to do with the Nazi party. It was a good name. I should have burned the papers, but I couldn't. Then, the bank was moving premises, and they contacted me a few years ago, just after my husband died, and I put them in my safe here at home.' Elsa sat back and closed her eyes.

'When did Marissa start to blackmail you?' asked Moss.

'Yes. I let her have those diamond earrings, to begin with. I thought it would be enough to keep her quiet, but it wasn't. She realised what the consequences would be for my family, for

Charles and his family, if people found out. The Litman's have a lucrative jewellery business in Hatton Garden, which is histori-cally a Jewish place of business. Think what would happen if it was made public that his mother…' her voice trailed off. She looked weary now, resigned to her fate.

'You told us that Marissa had been grabbed by a man wearing a gas mask, a few weeks before Christmas,' said Erika.

'Yes.'

'You wanted to make us think that she had been targeted by him before?'

'It was the perfect opportunity. He was making headlines, the man in the gas mask; the public were afraid… It was around the same time that I heard people in our local shop talking about a young woman who he had attacked, late at night, on her way home from the train station.'

'It was feasible that he could have attacked Marissa,' said Moss. Elsa nodded.

'To commit the perfect murder, you need the perfect cover,' said Erika. 'And Taro Williams was your perfect cover.'

'It's taken us some time to access Marissa's mobile phone records. We now know she phoned you, Charles, shortly before she boarded the train to Brockley on Christmas Eve.'

He looked up from where he was slumped on the sofa. 'She phoned me to say she wanted more money, or jewellery, whatever was quicker,' said Charles, putting his head in his hands. 'She said she was going away, she needed it fast… We had already given her the earrings and money. I didn't have a choice. It would never have stopped; she would have gone on blackmailing us and threatening us.'

'Where did you get the gas mask?' asked Erika.

'It was from a second-hand shop in Soho,' said Charles. He hung his head and started to cry.

'The only problem, Charles, is that you have an alibi for Christmas Eve,' said Erika. He looked up at her. 'We have CCTV footage of you on a petrol station forecourt in North London, eleven minutes before the CCTV images we have of Marissa's murder. There is no way you could have been here.'

They looked back at Elsa.

'No one will believe that a ninety-seven-year-old woman had it in her to kill a strong, young twenty-two-year-old,' Elsa said, giving them a nasty, sly smile. A chill descended over the room.

'Are you admitting you did it?' asked Erika.

Elsa shook her head, still smiling.

'The post-mortem showed that Marissa was killed by a particular kind of paring knife. An eight-inch blade, with a serrated edge at the top,' said Erika. 'When the police searched your house with the warrant, one of my officers took away an identical knife… It wasn't classed as valuable, so you weren't informed. I'm sure you washed it, but you'd be shocked to discover what tiny amounts modern forensics can work with. We found microscopic amounts of Marissa Lewis's bone and blood on that knife…'

The smile had now been wiped from Elsa's face and her mouth was agape in horror. Erika went on, 'Not only that, we were also able to match the knife to the cuts and slashes on Marissa's body. Your knife is the murder weapon. We've also used the latest technology to study the CCTV camera opposite Marissa's house, which caught the murder. We can match your height with the height of the figure in the gas mask.'

'No… No!' cried Elsa.

'And the last piece of the puzzle, well, it's the best yet. On Christmas Eve, when Marissa got off the train at Brockley, she was wearing those diamond earrings,' said Erika, indicating the box which was still open on the table. 'Jeanette Walpole has confirmed Marissa was wearing them, and we also saw, again, on CCTV at Brockley station, that Marissa spoke to two drunken young men at the bottom of the footbridge. They were sleaze bags, and were trying to chat her up, and they asked her for a selfie, no doubt to show their mates.'

Moss took another photo from the folder. It was the selfie, in very high quality, of Marissa with the two young men. Marissa could be clearly seen wearing the earrings.

'It was taken around fifteen minutes before she died,' said Erika. 'We tested the earrings for DNA, as you said we should. As well as small amounts of sweat and oil, they were covered in blood. They had been wiped clean to the naked eye, but we used a chemical called Luminol, which shows traces of blood on objects. You have probably seen it on police TV shows. It glows blue under the right light. We found that both earrings were saturated with blood. Far too much for it to have been from a simple cut. You killed Marissa, Elsa. You slashed her throat with your paring knife, and then as she lay dying, you removed the diamond earrings.'

The front door bell rang, and then it opened. Peterson came into the living room with McGorry and three uniformed officers. Erika looked over to them and nodded. Elsa sat back in the chair. Her face had sunken in on itself and she looked ashen. 'No... No...' she croaked, but all her bravado and confidence had evaporated.

'Elsa Fryatt, I'm arresting you for the murder of Marissa Lewis. You do not have to say anything, but it may harm your defence if you do not mention when questioned something which you later rely on in court. Anything you do say may be given in evidence against you. I'm also informing you that a lawyer from the international war crimes court, and the German government, have requested to speak to you under caution regarding your time working as a guard at the Mathhausen-Gusen concentration camp, and the crimes you committed against humanity during the Second World War.'

Mrs Fryatt stared up at her. Then she grabbed a gold letter opener from the coffee table and lunged across at Erika, holding it in her fist. Peterson ran forward and caught her wrist, the tip of the blade inches from Erika's face.

'Black hands. Get those filthy black hands away from me,' hissed Elsa, her eyes glittering with hatred. Peterson prised the letter opener out of her grip. He pinned her arms to her side, and McGorry handcuffed her hands behind her back. Elsa stared up at Erika. 'You people will never understand. If I had my time again, I would do the same.'

'Take her away,' said Erika. Peterson led Elsa from the living room and out to the waiting police car.

EPILOGUE

Erika, Moss, Peterson and McGorry watched as Elsa and Charles were loaded separately into waiting police cars. As the car containing Elsa pulled away, she sat upright, with her head held high, looking straight ahead. As the second car followed, Charles was slumped with his head down, and he was weeping.

Across the street, the neighbours had come to their gates and front doors, and others were peering through net curtains.

'I wonder what they'd think if they knew they'd been living beside a murderer and a Nazi war criminal,' said McGorry.

'They'll be shocked, I'm sure. She was always dressed head to toe in Marks and Spencer,' said Moss. 'Covers a multitude of sins.'

Erika smiled.

'What's going to happen to her now?' added McGorry.

'Even though she's old, we'll push to go to trial for Marissa's murder,' said Erika. 'And Charles will be charged with conspiracy to murder. I'm just concerned about the other charges. The historical war crimes. I want her to live long enough to pay for what she did during the war.'

'Let's hope she lives for a long time, and gets to rot in prison,' said Peterson.

A black van pulled up at the kerb, and a team of forensic officers got out and went to work on the house. Erika took out a cigarette and lit up. Peterson gave Moss a look.

'Come on, John,' she said. 'Let's go get some coffee.'

'I've already had two coffees…' he started, but Moss gave him a look and he followed her through the gateway.

Peterson shifted on his feet and looked at Erika.

'You okay?' she asked.

'What?'

'Elsa, and what she said.'

'You never get used to racism. It's always there. Every day, in some shape or form…'

Erika nodded, and didn't know what to say.

'I wanted to talk to you, about something different. Not work,' he said.

'What?'

'I should have told you straight away about Kyle and Fran… I tried to tell you the night we went to the club, but… I wimped out.'

'After all these revelations. The fact you're a father doesn't seem so shocking now.'

'If you put it like that…' he said.

'I can't say I'm over the moon for you, James, but I'll get there,' said Erika.

'OK.'

'You always wanted kids, and you've been able to miss out on all the nappy changing…'

He shook his head.

'Sorry, that came out wrong,' she added.

'It's okay. I know what you mean.' He smiled at her. 'Are we cool? Can we be cool?'

'Yeah. We can,' she said. She was glad when his phone rang, and he indicated he had to take it. 'Shall I meet you in the coffee shop?'

She nodded and watched him go off and answer the phone, a big smile on his face.

She stayed at the gate, smoking. The feeling of relief and elation washing over her that she had nailed a case. She wasn't sure how long she was there, until she looked down and saw four cigarette butts on the ground.

'Screw it,' she said to herself. 'It's not every day you catch a murderer and a Nazi war criminal before lunch.' She took out her packet of cigarettes and lit another. One of the uniformed officers came out of the house towards her.

'Sorry to interrupt, ma'am. We think we've discovered the coat the murderer wore, stuffed under some floorboards. And there's a gas mask. Both look to be encrusted with blood.'

'I'll be there in a second,' she said. The officer went back in the house, and Erika took a moment to savour her success. A bird was singing, high in one of the surrounding trees, and she looked up at the bright sky, savouring the soft sound. She took a drag on the freshly lit cigarette, before stubbing it out on the bottom of her shoe and slipping it back in the packet.

Then she made her way back into the house.

A LETTER FROM ROB

First of all, I want to say a big thank you to you for choosing to read *Deadly Secrets*. If you are picking up one of my books for the first time, or if you are back again for more Erika Foster, I would be very grateful if you would consider writing a short review. It needn't be long, just a few words, but it makes such a difference and helps readers to discover one of my books for the first time.

I love hearing all your thoughts, and reading your messages. Thank you to all those readers who have been in touch, I read and appreciate every message. You can get in touch on my Facebook page, through Twitter, Goodreads or my website, which you'll find at www.robertbryndza.com. There are lots more books to come, so I hope you'll stay with me for the ride!

Robert Bryndza

P.S. If you would like to get an email informing you when my next book will be released, you can sign up to my mailing list using the link below. Your email address will never be shared and you can unsubscribe at any time.

www.bookouture.com/robert-bryndza

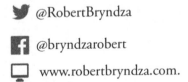

@RobertBryndza

@bryndzarobert

www.robertbryndza.com.

ACKNOWLEDGEMENTS

Thank you to Oliver Rhodes, Claire Bord, and the wonderful team at Bookouture. Thanks also to Rebecca Bradley for your feedback and advice on police procedure. Any liberties taken with fact are mine.

Thank you to my amazing agent, Amy Tannenbaum Gottlieb, for guiding me through the last few months with such grace and wit. Thank you also to the equally amazing Danielle Sickles, and all at The Jane Rotrosen Agency. Thank you to Jan Cramer, for your wonderful audiobook narration of the Erika Foster series.

Thank you to my mother-in-law, Vierka for all your love and support, and for the line drawing of the gas mask. You did me proud, and came up with something chilling. A massive thank you to my husband, Ján for reading endless drafts, and putting up with my crazy writer behaviour. If there was a literary awards category for writer's spouses, you would win it every year. And thanks to Riky and Lola for the unconditional love, and for making our days so bright and full of fun.

And lastly, to all my wonderful readers, all the wonderful book groups, book bloggers and reviewers worldwide. A writer is nothing without his readers. Thank you.

ACKNOWLEDGEMENTS

Made in the USA
Monee, IL
06 January 2024

51292150R00181